"What ... ... prowling out here?"

Bracing herself, Erin whispered, "I didn't know where to sleep. I guessed this was your room and—"

"You're not sharing it," he stated harshly against her ear. Mace knew he had made another mistake to add to the long list he was compiling. The air was filled with warm woman, and it pierced him as he breathed it in. "Damn you," he muttered, releasing her skirt only to take her arm. "I'll show you where. Far enough away from me."

Down the darkened hallway he strode, unmindful of his naked state, until at the end he threw open the door. "This is your room. Learn where it is so there's no mistake. I don't ever want to find you in my room again. You hear me?"

"Yes, Mr. Dalton. I hear you, and I'm sure everyone else in the house does, too."

He let her go and glared down at her shadowed features. "Won't matter, will it? They'll all know soon enough the reason why."

Dear Reader,

This month we bring you award-winning author Patricia Hagan's latest Harlequin Historical, *The Desire*. The novel is the sequel to *The Daring* (HH#84) and tells the story of Belinda Coulter, a troubled young woman who finally finds happiness as a Confederate nurse, only to come face-to-face with a man from the past.

Columbine is the second book by Miranda Jarrett, one of the first-time authors introduced during our 1991 March Madness promotion. The story sweeps from busy London to the wilds of Colonial New England, where a disgraced noblewoman finds a new life full of hope and promise.

Theresa Michaels's *Gifts of Love* is an emotional tale of a grieving widower and an abandoned woman whose practical marriage blossoms into something far more precious than either of them could ever dream.

Lucy Elliot has been writing books for Harlequin Historicals since the introduction of the line. *The Conquest,* her eighth book, is a sequel to *The Claim* (HH#129). It's the story of a tempestuous Frenchwoman and a cool-headed American soldier who fall in love against the backdrop of the American Revolution.

Four intriguing heroines. Four unforgettable heroes. We hope you enjoy them all.

Sincerely,
Tracy Farrell
Senior Editor

Gifts of Love

Theresa Michaels

Harlequin Books

TORONTO • NEW YORK • LONDON
AMSTERDAM • PARIS • SYDNEY • HAMBURG
STOCKHOLM • ATHENS • TOKYO • MILAN
MADRID • WARSAW • BUDAPEST • AUCKLAND

Harlequin Historicals first edition October 1992

ISBN 0-373-28745-3

GIFTS OF LOVE

Books by Theresa Michaels

Harlequin Historicals

A Corner of Heaven #104
Gifts of Love #145

THERESA MICHAELS

is the pseudonym for an award-winning historical romance author. Avid reader turned writer, Theresa collects old Western newspapers and antique books on Western lore and Victorian Americana. A former New Yorker, she writes full-time and lives with her family and one cat in Florida.

To Tuesday's Group—Marilyn Campbell, Nancy Cohen, Nancy Grant and Debi Shelgren, for all their support and all those calories.
And to Elizabeth Bass, who made working together a pleasure.

Chapter One

November 1, 1873
Washington Territory

Ketch Larrabee guided the buckboard team around the sprawling log ranch house and down the lane to the barn. The high-stepping team showed little trace of their seventy-mile round trip to Walla Walla. A bitter winter chill cut through his sheepskin coat and he cursed the glaciers that had gouged and sculptured this valley where Mace Dalton had carved a home for the Diamond Bar D. But the wind was no more bitter than the look his boss shot him when he pulled up and wrapped the reins around the pole brake.

"She gone, Ketch?"

"Yep. An' that's the last time, Mace. Ain't haulin' no more female dragons. Ain't doin' the cookin' for this outfit. Ain't playin' nursey maid to your young 'uns. Ain't—"

"Spare me, Ketch. I've heard it all before."

"Heard me? Maybe. But you ain't actin'."

"And I won't. *I don't want a wife.*"

Ketch shot him a narrow-eyed look. Mace was on edge.
The words had come from between gritted teeth in a voice
as cold and cutting as the sharp wind that came up from
the Blue Mountains to the south. Ketch shook his head,
jumped down and set about freeing the horses from their
traces.

After a moment, Mace began to help him. Ketch had
his own notions of why his boss refused to marry again.
But he kept silent. Mace could be as hard as a whetstone,
with a temper that, if crossed, would have a body believing that he had grabbed himself a snarling wolf by the tail.
Ten years ago Ketch had come up from Oklahoma with
twenty-year-old Mace, who had more savvy about cattle
and horses than men twice his age. He thought he knew
Mace about as well as any man could ever know another.
It was that knowledge that made him back off now.

Mace led the near perfectly matched pair of bays into
the barn toward their stalls. He heard Ketch moving
around behind him, and knew the other man would finish taking care of the team. He wanted to walk away, but
Ketch was right. He had to think of a way to solve his
problem. But he did not lie to himself or Ketch. He did
not want a wife. He never wanted to need another woman
again. With a weary sigh, he rubbed the back of his neck
and waited until Ketch had spilled grain for the horses.

With a lazy, off-centered smile, Mace took up the curry
brush. "I'll tend to them," he offered, and then asked,
"you real sure about not cooking for us?"

"Said so, didn't I?" Ketch snapped.

"Now, Ketch—"

"Save all that sweet talk for some gal. Ain't gonna do
it. You had yourself eleven females in five years an'
couldn't hang on to one of them. Never hired me on as no

cook. Get Dishman to do it. Get Cosi or Heppner, but you ain't gettin' me.''

Mace tossed him the brush. "Fine. I'll do the damn cooking."

Ketch grabbed the brush and stomped off to the bay's stall. He stopped and made an abrupt turn as Mace's words sank in. "Now, jus' you wait up, Mace. You're like a flounderin' stud in the kitchen."

Mace shot him a wide grin. "I know."

"Can't make biscuits worth a damn. Your porridge always has lumps that'll choke a man, an' you can't pick feathers off a chicken."

Mace didn't answer him. He hooked his thumbs in his belt, rocked back on his heels and waited.

"Figure we can strike us a deal?"

Once again, Mace didn't answer him. Ketch was the best hornswoggler he knew.

"I'll do the cookin', but you start lookin' for a wife."

"No wife."

"Gotta be that way, Mace. It ain't stablizin' for your young 'uns. Ain't too stablizin' for my constitution." Seeing the implacable stare coming from Mace's eyes, Ketch muttered, "Hard-nosed, cow-hocked longhorn."

Mace cupped his hand around his ear and angled his head forward. "What was that, old-timer?"

"You heard me well enough. You strike that deal with me or you can flounder till hell freezes."

The grin disappeared. The teasing mood vanished. Ketch knew what was coming and braced himself.

"Remember, Ketch, I live there. It's already frozen me to the bone."

"Mace, I'm an ole polecat that ain't got sense. Stay out of the kitchen."

Mace watched Ketch's rolling gait take him toward the main house. He couldn't deny that Ketch had a point. But marry again? The lump in his throat prevented him from swallowing.

"Papa, are you in here?"

The soft questioning voice of his daughter, Rebecca, forced him to move out of the shadows, not only the physical ones, but the shadows from the past that held him in their grip.

"Right here, Becky."

"Ketch said Miss Nolie is gone and that we won't have anyone to watch us again."

Mace hunkered down beside his daughter and smoothed the braided black silk of her hair. Even in the dim light filtering from the open doors, he could see that her wide brown eyes were filled with resignation. He sought the words to dispel the anxious note in her voice and found that another image imposed itself on his eight-year-old child's face. He closed his eyes, fought the tightening in his chest and the pain that pierced him. He released a breath when he knew the leashed control he kept on his own emotions would hold.

"Does that make you unhappy, Becky? You and your brother will be fine. We don't need a woman to clutter—"

"But Jake won't mind me." She bit her lower lip and shrugged her shoulders, nervously twisting her thin body from side to side. "I liked Miss Nolie and Miss Jessica and Mrs. McKenize. They taught me things."

"You forgot Mrs. Quincy and Ellen Clayton and..." Mace shook his head. He couldn't remember the rest of the names or faces of women who had come, stayed a few weeks, then left. He certainly did not want to think about the talk that followed each one of them. He didn't give a damn about the speculations people made concerning why the hired women wouldn't stay on here. And he didn't have the courage to ask his daughter what things some of these women had taught her. He still hoped that she never noticed Mrs. McKenize tipping her flask all day, or the repeated tries Miss Jessica had made to enter his room in the middle of the night until he had been forced to bolt his door.

Rebecca placed her small hand on her father's arm. "Papa, I really don't like Ketch's cooking."

"You like mine even less." Mace rose and took hold of her hand. "This one of the times you're feeling like clouds adrift in the sky?"

Becky offered him a solemn look and nodded.

Mace reassured her with a light squeeze of his hand. "Guess it's up to your papa to fix this one up."

"Ketch said you should marry again," she suggested in a timid voice. "Why don't you want to, Papa? I think it would be nice to have a mother. And I promise to be very, very good so she wouldn't leave us. I'd even make Jake obey."

"No one left because of you or Jake," he reassured her, but his voice was strained. Mace hid his guilt—guilt and the belief that because of him his children had lost their mother. No matter how he tried to stop blaming himself, the thought was ever present, ever near the surface.

Mace kept silent and shortened his long strides to match those of his daughter as they left the barn. Ketch was right. He'd need to make a decision, and soon. Thanksgiving was coming, and before he knew it the Christmas season would be here. It wasn't fair that his children should be denied knowing how a woman's touch could make those days special. But a wife...somehow he couldn't force himself to see another woman by his side.

But the idea had been planted. The Diamond Bar D profits were good these last few years, he reminded himself. He could afford to offer a generous settlement to someone, if he found himself a plain woman who wouldn't expect anything from him. He would be blunt about his terms of marriage so that there could be no recriminations later.

The good Lord knew that he was damn tired of worrying about the laundry, cooking, order in the house and care of his children. None of his men wanted to milk the cow, feed the chickens or slop the hogs, believing that these were women's chores and beneath their dignity.

And Ketch was right about Becky and Jake needing a woman to look after them. A sober, respectable woman, that is.

If he married her, she couldn't run off if things were not to her liking. He'd cut himself a deal as if he were going to buy another prize breeding heifer. Nothing more than money in exchange for services rendered.

Breeding? What was he thinking of, he asked himself with a shake of his head. He'd never put himself or another woman at risk by trying to have her walk the lines of wife and mother-to-be. It was the only justification he could offer himself for the betrayal he felt just from thinking of another marriage.

Opening the back door to the kitchen, he called out, "Ketch, tomorrow you fetch me every damn territorial paper."

San Francisco, California

"Just tell me you'll think about it, Erin. It's a choice, at least. You can be flat on your back for one man or many."

"But, Maddie, marry a stranger? Be a thing that's ordered and paid for like a—"

"Whore like me?"

Erin's fair skin colored. "I meant no insult," she hastened to explain. "You know how grateful I am for all your help. But marriage?" Erin Dunmore shivered at the thought. The weak afternoon sun did not penetrate the gloom in her third-floor room. Her mood became reflective as she stood near the grimy window. Looking down, she again heard the constant drum of traffic, shouts and curses along with drunken songs from men in the street. Wrapping her arms around her waist, an unconscious protective gesture, she knew it would not be long before she was serving drinks to the same sort of rough men in the downstairs parlor.

Shivers once again chilled her flesh. She hated singing for them, hated their lewd suggestions, their fetid breath, their sly touches. And she despised them for thinking that their money would buy them whatever they wanted.

No city in the country could boast more men of solid wealth than San Francisco. They built palaces from their silver bricks and could sell their holdings for five million dollars each as mines of fabulous possibilities poured their dividends into the pockets of the Licks, the Lathams, the Sharons and the Haywards.

Erin knew them well. She had worked for several of them.

The bedstead frame groaned in protest as Maddie Darling shifted her weight. "You know you've got to decide on doing something else for yourself soon. The coast is no place for the likes of you."

Erin closed her eyes for a moment. If Maddie knew the truth, she would not be able to make that claim.

"What else can you do, Erin?"

"I wouldn't be knowing for sure," Erin replied in a soft, defeated voice. She leaned her forehead against the window. Even though she knew Maddie's badgering came from concern, she found it hard to bear.

"You said you got turned out of your place without a penny or a reference. And you've no family to help."

"You know I wouldn't lie to you. There's no one to turn to and I can't see what good it does to repeat all this, Maddie."

"Good? I'll tell you, Irish. It reminds you that you can't be letting the days go by. How long can you figure to keep Jaffery out of your bed? Lumpy as the damn thing is."

Erin shook her head. She didn't know the answer. "I try to keep out of his way. All of the downstairs is cleaned long before he awakes. But you know that." She turned to face Maddie, who was sprawled across the bed, draped in a satin wrapper of the palest pink. The cut and the delicate embroidery trim could have graced any respectable matron's wardrobe. But this was a Maddie few, if any, were given the opportunity to view. When she was working, Maddie wore bright, flamboyantly styled gowns that brought her attention, and full pockets.

And Erin was in no position to judge Maddie. Erin rubbed her head, which seemed to ache constantly, and glanced down at the shapeless gown she wore. She avoided the sight of her reflection in the hazed mirror hung over the bureau with its missing legs and two holes gaping where drawers should have been. Not that she had possessions enough to fill four drawers. The room was squalid, no matter how much effort she made to keep it clean.

"Erin, you listen to me and stop feeling sorry for yourself."

"I'm not feeling sorry for myself. I'm tired of being alone. You had a family. You could go back. For me there is an emptiness of wondering why my mother never wanted me. You can't understand the haunting I feel in not knowing who she is, or who my father is. Were they married? Was I an extra mouth they couldn't feed? Was I—"

"Stop it, Erin. You hurt yourself every time you think about this. No one can go back and change the past. You need to think about today and tomorrow. Jaffery is watching you all the time. It won't be long before he'll be making you choose. He'll tell you it's him or the street. And when he's done with you, you'll find yourself working one of the rooms." With a toss of her head that sent the thick honey blond curls tumbling over her shoulders, Maddie gave Erin's figure a thorough once-over. "You're getting too thin. You don't sleep, and the food you eat wouldn't keep a cat. Putting an advertisement in the western territory newspapers is a choice you can't ignore. You could pass yourself off as a respectable—"

"I was that, Maddie."

"Sure you were…are, I mean. Damn every one of those moneyed matrons for blaming a girl sweet as you."

Erin stared at the floor. She knew it was true. She had worked for a respectable banker's family as a parlor maid until she fell for a line of blarney from one of the bank clerks that wouldn't have fooled a child. If she hadn't been so lonely, so needing of love, of someone to care about her who would make her dreams of having a home and a family of her own come true, if only—ruthlessly she stopped herself. She had been foolish to believe, she had been turned out, and if it weren't for Maddie's kindness, she didn't know what she would have done. Perhaps this was the choice that had faced her mother? Stop it! Stop it, she warned herself, knowing this way led to unbearable hurt.

And she couldn't deny the threat that Jaffery presented. He owned the house and would press her for an answer soon. The only nice gesture she could say Jaffery made was to give her a choice.

A feeling of being trapped overcame her. She could never let another man use her. She had given Silas Duelle what he wanted, but only because he had pressured her. Erin knew she had enjoyed the hugging and gentle caresses that came before. She had needed the human warmth, the knowledge that here was someone who cared about her. But those had been lies. Lies she had fed herself, just as Silas had. Lies she had believed out of a desperate hunger and loneliness.

"Erin, you told me that you want a home of your own and a family to love more than anything. Marriage is the only way for you. And you won't be finding that if you stay here."

"I will think about what you said, Maddie."

The other woman rose from the bed, tightening the ties on her satin wrapper. Erin envied Maddie for being all that she was not. Tall, lovely and lushly figured. Men seemed to set great store by a woman's looks. Another strike against her, Erin thought.

Maddie fluffed out the wild tangle of her hair and walked toward the door. "It's time for me to get to work."

"Maddie, don't you hate it? Does it—"

"Honey, I keep telling you, for me it doesn't matter. I lost—well, what I lost don't fit in a thimble. But you matter. There's still hope left in you."

With an unconscious gesture Erin slid her hand across her stomach. She wanted and needed to say something that would ease Maddie's troubled look.

"I'll think about doing it and try to eat more. From the first day you found me wandering around, you've been very kind to me, Maddie. I'll never forget you."

"Oh, you get yourself married to a fine, respectable man and forget you know my name. And don't be getting all teary-eyed on me. No one ever gave me a chance to be anything but what I am. Maybe I want it to be different for you." She shrugged and opened the door. "Maybe I know something you don't, Erin. You're different from the rest of us here. Don't be long, or Jaffery'll come looking for you."

Maddie started to close the door after her, then stopped. "If you need pen, ink and paper, Jaffery keeps them in the top right-hand desk drawer."

"Thank you, Maddie."

"Honey, thank me when you're out of here and safely married far enough away that no one knows you."

Erin did think about Maddie's suggestion of placing a notice in the newspapers. She also thought of the lies she would be forced to tell. Lies that would go on and on.

Two incidents made up Erin's mind. The first happened the very next night. Two drunken miners came into the parlor where she stood alone, arranging her sheet music. Scooping her up between them, ignoring her struggles and cries, they managed to get her halfway up the stairs before Jaffery came out of his office.

He didn't order them to release her. He stood there, his unlit cigar hanging from one corner of his mouth, and finally, when Erin stilled, he spoke.

"You boys must be new to the city. Rules here say you pay up first, then have your fun."

One of the men tossed him a poke bag. "There's gold enough for four frail sisters, but this one'll do for us. Ratail and me like sharing."

"No! I'm not one of the—"

"Erin," Jaffery snapped, giving her a warning look while he hefted the small bag.

She waited, knowing that Jaffery would do all he could to avoid a fight. She begged him with a look to hurry up. Panic began to close her throat. He wasn't saying a word. She stared down at Jaffery's dark hair with its thick layer of pomade that reminded her of the sleek wet coats of the seals that could be seen in the bay. Her heartbeat thudded until she heard its pounding in her ears. Both miners had firm, bruising grips on her arms. Their bodies, encased in new, stiff suits, but smelling as if months had passed without a bath, pressed tightly against either side of her.

A sweeping hot flush rose from inside her body. Sweat broke out on her brow and Erin began to gag. She couldn't stop. Then she was chilled and nausea churned her stomach. Bile burned its way up her throat. She managed a strangled sound that caught Jaffery's immediate attention.

"Don't you dare!" he shouted. "Let her go, you damn fools!"

Erin got free and ran up the three double flights of stairs. She barely made it inside her room. Dry heaves kept her kneeling beside the honey bucket all night. It was almost dawn when Maddie came to check on her.

"I heard you had yourself a close call, Erin," Maddie said, entering the room and flooding it with light from the kerosene lamp she carried. One look at the figure huddled on the floor and Maddie set the lamp aside, coming to her knees beside her. "Did they hurt you?"

Erin couldn't speak. She shook her head weakly. She didn't think about the bruise marks that would be livid on her arms. She had endured harder pinches, ones that left her skin purpled, from the home's matrons, and the cooks, upper maids and housekeepers she had worked for.

"Let's get you up and into bed." Shaking her head and muttering about men, Maddie managed to strip off the sweat-drenched shapeless gown that Erin wore. The petticoat, chemise and drawers were so worn she could see Erin's fair skin through the cloth. All were tossed into an untidy heap on the floor. Tucking Erin under the covers, she warned her to stay there until she came back.

Erin could do little else. Her hands still shook and she could feel her pulse beating at an alarming rate throughout her body. Shivers racked her, but they were from the deep feeling of despair that welled up inside her. What was she going to do?

Minutes later, Maddie returned with a cup of tea in one hand and a fresh pitcher of water in the other.

"Maddie, don't," Erin protested when she began to wash her face. "I know how tired you are."

"Sure. I won't deny it. But you're weak as a kitten and about half as smart."

"And you're trying out for mama cat."

"Don't give me your sass. That's a role better suited for you," Maddie said, forcing Erin to sit up so she could drink the tea.

Erin closed her eyes in appreciation of the warmth stealing through her. She was thankful that Maddie held both her and the cup, for she didn't believe she had the strength to do either one. But once the cup was empty, there was no way Erin could avoid Maddie's probing gaze.

"Erin, if you want to tell me, I'll listen. There was more reason than that bank clerk courting you that caused you to lose your job, wasn't there? If you don't want to talk, say so."

"You know?"

Directing a piercing look at Erin's pale face, Maddie met the startling clarity of her green eyes. "No. I didn't know for sure. I figured that might be your problem."

"Problem? That's a fine word for what's wrong with me."

"It can be a fine thing, Erin. And maybe it's true that you're all Irish, but don't try handing out any of that blarney to me. You care, don't you?" Maddie set the cup and saucer down on the bureau top.

"Right now, I'm scared, Maddie. I don't know what to do. I don't want this baby, my baby, to grow up not knowing who its parents are. I want this child to have a home where there is love."

"Did you love the father?"

"I'm not sure I know what love is. I've never had any, you see. I liked being with Silas. He seemed to care about me. But when I told him, he just laughed and said I wasn't the first one to try to lock him in that cage. I think he told the housekeeper and that's why they let me go. I never saw him again."

Erin's sad, pensive mood touched Maddie. She came to the side of the bed and sat down, fussing with the covers until she had Erin tucked tight beneath them.

"Do you see why you've got to get out of here? You'll never find love in this place, Erin."

"But to do what you suggested means I would have to lie." Erin reached out for Maddie's hand and squeezed it. "You've been a good friend to me. The first one I've ever had."

"Why don't you try to rest? We can talk again in the morning."

Erin was only too willing to close her eyes, but her mind was in a turmoil now. She would never do to her baby what her mother had done to her. She would never allow her child to be raised the way she was, in an orphanage where the only woman who had time to be kind, to hug and kiss, had been fired for her mollycoddling. Her child must not know what it was like to fight over scraps of food, or to pray that when special treats were distributed by the church ladies, she would be deserving of one. And when she wasn't deemed worthy, to stand aside and watch, longing for what others had.

Restlessly she turned on her side, wrapping her arms around her waist. Now she was warm, but she remembered when a too thin, too small blanket was all she had. No matter what she had to do, she vowed, her child would never feel the heavy weight of a brush three times the size of its small hands while being told to kneel and scrub floors already cleaned and so carelessly soiled by someone's entrance to the home.

And the nights... She would never forget the nights when she cried herself to sleep, feeling unloved and unwanted, only to wake and have those feelings reinforced time and again.

Erin tried to block her mind to the images that formed. She tried to think of her precious dream—of a home, warm with laughter and love, the vague shape of a man beside her, children's smiling faces looking up at her. But as morning came, the dream failed her.

She could only murmur over and over that she would find a way.

Three days later she was no closer to a solution to her problem. But when Jaffery refused to pay her, claiming that room, board and the charges for a bottle of whiskey she had broken left her with nothing owed, Erin knew she had to act.

With Maddie's help, she wrote an advertisement to be put in the newspaper. Maddie wanted her to state that she was a recent widow, but Erin argued against that. She couldn't lie while there was hope she might have many choices.

"Besides, Maddie," she said, sealing the letter, "would you marry a man who was looking for a wife immediately after the death of his first? We'll see what response I have and proceed from there. Someone may be kind, and I won't need to lie."

So Erin prayed. It was not for a wealthy man, although she hoped he would be able to provide a modest home. She prayed for kindness and understanding, for a man who might come to love her and the child she carried. That was the man she wanted to answer her.

Chapter Two

"Mace. Mace! Where in tarnation are you?" Ketch yelled, entering the house. "You still sulkin' over the turkey I burned?"

"Papa's not here, Ketch," Becky said, coming into the kitchen. "Tariko is foaling."

"Say no more, little miss." Ketch ran for the barn still clutching the newspapers he brought with him from Walla Walla.

Mace, all six foot two of him, was slumped against the big box stall when Ketch found him. "She all right?"

"Tariko is fine. Her colt is better."

"Looks to me like you could do with a shot of whiskey," Ketch suggested, peering at him.

"Heard you yelling, old-timer. What's got your tail afire?"

"Think I found you a woman, old son," Ketch snapped back, but he was smiling as Mace pushed himself up and stood to tower over him.

"A woman, huh? Figures you'd come back plaguing me. Well, don't stand there. Tell me."

"Come on up to the house with me, Mace. I could use a cup of coffee to warm my bones." Ketch didn't wait for him, nor did he leave the newspapers behind.

When he and Mace settled at the table with coffee laced with whiskey nearly gone, Ketch presented the ads he had circled.

Mace's lips twitched beneath his mustache as he began to read, then toss aside without comment each of the papers. For the past three weeks, Ketch had gone to town on Friday afternoons to get the local paper along with any others he could beg, borrow or steal. When he was finished, Mace leaned back in his thick oak chair and rested his folded hands across his stomach.

"Well, ain't you got somethin' to say? Can't be tellin' me there ain't a one that sparks some interest."

"Ketch, that about sums it up."

"You're a hard man."

"So I've been told. I agreed to this fool scheme of yours, but I aim to please myself, too. Widows with their brood won't have time for Becky and Jake. They'd likely be siding with their own every chance they could and make more trouble than I've already got." With a sigh, Mace leaned forward and enclosed his cup with his hands. "I don't think this is going to work out. I'll have to think of another way, Ketch."

"Well, jus' hold on there, son. I've been savin' the best for last." He produced a folded copy of the *Spirit of the West,* Walla Walla's own newspaper. "Now, look right here, taken out of the San Francisco paper."

Mace looked where Ketch pointed and began to read aloud. "'Wanted, gentleman of honorable intent to enter into correspondence with woman of modest manner, home educated, excellent cook and seamstress, of trim figure and of good nature. In good physical health.'" Mace stopped and looked at Ketch's anxious expression. "She's so good, I'm getting queasy reading this."

"Hush up and finish. You ain't got to the good part yet."

"Good, huh?" Mace shook his head and glanced down to find his place again. "'Children welcome and wanted. Desire to make home away from city. Serious inquiries only. Object matrimony. Erin Dunmore.'"

"Well, ain't that a right one?"

"Ketch, all the riding back and forth you've been doing has scrambled your head. What's right about this one?"

"She can cook. She likes children. She don't want to live in no city. She sounds right pleasing to me."

Mace drained the last of his coffee and set his cup down slowly. "Good. You marry her." He scraped back his chair and stood up. "I've got work to do. You've got supper to cook."

"Don't be so blamed ornery, Mace. You can't be puttin' this off. She's the best one yet an' you know it, even if you're too stubborn to admit it."

Mace settled his new flat-crowned Stetson on his head. "I know you're disappointed, Ketch. But if you think about it, she didn't even mention how old she was. She could be thirty."

"From where I'm sittin' that ain't so old. 'Sides, I got the feelin' that didn't matter all that much to you. Noticed how you don't mention it don't say here what color eyes or hair she's got. 'Course, that wouldn't interest you none."

"You won't let up, will you?"

"Nope."

"All right. I'll write to her tonight. Leave the paper on my desk."

"Right, boss. An' I'll even fix fried chicken for your supper."

Mace started to walk out then backtracked. "Gravy, too?"

"Yep. An' biscuits." Ketch waited until he heard the door close behind Mace, then he called out, "All right, you young 'uns can come out."

"Is it true, Ketch?" Becky asked, eyes alight as she pulled aside the skirt that covered the dry sink. She stood up and held it aside while Jake crawled out after her.

"You ain't supposed to be hidin' an' listenin' to men's talk, Becky."

"But how will I ever find out what is going on around here?"

As a reason, even Ketch couldn't argue with her. But he knew he should not let it pass. "Jus' ain't a right thin' to be doin'. Now, wash up an' help me get supper."

She pulled the small stool over to the pump and helped Jake to stand on it. "Papa really is going to find us a mother," Becky explained in her best grown-up manner. "Now, when she comes, you have to promise to be extra good."

Ketch listened as he cut up the chicken he had killed and plucked before he went to town. He didn't have the heart to tell them that it wouldn't be any time soon. If Mace had his way, it wouldn't happen at all.

"Tell us what modest manner means, Ketch? Do we have it, too?"

Ketch answered their questions as best he could, but he was swearing to himself the whole time. And when Mace came in for supper followed by Cosi Sawtell, Ray Heppner and Dishman, his mood resembled that of a surly bear wakened too early from his winter's sleep. He served up supper, grunting whenever anyone asked him to pass a dish, grunting when they all sat back, full and pleased and praised his cooking, grunting when Cosi mentioned that there was a Grange meeting in town that night.

His grunting turned to sputterings when Mace said he was going.

"You got a letter to write first," Ketch reminded him. "Do it right now an' post it."

"You know something, Ketch?" Mace said, glaring at him. "A woman's henpecking might be a sight easier to take than listening to you."

"Remember that when you write up your sweetness in that letter, Mace Dalton, or you'll be eatin' your own fix-in's again."

The men's laughter followed him outside, but Ketch didn't care. He knew he had needled Mace into doing what he wanted, even if the stubborn bull couldn't see clear for himself.

With any luck, come the first of the new year, Mace would have himself a wife and Ketch would never see the inside of that damn kitchen except to set himself down for meals.

Thanksgiving had come and gone with little to mark the day for Erin. She had one reply to her advertisement, and even now, as she reread the letter, she did not feel encouraged to answer it.

Dear Miss Dunmore,
I reply to your advertised request to enter into correspondence with a view toward matrimony. I am a widower, own a ranch in the Washington Territory outright, and have two children. My daughter, Rebecca, is eight, and my son, Jacob, is five.
Walla Walla is a thriving town, but my ranch is in an isolated area east of it. We have no neighbors. The

work is hard. A woman must be of strong physical and mental constitution to withstand the demands made upon her.

You did not state your age or give details of your description. Should you reply, I expect to have some knowledge of these.

I will consider further correspondence with you once I have your letter in hand.

Mace Dalton
Diamond Bar D
Walla Walla, W.T.

"Erin, are you reading that letter again?"

"Yes, Maddie. There is something about it...almost as if this Mr. Dalton wished to discourage me from replying." Erin shrugged and folded the letter, placing it on the bureau. "Did you want something?"

"Not me. But Jaffery does. He sent me up here to get you."

Erin smoothed her apron. She quickly thought of all she had done today, wondering what he had found to fault her with this time.

Almost as if she had surmised her thoughts, Maddie said, "He seems pleasant enough, but that's when I trust him the least."

"I'll keep that warning in mind."

Jaffery's office was set beneath the staircase, so he could hear the comings and goings of everyone. The room was large, sparsely furnished, with his wide oak desk dominating the far wall. Erin knocked on the open door, nervous as she always was when summoned by him.

She wished he would let her open the window, for his cigar smoke hung in a thick, suffocating cloud in the room, even when he was not smoking. She tried to breathe through her mouth to keep the smell from upsetting her stomach.

"Come in, Erin. No need to fret. I've got news to share. Good news for you." He smiled, revealing a gap where his eyetooth should have been, while he took a leisurely survey of her. She was slender and young, and he derived pleasure from seeing the tremor in the hands she held stiffly at her sides.

Her looks did not matter, although she was passably pretty with her black hair, green eyes and pale skin. Her breasts were too small for his taste, her hips too narrow, but he knew he had to supply a variety of fresh merchandise to his customers or they would take their business elsewhere.

What did count for him was her age. She claimed nineteen years, but she looked younger. He could get three, maybe four good years out of her before he threw her out.

Erin didn't fidget. She stood and waited and knew he was silent for some deliberate reason of his own. In her first maid's position she had been subjected to a housekeeper who enjoyed lining up the staff for morning, afternoon and evening inspections. But she hated being made to feel as if she were no more than a piece of furniture.

And Jaffery made her wait, playing his own game as he chose a fresh cigar from the carved box on his desk. He clipped off the end, brushed the cigar beneath his nose, sniffing appreciatively, then rolled it between his fingers, listening with a deepening smile to the soft crackle of properly aged tobacco.

He stuck his match and puffed furiously until the tip glowed. "I do enjoy a good cigar as much as I enjoy a good woman." Leaning back in his chair, he dropped his gaze to the cigar. "Florence is leaving us. I'll have to find a girl to replace her."

Erin bit the inside of her lower lip, steeling herself for what was coming. Inside her, she screamed, *I need time. Just a bit more time!* But beyond the blink of her eyes, she offered no visible reaction.

"You appear to be smart, Erin. You could be making more money if you worked her room." Jaffery waited, and when she said nothing, he smiled once again. "Florence won't be taking her clothes with her. She's about your size, isn't she? Pretty girl like you would look even better dressed proper. Well, you think about it and let me know."

He picked up his newspaper and Erin knew she was dismissed. Without a word she turned and headed for the door, sweat beading her brow. She was going to be sick again.

"Erin," Jaffery called, stopping her at the door. "Don't make me wait too long for an answer."

Erin did not make it to her room. She was thankful that most of the women were still sleeping, so that no one witnessed her being sick. She hurried to scrub the wood steps, running up and down the flights of stairs to haul fresh water, and on her last trip brought a bucket up to her room.

She was splashing tepid water on her face when Maddie came in.

"Again?"

Shamefaced, Erin nodded, patting her face dry with a linen cloth.

"Erin, you've got to answer that rancher's letter. You can't keep this up or you'll lose that baby." Eyeing the dark circles beneath Erin's eyes, she added, "I don't think you can wait until something better comes along."

Folding the cloth, Erin took a few minutes to form an answer. "I agree. I can't wait, but I don't know how I can tell a man I don't know about the baby. If he's my only hope of getting away from here and making a home, I could lose him before I have him." Cupping her flushed cheeks, Erin shook her head. "Listen to me. What am I saying? I don't want to lie."

"Just for a little while, Erin," Maddie urged. "See if he writes you back again. Make it a point to stress how much you want children. He's not a god, but a man, and I'm sure he's looking for a wife and not a saint. Erin, don't you see what you're doing to yourself? You can't punish yourself over what happened. People make mistakes all the time."

Erin heeded Maddie's warning and suggestions along with a few of her own. Later that night, she labored over every word of her reply to Mace Dalton.

The luck of calm seas and fair winds placed Erin's letter into Mace's hands within three weeks.

Ketch grinned like a beaver eyeing up the first leaves of spring, but Mace was reluctant to open the letter. He waited until everyone was asleep, the fire banked and a small glass of whiskey half gone before he read her reply.

My Dear Mr. Dalton . . . Mace almost crushed the paper in his hands. Possessive already? He groaned in despair, his gaze frantic as he searched the darkened corners of the room, looking, always hoping that he would see or hear again the soft, loving voice of his wife.

"Sky?" he whispered, seeing her touch in the woven hangings on the windows, the rugs, the faded patterns of the pottery. But Mary Blue Sky was dead these past five years. Dead in all but her spirit, which lived within his heart and their children.

His hand brushed the small tabletop by the side of his chair, coming away with a layer of dust. The whole room, which Sky had taken such pride in, showed neglect. And Mace knew it would be the same in every other room of the house.

He didn't need or want a woman for himself, but he didn't deny that his children needed a woman's softness. And he certainly didn't deny the need for a housekeeper. That settled, he again began to read Erin's letter.

Since you have made my description a condition of further correspondence, I will supply what details I can first. I was born in May of 1854. My hair is black and my eyes are green. My coloring is called fair. It is most difficult to give you my weight measure, but I believe it is one and one quarter centals.

Mace paused and frowned. "Cental," he murmured, then grinned. "So she weighs a little more than a hundred and twenty-five pounds." His own weight was a fraction less than double hers. He read on.

My height is almost five and one-half feet. I do hope this information will suffice. I do not have a likeness to send to you. You made mention of hard work. I am not afraid of work, honest work of any kind. In my present employment I often toil from six o'clock in the morning until late evening.

Mace had to stop again, annoyed that curiosity about this woman's employment should interfere. What sort of respectable employment carried those hours? And why should he care?

With his free hand he lifted his glass and sipped his whiskey. He didn't like the vague image his mind was creating. Erin Dunmore mustn't be real. What was deviling him that he should wonder how long that black hair was? Or how thick? Was it straight with almost blue-black light when the sun was caught within?

Like Sky's? his mind supplied. The whiskey burned his throat as he tossed the last of the drink down. He started to put the letter aside, but stopped himself. There wasn't all that much more. He could at least finish it.

Let me reassure you, Mr. Dalton, that the isolation of your home does not deter me. I admit, too, that I was greatly pleased to learn of your having children. I have longed for a family and would be most grateful if you would consider writing more about them. If you feel satisfied with my reply, I shall hope that you will answer me promptly. I must reach a decision shortly. Your response will have some account in my future plans.

 With all respect,
Erin Dunmore, San Francisco, California

Mace dropped the letter to his lap. Bringing his steepled fingers to rest against his lips, his thoughts took a serious turn.

The brief physical description did not satisfy him. He found himself tantalized with the vague image that kept forming. She had offered few clues to herself. This second letter was as neat as the first; not one ink blot marred the paper. Twenty years old and just now looking to marry. There was something wrong with that.

As his curiosity peaked, he found annoyance surfacing that she in turn had not asked personal questions about his habits or appearance.

With a grunt of deeper annoyance, he realized that he was put out because she inquired about his children and not himself. What was wrong with her? She was, as he had told Ketch, too *good*. He was the one she would be marrying. Living with. Sleeping beside.

But you never intended this to be a real marriage, a voice nagged from the back of his mind. He should be feeling pleased that she cared about the children. It was a point to lend weight in her favor.

Before he allowed more questions to plague him, Mace rose and lit the lamp on his desk. Drawing a fresh sheet of paper toward him, he sat, dipped his pen into the inkwell and began his reply.

He found himself glancing at the delicate handwriting time and again as he tried to put some warmth into his words. He was nearly done when he heard Cosi whispering his name.

"What is it?" Mace called out, turning the letter over.

"You'd better come, Mace. Tariko is down in her stall."

The Palouse mare took priority over some faceless woman, and his letter lay forgotten.

Tariko lifted her head when Mace entered her large box stall. Cosi had already lit several lanterns and hung them from the wooden beams. Mace spoke softly to his prized mare, her value not measured in money, but for being a gift from Thunder Rolling In The Mountain, the chieftain of the Nez Percé Indians.

Mace knelt in the straw by her head, his big hands gentle as they moved over her black-spotted coat, which whitened toward the rump. She was tough, game, a runner without equal, bred for a man to ride through rough terrain. Murmuring soothing words, he examined her forefeet, turned in so they could toe dance the narrowest pass and wide-heeled to make her surefooted, and listened to her labored breathing.

"It's distemper for sure," Cosi whispered.

"Seems so. It's a good thing she's been away from the herd. Take the colt out and I'll start making a purge for her." Mace smoothed Tariko's velvet nose. "Rest easy, girl. Ketch'll make you light bran mashes and have you fit in no time."

Cosi knew it was a measure of the mare's trust that she didn't stir as he led her colt from the stall. When he returned to Mace he offered to stay with her.

"No. You get some sleep, Cosi. I'll tend her."

Mace lost track of the days. He ate when Ketch or Becky brought him food, slept when exhaustion forced him to, and often woke to the morning's light with Jake curled by his side. When Tariko was able to stand on her own three days later, he stumbled out of the barn. He didn't remember falling into bed, sleeping around the clock, waking at Ketch's summons.

He grumbled. Something was nagging him, something that he had left unfinished. Blinking as Ketch pulled aside the thick curtains that covered the two windows in his room, Mace stretched and yawned.

"What's the day, Ketch?" Mace growled, fumbling with his quilt until he kicked it free. He felt a stab of guilt for the clumps of mud from his boots that had dried on the quilt and sheet.

"Nineteenth of December. But don't be worrying about the letter. I sent it off with a bank draft to cover Erin Dunmore's traveling expenses."

Mace rose in a controlled rush, scowling. "You did what?"

"You heard me."

"I wasn't going to ask her to come. I can't marry her, Ketch."

Ketch saw the anger that Mace was trying to stifle but refused to be swayed by it. "Little late to be letting me know that, boss. Letter's on its way. Soon she'll be here."

"Damn you! I don't want her. I can't have—"

"Papa," Becky said, coming into the room, "I brought you coffee." She came to where her father sat on his bed, holding his head with both hands. "Can we go cut our tree soon?"

"Tree?" Mace repeated, taking the cup she handed him.

"The tree for Christmas, boss," Ketch answered. He knew by the look Mace shot him that it was the last thought in his mind. "Might also think 'bout fixin' this place up a mite. Give it a sprucin'. Women set a store by those things."

"Oh, is the lady coming here?"

Mace glanced at his daughter's face. He had to close his eyes, unable to speak, thinking of his children, their need.

"Boss?" Ketch prodded.

"Yeah, Becky, she's coming here." Shooting another black look at Ketch, he added, "If you want her here so bad, you get the mop detail and spruce up." He burned his tongue on the hot coffee and ignored Ketch's mutterings about this place needing more than a mop.

"Might think 'bout sprucin' yourself up, too, boss. You look 'bout as black as an ol' grizzly comin' from his winter's sleep, an' you're snarlin' like that ole gray wolf that's been killin' calves."

Becky's hand on his arm stopped Mace from answering Ketch. "I'll help, Papa. I'll clean and make everything pretty for her. Jake'll help me. You'll see."

Mace nodded, but refused to look at her. Wolf, house, Christmas tree, kids and sassy-mouth Ketch were welcome to find a home down in Hell's Canyon. If he had a wife . . . Yeah, he told himself, if he had a wife he'd be rid of Ketch, kids, house and tree. The wolf would be his only worry.

Just the thought of being up in the mountains, riding alone through the forest that would thin as the timberline climbed, listening to the sharp cry of the wind in the trees or over the creased ridge tops that made a man feel small, was enough to bring a smile to his lips. Rubbing his bearded face, he turned to Becky, hating his selfish thoughts.

"Ketch is right. I'm mean as a grizzly. You lend Ketch a hand 'round the house and I'll take Jake out to look for a tree. Deal?"

"Deal, Papa." Becky offered him a too fleeting smile and a quick kiss on his cheek.

Mace suddenly realized that Becky didn't laugh or smile nearly as much as she once had. He looked up to see that Ketch was watching her, too.

"Like I said, boss, a woman's what you need."

"Need, but not want, Ketch. You fix up that room the others used. Chimney wasn't drawing well last I heard."

"But you're marryin' this one." Ketch stopped himself from saying more. Mace's eyes were bleak and painful to look at. "Sure thing, boss. Me an' Becky'll tend to it."

Taking the little girl by the hand, Ketch started for the door. He tried to wipe out the sight of Mace's fingers curling into a fist. The man had to let go of the past. It was eating him from the inside out.

With the Christmas holiday approaching, Erin's mood was as dark as the shortening days. She couldn't help but think of the delicious aromas that rose from the kitchen as the cooks set about outdoing each other with delicate treats meant for their employer's table. The household staff was allowed an extra afternoon off, but as the under parlor maid, Erin's best time had been to clean the morning room where the tree was displayed in all its finery.

Glossy beeswax candles in their round silver holders graced the tips of the weighted branches. Fragile hand-painted ornaments peeked from between the fragrant pine needles. Each day saw new boxes from the elegant shops in the city added to the growing pile beneath the tree.

But the sweetest and most painful memory came from the image of herself kneeling to feather dust the tiny figures of the crèche. She never understood why anyone would tell the Christmas story with a bit of sadness. Mother, father and child—poor, yes, she didn't deny that—but they were together. A family.

Rousing herself from looking into the past again, Erin finished folding the sheets, unable to understand why business seemed to be picking up, not slackening off in this holiday season.

With every day that passed, she heard the women talking and learned that she was not the only one Jaffery claimed owed him for his expenses. Each woman who worked in his house paid him a handsome share of her money for his operational costs. Every time a group of church ladies banded together and voiced an outcry against the houses of prostitution, political payoffs increased to keep them open.

To Erin, it appeared to be a vicious circle. The more money Jaffery demanded, the harder and longer the women worked. For most of them the alternative would be the street.

In the two months she had been here, she had seen a few fights break out, but these days were marked by increased drunkenness, fighting and violence against the women.

Daily, she prayed for her letter to come. She was exhausting herself trying to fight the desperation that hovered in the back of her mind.

She set a date of January fifth of the new year as the day she would leave here. Believing herself to be close to four months along, Erin knew the constant running up and down the stairs, too little sleep and her own nerves were draining whatever strength she had. Keeping this baby became the most important goal in her daily struggles.

Erin confided her plan to leave to Maddie, and the woman, once again coming to her rescue, took up a clothing donation from the others. Every minute that Erin could steal from her chores was spent tearing garments apart, stealing lace from this one, a flounce from another, and stitching them into more modest styles. All the clothes underwent a transformation, except for the lilac satin robe Florence had left behind.

Alone in her room, Erin slipped it on, feeling the smooth, lush weight of the robe. She blushed when she saw herself in the mirror. The robe had no fastening but for a tie. The sleeves fell open when she raised her arms to examine the rectangular shape of the material that formed them. The back was thickly embroidered with flowers of every color and shape. The hem trailed behind her when she walked. She felt soft, feminine and just a bit wicked wearing the robe.

For the first time, she gave some thought to the man behind the letters that might mean her freedom and the realization of her dream.

What was Mace Dalton like? She had never asked him to describe his own appearance. Not that his looks would matter. As long as he was kind, she didn't care if he were five feet tall and bald. Maddie's favorite customer, one of her steadies, was short, balding and portly, but he never hit her, always brought her a gift and left her a little something extra that Jaffery didn't know about.

Was he a good father to his children? Her mind supplied the answer before she finished asking herself the question. Of course he was. He had cared enough to keep them and find them another mother. He had made a home for them.

Would he like her? Erin didn't know and tried not to care. Freeing her thick black hair from its tightly pinned roll, she shook it until a few waves curled near the ends that brushed her waist.

She peered closely at her face in the hazed mirror, the shadows beneath her eyes marring the flawless skin she had been blessed with. Her hand curled and drifted down to rest on her stomach, which was still flat, she saw and felt, spreading her fingers.

"I'll keep you safe, little one. Mama will make us a home somewhere."

"Erin! Erin, it's here! Where are you?"

Erin heard Maddie screeching her name throughout the house, but she was outside in the alley emptying the honey buckets.

"Stupid name for the darn things," she muttered, gazing at the low water level left in the common water barrel that served four buildings. Scrunching up her nose at the fetid smell of the alley, Erin had to lean dangerously over the edge of the barrel to scoop up half a bucket full. She used this to wash out the soiled buckets. She had never liked the job of emptying chamber pots, but Jaffery was too cheap to supply them.

Trying to manage eight buckets to save herself an extra trip taxed her strength, but she toted her awkward burdens until each bucket stood before someone's door.

It was a wasted trip up to her own room, for Maddie was gone. Back downstairs, Erin knocked on Maddie's door, hoping that Jaffery wasn't calling for her. Wiping her hands on her apron, she slipped inside as soon as Maddie opened the door.

"Well, now I know where you were, Erin. Emptying the buckets." Maddie wrinkled her nose. Taking the letter up from the clutter of her dresser, she handed it to her. "Hurry and see what he's written," Maddie urged Erin, who seemed to be all thumbs.

Erin didn't notice the bank draft that fell. She quickly scanned the lines of bold masculine writing, which she had memorized from rereading his one letter. Maddie's unladylike whistle of approval meant nothing to her, for she reached the end and turned the letter over only to find there was nothing more and no signature.

"I don't understand, Maddie. He didn't finish it."

"Look at this and stop questioning."

Erin could do little else but look at the bank draft Maddie held up before her. Erin's eyes widened. "Maddie, it's for one hundred dollars."

"Sure is," she answered, smacking the flat of her hand against the draft. "Looks like you've got yourself a man, honey."

Erin flung her arms around her friend, tears brimming in her eyes. "He wants me, Maddie. Me. He really wants to marry me."

"And why not? You're likely gonna be too good for him."

"No, you mustn't think that." Erin pulled free, her voice and gaze pleading. "He's the one who is good and kind. He's the one who's offering me all that I've dreamed of. I'm afraid Maddie. How can I write and tell him about the baby?"

Gripping Erin's shoulders, Maddie gave her a little shake. "Listen to me. You are not going to write and tell him anything but the fact that you're coming. Once he sees you, honey, he won't care about the baby."

"How can he not? Don't men set a store by their children?"

"Sure they do. But he's got two of his own and this baby is yours. Don't let doubts lose this chance for you, Erin. I've got a ship's mate who'll get you passage as soon as you cash that." Maddie released her, hoping that she was right.

"I've never had so much money. But Maddie, we mustn't be reckless spending this. You'll ask your friend to find me cheap accommodations. I won't have Mr. Dalton thinking I'll be costing him more than I'm worth."

Biting her lip not to shout at Erin for her stubborn belief about her own worth, Maddie also had to refrain from asking her how she expected not to cost the man money with a baby on the way. The light in the room was poor, but she could see Erin's eyes shining with joy. This was no time to spoil it for her.

"Well, now that we have all the practical matters settled, we'll celebrate. You're the first one to marry and all the girls will send you off in style. Every bride deserves a few new things to take with her. Wait here, I'll tell the others." Maddie paused by the door. "And Erin, I want to be the first to wish you happy. I hope every dream you have comes true."

"You could come with me. You don't have to stay here, Maddie." Erin made no attempt to hide her fear. Maddie was her only friend and now she had to leave her.

"Honey, forget me. You take up your new life as the respectable Mrs. Dalton with her lovely family and, I hope, kind husband."

"I'll write you once I'm there. Please, Maddie, don't ask me to cut all ties with you. If I can escape my past maybe you can, too."

Maddie came back and hugged her. "You're good, Erin, deep inside where it counts. I'm happy that it all worked out for the best."

"Yes, it did. All for the best."

When Maddie left her, Erin tried not to think too far into the future. She reread the little that Mr. Dalton had written about his children, about the chores that would be hers.

Ignoring the work she would be expected to do, she dreamed about the quiet little boy named Jake and the sweet obedient Rebecca.

Erin refused to speculate about the man she would marry. The only thing she was sure of was that Mace Dalton would be told about the baby before they married.

It was not vanity about her looks that made her hold out hope that once he saw her, it wouldn't matter. It was the exacting list of chores that spoke of need for a woman's help.

With these thoughts in mind, Erin counted off the days before she would begin her new life.

Chapter Three

The room Mace occupied in the St. Louis Hotel overlooked Main Street. He stood by the window, but his attention was focused on the letter he held, announcing Erin Dunmore's arrival on or about the thirteenth of January. If she had taken a steamer up from San Francisco to Portland the trip would cover about four to six days. He guessed the stern-wheelers that plied the Columbia River's almost three hundred miles would take another few days, since they made frequent stops to unload cargo and discharge and pick up passengers. Ketch had insisted that Mace come to Walla Walla a few days early to arrange for the hotel room, a celebration meal and the wedding.

Mace had grudgingly agreed that he couldn't bring Erin out to the Diamond without marrying her first, but he did not swallow the idea with grace. He was restless waiting for her arrival, wondering what she looked like, telling himself he didn't care. He questioned how much of what she had written to him was lies, then thought of how he would explain his own rules for this marriage.

Mace tried to remember that his children needed her. Ketch had threatened to quit if he came back without her.

Moments later, phrases from her letter accepting his proposal drifted back to him. She hoped he possessed a genial disposition, that he shared her desire for a large family, and prayed that he would be generous in giving her time to accustom herself to his ways.

The opinion held by his hands was that he needed a woman to soften his disposition. Mace had already taken care of getting the woman, but he had no desire to have children with her. The last of her requests he could grant with ease. She could have all the time she wanted. Would have it, if she married him.

Yet his impression that Erin Dunmore was too good to be true still nagged him. There was that word again, *good*.

Was he going to saddle himself with a paragon of virtue? And why should he care?

There had been only one woman who from the first had invoked in Mace a sweet passion that was gently consuming. There would never be another.

He turned away from the window and the intrusion of the past. Ketch had warned him to bury the past, both for himself and this woman he would marry and share his life with. But Mace could not stop the feeling of resentment that flooded his mind. Why should he be thinking about her virtue, or the passion he had known, when he had no intention of this being anything but a marriage in name only?

It took a few seconds for him to realize someone was knocking at his door.

"Mr. Dalton, it's me, Donny. You said to come get you when she got here."

Mace opened the door. "Where is she?"

"Downstairs in the lobby. I told her to wait."

He handed the towheaded boy a dollar gold piece, thanked him and shut the door. The wait was over. He was about to meet his bride.

Slowly unrolling his shirtsleeves, Mace was beset by a sudden case of nerves. He buttoned up his shirt, tied his string tie and tugged on his jacket. Scowling, he took a moment to look at his reflection in the mirror, slicking back his freshly cut hair and smoothing down his mustache. His hand moved of its own volition to the bottle of bay rum and for a moment he felt as he were standing outside himself as he lifted the stopper and splashed a few drops into his palm. Rubbing both hands together, he patted his clean-shaven cheeks then realized what he was doing.

He was spit-polished and shined for Miss Erin Dunmore's approval. Shooting a look of disgust at his image, he swore, turned away and left his room.

There was only one woman in the lobby as he reached the top of the stairs. He came to a sudden stop and watched her slowly walk back and forth. He cursed Ketch to the bottom of Hell's Canyon.

Erin Dunmore had a walk that whispered she was all woman. She turned and the sight of her hit him like raw lightning. Every muscle in his body tightened. The breath he was holding left his body in a rush and he was thankful that she did not notice him.

He needed time. Time to reconcile the vague image he had of a good, plain woman of modest manner to the incredibly lovely woman who was sleek and graceful and arousing him like hell on fire.

She paused and looked out the wide front window and he stared at her profile. He needed to find fault with her. Why that was important, he could not fathom. Her chin angled up, revealing a rounded line, lips that hinted of passion in their defined fullness and a nose whose tip turned up a bit. Even from this distance he noticed the thick lushness of her lashes, the faint arch of her dark brows against the fair cream of her skin.

Mace wanted her the way he wanted sweet, cold spring water in the heat of summer. And he hated her for making him want her, for bringing his arousal so swiftly that its heat and speed stunned him.

"Mr. Dalton," the desk clerk called from below.

Erin jerked her gaze from the window. The instant her eyes came to rest on the man at the top of the stairs, she sucked in her breath.

His eyes, so dark they appeared black, pierced straight through her. But that was not what stole her breath. It was the hostile intensity smoldering from his gaze that held her still.

The rest of his face was as startling as his eyes. All hard angles, like the cut of the mountains that left her breathless when she first saw them. His cheekbones were high and sharp, his jaw perfectly square. Above wide, narrow lips, was the dark brush of his mustache. His nose was long, but slightly crooked as if it had been broken. He continued to stare at her as he slowly walked down the stairs, and the contempt in his eyes chilled her.

Erin wanted to cry out, but she did not make a sound. She had to stand there and wait until he stood beside her. The life of her baby as well as her own dream was at stake.

But as she stared at the tall, powerful man whose dark presence she found so intimidating, and whose eyes revealed nothing of what he was thinking, she wondered what the cost would be.

"Do you want Donny to take Miss Dunmore's bag to your room, Mr. Dalton?"

Mace jerked his head up and pinned his gaze on the clerk. Her bag? His room? Sweet suffering saints!

"Mr. Dalton?" she queried in a soft, musical lilt.

The sound of his name scoured his nerve ends. Before he could stop himself he was full, aching and ready, and he swore in disgust at his unruly sex. "Take her bag up to my room," he ordered, his voice a growl of frustration.

Erin glanced at his face then to one side. She was not reassured by this beginning. He was younger than she expected, and his voice, although deep, was sharp and cutting.

Mace turned his attention to her. "I hope you had a pleasant trip. We can spend the night here, but in the morning we leave for the ranch."

"But I had thought to have some time. We should...we need to talk...to become acquainted."

Mace looked at her eyes, as dark a green as the leaves of the alpine lilies, and listened to his body talk to him. There was no way he was going to spend time with her in town with everyone watching and expecting them to share a room. He had to get her to the ranch. He needed open space between them.

Erin knew his answer before he spoke. She was polite as she listened to his denial of her request, fighting her tiredness, fighting the feeling of being unsure of herself and determined not to reveal any weakness to him.

"Want me to bring hot water up now, Mr. Dalton?"

Annoyed with the interruption, Mace stared blankly at the clerk. The only word he heard was hot, because that described exactly what he was.

"Hot water, sir?" the man repeated.

"For what?" he snapped.

"Miss Dunmore might want to refresh herself." He glanced helplessly at the woman. "Ma'am?"

Erin wanted to do more than refresh herself. The thought of hot water and a bed brought a soft, dreamy look to her eyes, but she lowered her lashes and waited for this overwhelming stranger to decide her course.

"Won't have time now," Mace finally answered, ignoring the twinge of guilt he felt when he sensed that was what she wanted. "I've had the preacher standing by every day, waiting for you to arrive."

"A preacher? But I hoped to be married by a priest."

"Well, up here you can't always get what you hope for."

Erin flushed then turned pale. Her chin lifted a notch. "If you are disappointed and find fault with me, Mr. Dalton, there is no need for us to—"

"Oh, yes, there is."

He didn't elaborate and she couldn't bring herself to ask for an explanation. She felt threatened and drawn to him at the same time. His raw masculine appeal and its effect on her were new. She didn't have the experience to stop the heat shimmering through her from his presence. A small voice warned her to let him have his way. Hurry and marry him and then it would be too late. But Erin knew the cruel pain of lies; she would not inflict them on another.

Seeking to buy time, she glanced around. "Where are the children? I had hoped to meet them."

"You will, soon enough," he snapped, hoping that once they were married she wouldn't turn her anger for his lies on Rebecca or Jake. He soothed his conscience with the thought that he hadn't really lied to her, he had just omitted a bit of information. Information that prevented him from finding a wife from among the single women in Walla Walla or nearby towns.

Erin's thoughts ran parallel to his. Mace Dalton was attractive. Why didn't he seek a wife from nearby? She sensed he had a temper. Could he be a violent man? Was that why he had not brought the children to meet with her?

Mace offered his arm, feeling he had given her enough time, more than he wanted to.

Erin glanced down at the stained plum velvet box-pleated hem of her walking suit. The matching colored silk overskirt that gathered in an apron front was wrinkled. She didn't bother to look at the demi-train. She knew the velvet was crushed and marked by the careless boots of men who had continuously approached her in her travels. Erin felt his watchful gaze as she brushed the front of the long basquine, puffed up the dolman sleeves and straightened her plum velvet Normandy bonnet with its pale lilac silk ruche. Smoothing her buff gloves, she placed her arm through the crook of his elbow and looked up at him.

"Having second thoughts, Miss Dunmore?" he asked, his eyes warming as he looked from the delicate curve of her neck to her mouth and wondered how she tasted.

The taunting quality of his voice more than the words made her spine stiffen. Erin had been having second thoughts since she had left San Francisco. His unseemly haste was throwing her plan to tell him the truth once they had had an opportunity to meet and talk right out the door. She was unwilling to argue with him, afraid that he would send her back.

But Erin knew a sudden surge of panic unlike any other. She could not marry him with a lie between them. This was not a matter to hide. "Please, Mr. Dalton, there is a matter I must discuss."

"I'm sure there is. You'll be wanting to know about provisions for yourself should I die. Don't worry, Miss Dunmore, you'll be taken care of as long as you make a home for Rebecca and Jake."

"That is not what I wanted to discuss."

"Didn't you? Well, you'd be the first then who didn't. But we'll have plenty of time to talk later."

He obviously did not have any desire to know more about her. Whatever his reasons for this haste, he was intent on marrying her. But Erin found she had a streak of stubbornness and dug in her heels, unable to let it go.

"I must object and ask that you reconsider this unseemly haste. Marriage, sir, is a serious step."

Mace's amusement with her ruffled feathers faded. He was annoyed with the thought that she might have second thoughts about marrying him now that she had met him. He knew he was attractive to women as a marriage prospect. It wasn't vanity about his looks, but the certainty that his bank account and thriving ranch would overcome most female qualms. And he wanted Miss Erin Dunmore to realize that.

A warning cloud settled over his hard features. "I am well aware of how serious marriage is. I've already taken the step. Have you?"

"No, I've not been married," she whispered in a faint voice, wondering why his eyes had darkened and his mouth appeared somewhat harder.

"If you expected me to play the courting swain, Miss Dunmore, let me disabuse you of that notion right now."

The cold finality of every word pricked Erin and saw a bit of her dream die. Had she been hoping for that very courtship he would deny her? Drawing a quiet dignity from deep inside, she managed a curt nod. "I understand you perfectly, sir. You wish for a mother to your two children and a competent housekeeper. No more, no less."

His gaze lowered from her eyes to her shoulders to her breasts. The stare was bold and assessing, and he made no attempt to hide it. She was miffed, all right. But he did notice that she had been generous when she estimated her weight. About fifteen pounds too much was his guess, and every bit of it irritated female.

The heat of desire climbed high again, clouding his mind. He'd be a fool to let her back him into a corner with the belief—Mace stopped himself. He didn't want to share a bed with her, did he? He was the one who had set the rules of this marriage in his mind. He wasn't going to let her know that she had started an itch that wanted scratching—badly.

Erin licked her lips. She felt the muscles of the arm she held tense and swiftly removed her hand. The fight seeped out of her as exhaustion swept over her. She glanced away from him, closing her eyes briefly, undecided about what to do.

The insidious thought that this meekness she displayed concealed a deeper fear slid into Mace's mind and stayed. He knew he should give her some time; he wasn't an insensitive man. At least he hadn't been with Sky. But the tiny claws of desire were not retracting, they were stretching inside him, warning him to hurry and satisfy them or he'd have no peace.

Yet he found himself leading her away from the door, asking, "If you find me not to your liking—"

"I did not say that."

"You don't have a husband or irate father back in San Francisco that you forgot to tell me about, do you?"

Erin looked up at his face. "No, I don't have anyone. I'm an orphan."

Mace took note of the lack of emotion in her voice. A feeling of pity, which he somehow knew she would take exception to, rose in him but remained hidden. "I assume that you are old enough and free to marry?"

"I would not be here if that were not true, Mr. Dalton. But—" Helplessly, Erin glanced around the lobby again. The clerk had been joined by another man behind the desk. Two men were now engaged in an earnest discussion in one corner and a couple were coming down the stairs. She wished she could find the courage to tell him about her baby, but she couldn't, not here. Not where others could see and hear his reaction. Not when she was unable to sense what that reaction would be.

"Well? If there's nothing else, Miss Dunmore, let's go." Mace took the few steps to the door and yanked it open. "After you." But before she moved, he added, "You didn't lie to me about being able to cook, did you?"

"No, Mr. Dalton. I did not lie to you about my ability to cook, or clean, or sew, or work hard."

"Good. Then we have nothing else to discuss."

A tiny spark of temper flared and grew. Erin glared at him. The man had made it perfectly clear why he was marrying her. If she mattered so little to him as a woman, she would not care what surprises she had in store for him.

Erin sailed out of the door with her head high and her eyes sparking temper.

But the light of temper died immediately. She had to find some way to tell him about her child. Faced with the actual sight of Mace Dalton, not the vague image she had kept in mind, she knew this man had a great deal of pride. That certainty settled deeply inside her, although she didn't know why. She was almost four and a half months along by her closest reckoning. Time seemed to have run out, and she didn't know what to do.

Mace stood a moment, looking at the natural sway of her hips, and wondered if her little fanny was as tempting

as the rest of her. He tried to remember his vow. He surely
did try.

He followed her outside, knowing it was going to be a
long, long night.

Chapter Four

Mace took hold of her arm and led her along Main Street. Erin felt the enormity of what she was about to do settle like a cold, hard lump in her stomach. Yet for every warning that whispered to her to back out now, she countered it with the knowledge that she had no where else to go.

She had twenty dollars left of the money he had sent to her. Taking the cheapest accommodations made her journey a hell. She had never given thought to having to pay for food. The greasy fare offered to travelers wasn't expensive, but she couldn't eat it.

Besides, she had a strong feeling that Mace Dalton would ask for his money back. Erin felt the strain of the silence between them and nervously began to ask him questions about Walla Walla. She hoped that he would reveal more about himself to make him less of a stranger.

Mace answered readily enough, telling her of the town's beginning as a British fur trading fort called Fort Nez Percés, although this was the homeland of the Wallawalla and Cayuse Indians. Most white men still couldn't tell the difference between the tribes. And few wanted to learn.

Erin freed her curiosity and looked wherever she could, listening to the deep, lazy drawl of his voice as he explained the growth the town enjoyed as mining, farming and ranching interests spread in the surrounding area.

She was reassured to learn the town supported six doctors, a surprising number, and that two of them practiced obstetrics. Maddie had warned her to look for such a physician, for she had in her blunt way expressed concern over Erin's narrow hips and poor health. She would be pleased when Erin wrote to her and told her not to worry.

The town boasted two newspapers, *Spirit of the West* and the *Walla Walla Statesman,* along with two fire engine companies. Everything she saw spoke of a thriving community, and Erin felt hope bloom again that she would be a part of this.

Entertainment was not lacking, for Mace told her they had a theater group, skating parties and Grange dances along with church socials. Longing to attend each one filled her. She never learned to skate or dance. Erin had once attended the theater with Silas, but when she asked that they go again, he made excuses. Mace Dalton had not assured her they would be attending any of these offered entertainments, but she could hope for the future.

After a wagon and carriage passed, they crossed Third Street, and she noticed that Mace nodded to almost everyone. He made no attempt to introduce her, and Erin didn't ask him why. She knew what she looked like and couldn't blame him for being ashamed of her appearance.

There were two hotels beside the St. Louis, and Erin smiled when he told her the restaurant was called the San Francisco.

"I've made arrangements for us to have supper there this evening," he stated.

"But how did you know—"

"I've had a standing reservation for a table for the past week."

"That is kind of you, Mr. Dalton."

"Not at all, Miss Dunmore. It is a respectable place to take a wife."

Erin stared straight ahead and thought of how stilted and formal they sounded. Wishing wasn't going to change it. She spotted the small post office as they walked up Second Street. "Would I have time to send off a letter before we leave for your ranch?"

"I thought you said you didn't have anyone?" Mace realized he spoke quickly and harshly, too much so, for she glanced up at him with dismay. He stopped walking and gazed at her.

"As I told you, Mr. Dalton, I have no family. She is a dear friend, the only one I have, and I simply wish to write and let her know that I arrived safely. She was most concerned about my traveling alone."

Mace searched each word, each inflection of her lilting voice for the reprimand he was so sure would be there. But there was none. He found himself forced to acknowledge her quiet dignity as she stood and awaited his response. He apologized, adding, "Of course, there will be time. I'll make sure of it. And don't refer to the Diamond Bar D as my ranch. It is to be your home, too."

Erin's lips formed a smile, a smile that was reflected in her eyes, making him catch his breath. Suddenly aware that he was standing in view of several pairs of curious eyes, Mace once again took her arm and began walking.

Erin kept her smile in place as she saw the City Book Store. She had taken the stern headmistress's advice and did well with the little schooling the orphanage allowed her to have. She would dearly love to buy a book for her very own, but hesitated to ask him to stop now. It was embarrassing to need to ask him if she could spend the balance of his money on a book and small gifts for his children.

Fears that Walla Walla was a wild and rough town faded from her mind. Everything she saw led her to believe this was a thriving, civilized place. If only she could be as sure that Mace Dalton was civilized.

The Methodist Church was up ahead, next to the office and residence of a Dr. Simonton. A man hailed them from the front porch as they walked past.

"Glad I saw you, Mace," he called out. "Save you the trouble of going to the church. He's not there. Got called away almost two hours ago. Stopped here and said to tell you he's not sure when he'll be back."

Erin ignored the mutters that sounded suspiciously like swearing coming from Mace. He stopped, and she with him, as the man she assumed was the doctor came down the steps and walked across the front yard toward where they stood.

She greeted the news that the preacher was not waiting with a burst of fear. Was this an omen that she and Mace would not be married? Had the good Lord taken pity on her need to tell Mace about the baby first, and granted her time?

Mace dispelled the very idea. "Don't worry, there's still the J.P. at City Hall."

"Oh," Erin managed, missing his pointed look.

Mace counted himself lucky that no one he knew had stopped him to demand an introduction. Wil Simonton was not going to let him get away without one. "Miss Erin Dunmore, may I present Dr. Wilbur Simonton."

"Wil to you, Miss Dunmore."

"Then you must call me Erin," she replied, smiling.

"Mace, I've called you this before, but you are a sly devil, ordering yourself the prettiest gal for a wife." And to Erin, he said, "All the marriageable ladies having palpitations every time he came to town and spoke to them was good for my business. You've got yourself a prize catch here, young woman."

"Don't be filling her head with a lot of nonsense, Wil. Women aren't falling over themselves to marry me and you know it."

Erin wasn't looking at the doctor. She watched Mace and found herself surprised to see a dull flush creep into his cheeks.

"Figure you're in a hurry, Mace, marrying her right off the stage."

"Stage?" Mace repeated.

"Ain't you heard the river's nearly two inches down? Can't have river travel till the snows melt. With the weather warming like today to almost forty-five, we should have the snow melt soon and Hell's Gate open."

Mace glanced down at Erin. He hadn't even bothered to ask her how she had arrived. Knowing that she had a rough stage trip behind her made him feel guilty for rushing her out. But he was still uncomfortably aroused by her, even if he damn well knew she had done nothing deliberate to cause it.

"I hope you will be happy, young woman," Wil said, eyeing the delicate shadows beneath Erin's eyes. "You take good care of her, Mace. We'll expect you to bring her to the grand masquerade skating carnival at the end of the month. Folks'll want to meet your bride once I tell them how pretty she is."

"Won't be back to town that soon," Mace answered with an impatient note.

"I'm sure it would be lovely, but I don't know how to skate," Erin added, smiling to soften the rejection of his invitation. She knew by the shrewd look Wil Simonton sent her that she hadn't fooled the portly, bewhiskered doctor.

"Tickets are only fifty cents, Mace. Free skates if you come in a mask. Your children might like it. Don't get to see much of them."

Mace had enough to contend with, feeling that the mask he wore was about to crack. All this while they stood, he noticed that Erin had a habit of licking her bottom lip. If she did it one more time, he was going to lean over and take the tip of that pink little tongue and pretend he was a kid with an all-day sucker.

"You both give it some thought. I've got patients to get back to. Welcome to our town, Miss Dunmore."

"Thank you. You're very kind."

Mace once again took her arm and guided her up the street, across Main and into the City Hall. Jason Crawford, the Justice of the Peace, was in his office and more than pleased to perform the ceremony.

The stark office was not the place Erin had envisioned for her marriage. The dry, almost bored voice reading the vows for them to repeat made it all seem so cold. She truly felt as if she were merchandise ordered and paid for by the man who was promising to endow her with his worldly goods and care for her in sickness and in health. Erin was already attuned to the sound of his voice, and could not miss the pause, or the choked mumble he made of the word love. She began to tremble even as he recovered and spoke in a stronger tone that he would honor and cherish her.

This was wrong. She knew it. There was no way she could go through with this. But where could she go without money? Who would take care of her and her baby? She didn't think Mace had noticed her trembling, but his hand covered hers, which was resting on his arm.

"Erin is tired from her trip, Jason. She'll be all right now to finish." When her gaze locked on his, he added, "Won't you, Erin?"

The question was a warning for her not to embarrass him, and she took it. Erin didn't think she had moisture enough in her mouth to repeat one word. But somehow she did, somehow the cold band of gold found its way onto her finger, and then Mr. Crawford was smiling, closing his book and urging Mace to kiss his bride.

He placed both hands on her upper arms and drew her toward him. Mace lowered his head, angling for a brief touch of his lips to hers, but he found himself staring into her wide green eyes, which darkened as he watched with a strange sensual curiosity. Once more his muscles clenched and he found himself wishing they were alone and that he was free to take that dusky rose shaded mouth the way he wanted to. Completely. Deep. Hard. Fast. The temptation to slide his tongue into that sweet mouth surprised, then angered him. He pressed his lips lightly against hers, intending to pull back.

Good intentions went to hell.

With a tiny rush of breath, Erin's lips parted slightly. Her mouth softened with unconscious invitation as she felt the silky brush of his mustache, the warmth of his lips.

She could feel the hard lineup of their thighs, the crush of her belly and breasts against the unyielding hardness of his body. Her gaze seemed helplessly caught in his. The eyes she thought near black were dark brown splintered by flecks of gold. Every intake of breath brought her his scents, all richly masculine, so subtly layered she couldn't distinguish them.

Erin's breathing grew shallow. She didn't understand why she wanted this kiss. His hands, moving gently in tiny circular motions, drew her closer. With a breath-catching languor, his mouth caressed hers, his dark lashes drifting closed. And her eyes closed, too, the beat of her heart hammering in her throat, in her head.

The delicate swirl of their mingled breaths, the generous giving of her mouth, made desire explode through Mace. For one wild moment he deepened the kiss, skimming the seam of her lips with his tongue, urging her to open for him. She was satin sweetness, yielding with innocence that both infuriated and tempted him.

With a savage move he jerked his head back and stepped away from her.

Bewildered, Erin stared at him while he paid the justice. What had she done wrong? Her only experience was with Silas and he had never quite kissed her like that. But his had been a deliberate seduction. And she, whether out of need for love, her loneliness or whatever excuses she offered to herself, had given him what he wanted. But Mace Dalton seemed to want more. She had never felt the ache that this man, her lawfully wedded husband, stirred. As much as it excited her, Erin didn't deny that it frightened her, too.

He was silent and abrupt, taking her arm and leading her to the hotel. Once up the stairs to his room, he opened the door, but remained in the hallway.

"You should have told me you'd come by stage. Learn to speak up, Miss Dunmore. I can't pretend to be a fake and read your mind."

Miss Dunmore? The name stung, coming from the lips of the man she had just promised to love, obey, honor and cherish. She could barely nod in acknowledgment.

"Well? Go inside. Your bag is there and I'll have hot water sent up. When you're done, come down to the lobby and I'll take you to supper."

"Yes, Mr. Dalton. Thank you kindly, Mr. Dalton. Your thoughtfulness and consideration are overwhelming, if not too late." With that said, Erin stepped over the threshold and closed the door in his face.

It was going to be a long, long night.

Mace had thought so before and now knew it to be fact. He stared at the darker swirls of the knots in the wooden door, wishing he had never kissed her, wishing that the fierce elation that Erin Dunmore was as innocent as she was tempting would disappear.

Sliding his hands into his pants pockets, Mace rocked back on his heels. He was going to skin Ketch alive. She wasn't at all what he wanted. This was no plain-faced, levelheaded sober woman of modest manner. She had a temper. She was pretty. Her lips were too soft, too giving. And he mustn't forget that walk. Or that pink little tongue.

He could likely stand here all night and make a list of what was wrong with her. But he wouldn't. It was too late. He had married her. Taken her to wife. And the guilt began beating on him. Sky had been dead for five years; why did he suddenly feel as if he had cheated on her?

With a loathing directed at himself, he spun around and left.

Erin sagged against the closed door. He was gone. Repent at leisure. Well, she had all the time in the world to repent her mistake. She had been too hasty to enter into this marriage. Mace Dalton wasn't at all what she hoped for. He wasn't a sober, kindly man at all. He was arrogant. And hurtful. He shouldn't have kissed her as if she were fragile, courting her lips and body with subtle promises.

She mustn't forget the sense of danger in him. And she knew, if she were not exhausted, that she could and would go on.

But there was tonight to get through and all the days to follow. Miss Dunmore, indeed. How could the man be so callous? If he had no regard for her feelings, what would he do when he learned she was going to have a baby?

It was the fierce protectiveness of her child that finally spurred Erin away from the door. Somehow she had to survive her mistake.

Time. That was all she needed. Time to show Mace Dalton that she would be a good mother to his children, a good housekeeper and an obedient wife.

Removing her hat, she set the hat pins on his dresser top among his personal items. The brush and comb had been carelessly tossed down, the shaving brush was still damp in its mug and the bottle of bay rum uncorked. Erin replaced it and took up the crumpled linen towel, smoothing and folding it. She saw the rumpled bed reflected in the mirror, and averted her gaze.

She couldn't think about later. She didn't dare.

The knock on the door signaling the arrival of hot water put an end to her musings. She already knew Mace was an impatient man. There was no sense in irritating him by making him wait longer for her.

Chapter Five

Erin toyed with the scalloped lace edge of her collar. The meal that Mace had ordered was meant for those with hearty appetites. Neither one of them had done justice to the food, and she was thankful the last of it had been cleared. The return of barely touched food caused the proprietor, Mr. Philbrook, to come to the table, asking what was wrong, offering to make them something else.

Embarrassed by the attention they drew, Erin didn't listen to Mace's whispered explanation, but a bottle of champagne arrived with the man's compliments. Erin had never tasted the sparkling wine and, urged on by the feeling that if she didn't drink one glass, Mr. Philbrook would return, she indulged. Mace, she noticed, had no qualms about filling his glass before it emptied.

"Will you share the last of it?" he asked her, annoyed with the way she fidgeted and refused to look at him.

Erin did not look at him, but at the bottle he was holding midway across the table. She nodded, hating herself for being grateful that he broke the silence stretching her nerves raw.

Focusing on the tiny bubbles rising from the bottom of the glass, Erin wondered what he would have done if she had stated her preference for chicken instead of the thick steaks he had ordered. It was petty, she knew, but suggested to her that her likes and dislikes did not matter to him.

And then, as the floodgates opened on his transgressions, she had to remind herself of the curt introductions he had made for her when the curious stopped by the table to offer their congratulations. It was unfair of her to be angry with him for the brevity of his announcement that she was from San Francisco, had had an uneventful journey and was anxiously looking forward to ranch living. He had saved her from lying, and that was the only reason she held her tongue.

The few questions she had braved about the children and his ranch earned her a repeated, "You'll see for yourself when you get there."

She didn't understand his cutting her off before she had been able to utter a word to the two women who ventured to suggest that she might join their church and sewing circle, for they had the best socials. Did he intend to keep her imprisoned on his ranch? Or was he ashamed of her? Erin wished for the courage to ask him, but one peek at his face revealed the same hardened expression that had greeted her on their first sight of each other.

Beneath her napkin, her hand crept to curve over her belly. She knew before long she wouldn't dare let anyone see her, for everyone would know that the baby wasn't his. And that was all she should be worrying about. What his reaction would be.

Her gaze pinned on his hands. Small scars that bespoke his hard living marred the skin of large, strong fingers. The glass appeared almost fragile-looking when he lifted it; Erin refused to think of those hands touching her.

With the same recklessness that set her on this path, Erin lifted her own glass and fixed her gaze on the flame of the candle burning steadily inside the glass chimney of the table lamp. She sipped the champagne until it was gone. Carefully setting the glass down, she hoped the tiny bubbles would rise inside her with a flush of lightness to dispel the dark mood the brooding man she married had created.

Within seconds, Mace finished his drink, settled the bill and came around to help her on with her serviceable black coat that had seen better days. When his hands stilled on her shoulders, Erin was sure he was staring at the mended tears on her sleeve. If he dared to say one word, she would tell him about her *uneventful* trip, which resulted in those tears. He didn't utter a sound.

Taking her arm once more, he led her outside. Erin shivered in the cold. The coat was thin, and the green silk gown, so carefully made over to a modest style to be her wedding gown, offered little protection against the chill. She inhaled deeply and knew she had been granted a part of her hope. The champagne had brought a lightness, for her head felt as if it were drifting off somewhere.

Watching where they walked, she began to hum softly, ignoring the man at her side. All too soon they were at the hotel door. The lobby was deserted when they entered; even the desk clerk had abandoned his post. Two wall lamps spread a dim light to see by.

Erin glanced across the lobby to the stairs looming before them. Fear surfaced. The fear she had succeeded in almost burying throughout the day. She had entrusted her life and that of her child to this man. This stranger.

Her shoe seemed to stick to the rug and she lost her balance, pitching forward.

Mace caught her and swung her up into his arms. She found herself staring owlishly up at his face. His cheeks were already darkened by the shadow of a beard. A slow smile broke the hard line of his lips. Erin closed her eyes. His body warmed hers, and beneath her hand she felt the strength of his shoulder. Curiosity forced her to look at him. She hadn't imagined it; he was smiling at her. A small corner of fear snapped off and she thought of how he must feel, married to a woman who was as much of a stranger to him as she felt he was to her. The corners of her mouth lifted as she hesitantly slid her arm around his neck.

"I thought you said you wouldn't play the courting swain," she teased, trying hard to release the tension between them.

"I'm not. Couldn't let you fall and hurt yourself, Miss Dunmore." But he didn't even think about setting her down. He liked the feel of her in his arms, enjoyed the sensation of being stronger and powerful enough to protect her. But he didn't understand why her smile faded and she looked away.

Intoxicated by the unaccustomed champagne and sense of being soft and fragile in his arms, Erin no longer guarded her tongue. "I must beg your pardon, Mr. Dalton," she intoned in a voice that would have done a society matron proud. "I'm no longer Miss Dunmore. I am your wife, sir. Entitled, I believe, to all the rights and privileges of that position." With the last said, she nestled her head on his shoulder, closed her eyes and waited.

Rights and privileges? Mace repeated silently, having spent the last uncomfortable hours brooding over the fit of his pants and the coming night. Well, he wasn't about to deny her any one of them.

He took the stairs so quickly that Erin was forced to cling to him. She averted her gaze from him when he set her down to get the key from his pocket.

She knew when he opened the door and disappeared into the darkened room. She heard him move around, but made no attempt to follow him. With both hands, Erin held her head. She wanted the spinning sensations to stop.

Her mind was intent on replaying the very moment she had lost her balance and he swung her up into his arms. The man had been cold, rude and silent, but she had felt the protective strength he offered.

As if she were standing apart, watching herself, she heard again exactly what she had said to him.

Clasping her gloved hand over her mouth, Erin sagged against the wall. Mace Dalton must think her a brazen piece of baggage. She had practically demanded that he bed her.

The thought was more than sobering; it was horrifying. The pleasant sensations she enjoyed from the champagne dissolved like her backbone. She had presented herself as a respectable woman and he would know as soon as she told him about the baby that she wasn't. There had been no need for her to foolishly plant the wrong idea in his mind. Lord, grant me time, she prayed. Let me be everything he wanted before I tell him my secret.

"Do you need help?"

Erin looked up at him, partially framed in the doorway. The spill of light from the room behind him enhanced the darkness of his hair. He had removed his suit jacket. The cream linen shirt stretched across his shoulders, and the ends of his black string tie trailed alongside the now open buttons of his shirt. She tried not to stare at the strong brown column of his throat, but curiosity held her gaze to the spot where his pulse visibly beat. With an unconscious gesture, Erin raised her hand to touch her throat.

"What's wrong?" Mace asked, answering himself with the next breath. She claimed that she had never been married. He didn't think she was lying. He knew, likely better than she did, that society's rules demanded a woman be kept ignorant about sex. Did she suddenly find the thought of intimacy with him distasteful? What the hell did she think marriage meant? The remembered feel of her lips softening, parting slightly for his kiss made him dismiss his questions. Erin hadn't been the one to pull away, he had.

Tunneling his fingers through his hair, he tried to stem the flashes of another wedding night from coming to mind. Sky, lovely and innocent, had not been shy with him. She had been as eager as he to consummate their marriage. Her gentle manner had been no less passionate than his fierce tenderness to claim her as his wife. But Sky was dead. And he was very much alive. He could no longer name Sky his wife. Erin Dunmore held that place in his life now.

"Is the room not to your liking? Are you sick? Do you need something? Good lord, woman, tell me what's wrong?"

He offered her the opening she needed. Erin gazed at his face and found nothing soft. His eyes drew hers, and there was no mistaking the desire within those dark eyes. The words she needed to say stuck in her throat. He repeated his question.

"Nothing," she whispered.

Stepping closer, he gently grasped her arm, drawing her near. "Come inside."

The warmth of his breath brushed her cheek. Erin hoped for gentleness and preceded him into the room. She refused to look at the bed, but she wished he would leave.

Mace had no intention of leaving. He knew he was deliberately misconstruing her remarks about being his wife. But there were times, he was learning, when a man boxed up his conscience for other needs.

Survival needs. Like today, when he didn't mention that his children weren't accepted by society before he married her. And now he was doing it again. He wanted this woman. Wanted her before he had teased himself with the taste of her mouth. The impossible demands his body had been making since he had first seen her were intensifying.

Instinct told him that once he had bedded her, she wouldn't leave him. It wasn't from vanity for his skill as a lover that this certainty came, but from the woman herself.

His patience was in short supply at the moment. He wasn't going to try to figure all the reasons this strength of conviction about her was there. He knew he couldn't wait much longer when passion upped a notch from heat to burning.

He watched her withdraw the pins from her hat, then the hat itself. He attributed her continued silence to nerves. Uncertain what he could say to put her at ease, he gave in to his need to touch her and stood behind her, cupping her shoulders. Feeling the tension in her body, although she made no move to pull free, he finally realized that she would like, even welcome, privacy.

A rueful smile creased his lips. With Sky he had shared everything. There had been no shame for the passion that claimed them wherever they were. But Erin was a lady, he reminded himself. She was unused to a man's ways, his ways. With a cynical twist of mind, he knew that every kindness and consideration he offered her now would pay off once he brought her home.

From behind her, he reached out to touch the small feathers on her hat, gently crowding her body with his. The tiny catch her breath made told him she was aware of him as a man. His lips brushed against the delicate shape of her ear. When he took a breath, he inhaled the faint smell of flowers and her skin. The scent went through him like lightning, for it carried a promise of warm woman, a promise repeated in the soft press of her back against his chest.

"Am I wrong in believing that you'd like a few minutes alone?"

Erin turned her head so fast her lips grazed his cheek. Her green eyes had darkened. She stared at his mouth, far too close, and a fine tremor rippled over her skin. "Please," she managed to whisper, moistening her lip with the tip of her tongue.

Desire knifed through him, hardening him with a speed that shocked him. "Then I'll wait outside until you're ready. But Erin," he murmured, brushing his finger over the arch of her brow, "don't keep me waiting long."

His slow smile made a warmth awaken and shimmer deep inside her. "No. I won't be long." Heat climbed into her face at the breathless sound of her voice. For a moment she thought he would kiss her and her breath rushed in, wanting the touch of his mouth again. Her lashes drifted closed, but as her breath sighed out, she heard the door close softly.

Erin never tried undressing so fast. The more she hurried, fed by an urgency to be fully covered in that bed before he returned, the more clumsy she was. The ties on her corset knotted, her fingers frantic to get them undone. She couldn't find the buttonhook for her shoes until she searched the second valise. Throwing a panicked look at the still shut door, she slid the voluminous flannel nightgown on, unpinned her hair and quickly braided it. With pounding heart she gathered the thick folds of the night-gown and ran for the bed.

Mace opened the door seconds later and glanced at her, hiding with the covers pulled up to her chin. Her eyes were closed, but with the soft glow of the lamp, he could see the faint flutter her lashes made as she watched him. He stripped off his shirt, tossing it on the chair. And Mace knew then that he didn't just want to satisfy the desire obsessing him, he wanted Erin to want him. Kicking off his boots, he smiled to see how hard she was pretending not to watch him. Since he didn't need her screaming at her first sight of a naked man, he turned his back toward her to unbutton his pants.

With the carelessness of a man who more often than not worked eighteen hours a day, fell asleep in his clothes and didn't have a woman nagging him, Mace left his socks and long underwear where they fell. He came to the side of the bed and tossed back the covers.

Erin's eyes flew open and were snagged by his intense gaze. "Please, the lamp. You can't mean to leave it on."

The crude words of wanting to see exactly what he had bought himself remained unspoken. She lay there, rigid as a board and terrified. She stared up at his face, giving him the feeling that if she dared look anywhere else she'd fall to pieces. Ladies! Hell! He strode to the dresser and turned down the wick until dark enfolded them.

Erin felt the bed dip beneath his weight. The soft feather mattress depressed and she had to clutch the side so she wouldn't roll up against him. With her free hand she grabbed for the quilt and pulled it up to her chin. She had never thought about this part.

"Listen to me," he began, hating the feeling that she was cringing away from him. "Erin?" he asked softly.

She saw the faint outline of his body looming over her and her chest rose and fell with the erratic breaths she drew.

"I won't hurt you. We can take this slow and easy." Mace groaned hearing his promise. Slow? Easy? What the hell was the matter with him?

What was he talking about? Erin asked herself. Slow and easy? Maddie had not neglected to inform her of all the ways a man took his pleasure. Slow and easy was not one of them. Or had Maddie mentioned it and she, flushing with embarrassment, hadn't listened? He seemed to be waiting for her to say something.

"Fine. That will be fine."

A sigh of pure disgust that he didn't attempt to hide escaped him. Mace leaned away from her but not far enough. He heard the small frightened sound she made. He strove to take control of his body, but need came clawing like a steel spur over his skin. He punched up his pillows and rested against the headboard, knowing he should have given this more thought.

But he wasn't good at talking. He'd never had any complaints when he left a woman's bed. Flo Jamison could attest to that even if she refused to marry him. With Flo it hadn't been the children, just too many years of being under a man's hand and wanting her freedom. But Flo was part of the past, and Erin, shaking rabbit that she was, was all he had for a future.

And he wasn't about to start this marriage off with her having any control. "Erin, come here."

He counted off the seconds before he felt her wiggle a few inches nearer. At this rate the night would be half gone before she managed to get next to him. Mace reached for her and drew her tense body to his side. Again he began to count, striving for patience, but by five, he turned, one hand on her waist the other stroking her hair.

He lowered his head, feathering kisses across her temple, brushing her cheeks with his lips, tracing the rigid line of her jaw. Lifting her arm, he placed it around his neck, fitting his mouth to hers. He kept the kiss light, finding the corners of her mouth with the tip of his tongue, stroking over her bottom lip, coaxing her response.

Mace refused to believe she was cold. The thick flannel nightgown had enough yardage to make a man-size tent and he wanted it gone. Sky had never slept with anything wrapped around her but him.

But when his fingers touched the top button, her hand snaked between him and the cloth, stopping him. "What in the Lord's name are you doing?"

"Something the good Lord intended when he made you a woman and me a man."

Rather than fight her to open the button, Mace lifted her hand to his mouth. Turning her hand over, he kissed her palm, sliding his tongue over the chilled skin until his teeth gently bit the fleshy pad at the base of her thumb.

With a tiny flip, Erin's stomach turned over. She felt the silky brush of his mustache against the pulse in her wrist. His body heat surrounded her, making the shimmering sensations inside her turn to an ache. Her heart increased its beat and she didn't resist when he pulled her fingers to the warm curve of his neck. Her hand measured the strength there and, unable to deny her curiosity, she explored the thickness of his hair.

Their breaths mingled, growing deeper, keeping a cadence that was rife with tension. The scent of him filled her, and when he brought his mouth to hers, she wanted his kiss. Behind closed eyelids, the sight of his naked strength sent flutters from her breast to her knees. She had been too afraid of him catching her staring to open her eyes and look her fill. But what she had seen fascinated her. Without realizing it, Erin began to explore that strength, sliding her hand over his shoulder, down his muscled arm, feeling the soft hair that covered his forearm and working her way up again. Her mouth swelled and parted, her body turned to his and she wanted more of the kiss that was so gently coaxing her into a dreamy feeling of being cherished.

She had been so wrong to fear him. There was nothing frightening about the skim of his tongue over her lips. He wasn't ripping the protective cloth from her. He wasn't moving at all.

Mace thought about racks. In particular, the one he was on. The cool slide of her hand over his burning skin made a wildness flow through his body. Blood heated and pooled. Hunger prowled like a winter-starved wolf, and he tested the limit of his control not to take her mouth the way he wanted. Man hungry. Hard. Deep. Fast. As the seconds passed and brought his body to a shocking hardness, hers softened.

A shudder ripped through him. She made a tiny sound and opened her mouth. Sweet velvet warmth beckoned him to taste. And the tiny sounds came again. He rocked his mouth back and forth over hers, drawing her closer, dipping his tongue into the honey sweet taste of her mouth. He held the kiss until their breathing was broken, her heart pounding as hard as his own. He stroked her fragile collarbone, mentally cursed the thick cloth as he shaped her shoulder and scored his blunt fingers down her spine.

Patience was rewarded. Erin followed the lift of his mouth, clasping her hand to his head so he couldn't back away, and pressed against his chest.

Shivering with the strange pleasure streaking through her, Erin felt the flex and play of his muscles with her every touch. The fear of his strength and power was fast disappearing. Timidly, she touched his lips with the tip of her tongue. She felt his powerful body tremble just as hers did. Erin thought she was balanced on the edge of a cliff; fire was waiting, enticing her, if only she had the courage to reach out for it.

Her palm caressed the beard stubble on his cheek, her tongue growing bold, seeking the warmth beyond the edges of his teeth, shivering now, and feeling the shivering of his body in return.

Erin lost herself in the deepening kisses, in the feel of his hand kneading her back, sensations shimmering and heating until she couldn't separate them. The retreat and penetration of his tongue was repeated in the caress of his hand up and down her back, her legs, easing and shifting her body closer, all with gentle pressure that brought her nothing but pleasure.

He tried to bite back a groan as she rocked softly against his aroused flesh, but it escaped him only to be drunk by Erin just as he drank her small cries. His hand knew her back intimately, knew the slim curve of her hip, but he wanted to touch her skin. Scattering kisses over her flushed cheeks, he worked his way to her ear, suckling the lobe and taking tiny bites of it. She was distracted enough to allow him to get most of the buttons open. He wasted no time, refusing to allow her to shy away from him. His lips slid down her throat, the fevered pulse in the hollow of her throat drawing his tongue, but his need was to taste more of the skin that was as smooth as cream and just as sweet.

Using his teeth, he drew aside one fold of the night-gown, his finger edging aside the other. He swore at the darkness that prevented him from seeing her.

The ache that was growing in her breasts made Erin twist against him. She wanted to tell him but the laving heat of his mouth only brought a sound of need from her.

A need that Mace increased. He took the tip of first one breast then the other with his lips, then carefully with the edge of his teeth. The arch of her back told him she wanted more, and he drew the nipple into his mouth, tugging it into a taut peak. Her whimper of protest when he released her sent a violent shudder through him. He welcomed the restless movements of her legs, wanting to cover her body with his and bury himself so deep inside her that she wouldn't know where she began and he ended. But he knew it was too soon.

The dragging motion of his hand had bunched the thick cloth of her nightgown between them. He wanted it gone.

"Erin," he whispered, his voice husky, "let me take this off you."

He savored the slender curve of her hip, the faint tremor rippling over her skin, and took her mouth the way he had longed to do.

The hungry urgency of his kiss left her without the chance to breathe. But she wanted to please him, needed to do so, and she fought the fright that started to spread through her. He broke the kiss and pulled back before she could move, deftly turning and lifting her to strip off the nightgown.

Mace tossed it behind him, taking her mouth again, dragging her against him so that her softness fit every hard inch of his body. With a lean, strong hand, he stroked her from breast to thigh, love-biting a path down to the taut nipple nestled against his chest. He kneaded her hip, fingers spreading toward the soft curve of her belly, her moan bringing his leg to anchor her legs still.

He drew her nipple deep into his mouth, suckling hard, knowing she was aroused enough to handle a man's hunger. Her fingers dug into his back and he brushed the soft hair concealing the feminine heat he was on fire to claim. But he didn't linger, although he wanted to—he wanted to so badly that he was shaking. She was twisting beneath him and he stilled her with his hand spread across her belly.

"Talk to me, Erin. Tell me what you want." The demand was filled with hunger and she stilled, her hand pressing against his chest, the other gripping his arm.

The violence of passionate need seething through him made Mace doubt his mind when he felt the slight flutter under his hand. But he didn't mistake the sudden tension that ripped through Erin.

For a moment he couldn't drag air into his lungs. He propped himself up on his elbow, cursing the dark but staring down to where his hand lay against the paleness of her body.

He shook his head as if that would clear it. But the slight movement came again, sending him a message only a damn fool would ignore.

His mind knew what it was he felt. His body refused to listen. It demanded the heat and softness and pleasure he had been promising it. But while his body had ruled the day, had commanded him the past hour, his mind exerted a pressure and demand that he couldn't fight, could not ignore.

If he had any doubt, he remembered Sky. Memory eagerly supplied him with the first time. Memory dragged up the incredible joy they had shared to feel the first flutters of their child's life. Cherished memories they repeated with Jake. But Sky had been his wife. He had been her first and only lover. She had carried *his* children.

Erin Dunmore became his wife today. Hours ago. She had married him knowing she carried another man's child.

Chapter Six

"**Y**ou lying bitch."

The very softness of his tone tore through Erin.

Fear doubled the tension that froze her beneath his hand. At first she hadn't understood what had happened, but his stillness and the repeated tiny fluttering against the hard press of his hand warned her that time had run out. She didn't know she would feel life this soon. No one had told her.

The tightening clench of his fingers on her belly sent new fears splintering through her. She wanted to shove his hand away, afraid he would hurt her, afraid that if she moved he would explode.

Mace shook. His body hadn't cooled; it was reacting to the rage that erupted with a series of explosions, each more violent than the last. For minutes he saw nothing but a red haze. Heat seeped out of him. A bone-chilling cold replaced it. He couldn't think, couldn't speak. A feeling of betrayal ran deep, down to the marrow. He tried to concentrate on breathing, so he could do something about the knots twisting his gut.

Suddenly he wanted the lamp lit. He had to see the bitch who had trapped him, then slammed the cage door shut. And it was good that he could move away from her, for he no longer trusted himself to hold back the rage that was screaming inside him.

He needed to get to the lamp. He refused to talk, knowing it would tax what little control he had left.

Mace had never questioned his own strength. He had tested it more times than he could count. He had lived when Sky died and that had taken the greatest strength of all. But his legs felt weak as a newborn foal's, his hands shook, and he staggered across the room until he felt the hard, solid edge of the dresser under his hands. With his head bowed, he rocked back and forth, fighting the need to strike out at something, anything, to release the treacherous fury ripping inside him.

The tension in the room suffocated Erin. His silence threatened her more than if he had shouted. "Mace?" she whispered, afraid to say more, afraid to move.

There was no answer. She strained to hear him. All she could see was the faint outline of his body. Erin called out his name again. He didn't answer. The tiny flutter came once more, but this time Erin gave in to her intense need and her hand covered her bare stomach. She forgot Mace, forgot everything in the joyous wonder of feeling her child move, stretching inside her, testing the bonds of its safe nest, telling her she was not alone. Would never be alone again.

Mace lit the lamp and turned slowly to look at her. For a moment, the enchantment of her expression arrested him. Her eyes were wide, her lips, swollen from his kisses, parted. He stopped himself from really seeing her. But his eyes targeted hers, and he knew it was the hate pouring out of him that held her gaze to his.

Erin wore nothing but goose bumps. No, she corrected herself, that wasn't true. If hate could be worn, she was smothered in it.

Her throat constricted. She knew she had to talk to him, try to explain. She swallowed repeatedly, unable to look away from the scorn in his eyes.

He stood motionless, tall and hard as stone. The male power she first sensed in him took a dangerous turn. Mace Dalton was a stranger. And she had married him. Suddenly the risk she had taken to gain a home for her child and herself carried too high a price. He frightened her.

"Please listen," she begged, "I tried to—"

"Shut up," he grated from between clenched teeth that made his jaw ache. He could feel the muscle in his cheek twitch. But clenching and twitching didn't compare to the murderous fury that held every muscle in his body within its grip. The battle wasn't over inside him; he had a feeling it was just beginning.

As long as his contemptuous gaze remained focused on her face, Erin didn't attempt to move. But when those dark, pitiless eyes narrowed and she felt as if he were touching her, shame for her nakedness flooded her. She couldn't lie there, vulnerably exposed to him, not when he made her feel soiled. Even as the thought struck her she knew he was right. She was soiled. But even an animal tried to find shelter when a predator was closing in for the kill.

Stretching out one hand, she prayed to feel the edge of the quilt, but no one was listening to her prayer. Or if the Lord was, he decided to side with Mace Dalton and punish her for her deceit. To cover herself, Erin had to sit up. But his piercing gaze froze her. Her own eyes would not drop below the square jut of his dark stubbled jaw. He didn't seem to realize that he stood before her as naked as Adam and twice as proud, his silence condemning her for betrayal.

But she wasn't Eve and this was no garden of Eden. She accepted her guilt for deceiving him, but not for tempting him. But no word in her own defense escaped her lips.

"For Christ's sake, cover yourself. You've played the whore and got what you wanted."

His savage attack made her cringe. Feeling the bonds that had frozen her snap, Erin grabbed for the quilt. She didn't hide beneath it the way she longed to do. She sat up, wrapping it tightly around her chilled body, focusing her gaze on the flocked pattern of interlocking leaves on the wallpaper. And she waited for the next blow.

He didn't make her wait at all. "Why me?"

Erin didn't even think about lying. "You were the only one who answered me," she stated in a deadened voice. Bit by bit, she dragged up a fragile shell to protect herself. It had served her well in the past. She needed it to work now.

"The only one fool enough." Mace didn't think he could stand the sight of her. He wanted to bolt from the room, wanted that freedom so bad he could taste it. But she wasn't going to get away from him without paying. And she bore his name. He couldn't get rid of her by walking out. Stuck and tied. With her and another man's child.

The silence grew and thickened.

Mace drew in a deep breath and felt it shudder from his body. *Too good.* That's what he'd told Ketch. Knowing he'd been right didn't ease his feelings. She had used him. The words in her letters slammed into him. *Modest manner. Children welcome and wanted. Longed for family. Answer me promptly. Your answer... future plans.*

But then he thought of the woman he met hours ago. She dressed like a lady; her manner had been modest. A little sass that intrigued him. A woman's walk. Her mouth . . . Stop it!

But he couldn't. His body recalled what his mind wanted to bury. She had been frightened. Either she was a damn good actress, which made her a classy whore, or . . .

"Were you raped?" The moment the words left his lips he hoped they were true. Whores protected themselves against pregnancy. If they didn't, they were smart in knowing how to rid themselves of the one thing that prevented them from earning money. She was young. Pretty enough and tempting enough to raise his blood. If she had been raped, he could find a way to live with that. Mace knew his thinking was not that of most men, but he'd never forced a woman. If a female couldn't come willingly to him, wanting to share God-given pleasure, there wasn't any pleasure at all for him.

Rape would make a respectable woman flee from her home. A sop to his pride, perhaps, but better than knowing she was the whore he had called her. But she wasn't answering him, and he was forced to look at her.

The colorful pattern of the quilt rested against her cheek, as white as new-fallen snow. The paleness of her skin made her hair appear blacker than night and the soft line of her mouth barely showed. There was no color; it was as if the blood had drained from her.

He had no room for pity. Not for her.

"Were you raped?" he repeated, fury shaking his voice.

"No."

He didn't hear her, not really—he saw the word formed by her lips. His fingers curled into fists and the need to strike out came back with a slamming force. But Mace had never used his brute strength against anything smaller than himself. He had never hit a woman. But even as he watched, he saw her shrink before his eyes, hiding as though she sensed his thoughts.

"Stop burrowing like a rabbit down a hole. I wouldn't touch you. I don't dare." She didn't look at him, didn't move, but instinct said she had walled herself off from him. He was raw, hurting and seething for release. She wasn't going to run or hide.

"If you weren't raped, then tell me why you had to go looking for a sucker."

"It doesn't matter," she answered, chilled by the cold venom coating his every word.

"It matters, all right. To me. Me, Mace Dalton, the man you took for a fool."

"No. I never thought that. I never—"

"Lying isn't going to help you now. *I married you.* It's my name, my honor that you're dragging in dirt." He raked his hand through his hair, hanging on to a thread of rational control. "You'll tell me anything and everything I want to know. You owe me that much."

Owe. Erin closed her eyes and shivered. So the price began its accounting. She found that her protective shell, the tiny walled space where nothing could touch her, wasn't going to save her now. In the past she could forget cold, hunger, scathing voices and hard hands. Mace Dalton was too powerful a force, too dangerous. What would he deem payment enough? Tears? Begging? But what right did a woman like her have to question his costs? She had taken a risk, more than she knew, and her future, her child's future, all rested in his hands.

"Don't—make—me—wait."

The grated command forced her to open her eyes and once more stare at the wall. "I am an orphan, Mr. Dalton. I did not lie to you about that. I worked as a maid for a banker's family. One of the clerks began courting me. I thought he cared for me. He spoke often of marriage as soon as he had saved enough money. I believed him. If you had ever in your life hungered as much as I have for a home and family of your own—''

"Stop trying to arouse my pity. I've none for the likes of you."

Erin laced her fingers together so tightly she could feel them go numb. "I wasn't trying to arouse your pity or anything else. I wanted a home and did not refuse when he told me he loved me. When I was certain there was to be a child, I told him. He—'' Erin stopped, unable to admit to the laughter that had greeted her announcement.

But Mace wasn't satisfied. He wanted to hear her tell him every bit of it. Especially how she conceived of the idea to hunt out a fool. He needed to hear her admit the deceit she played out on him. His pride demanded it.

And that demand was in his voice. "Finish it."

"There isn't much more. He refused to marry me or take care of me. I believe he told the housekeeper, who told my employer, and I was fired. If it wasn't for Maddie taking—''

"Who's Maddie?''

"The friend I told you about. The one I want to write to.'' Erin silently added, *To tell her I arrived safely.* She couldn't write to Maddie now.

"Why didn't you stay with her? Why the hell did you have to—''

"Maddie earned enough to take care of herself. I had to work," she continued, speaking softly, feeling the strength seep out of her. "Hard work, maid's work. I feared losing my baby. There were few choices for me.''

"Why should keeping a man's baby who didn't want you matter at all?''

There was a deep curiosity behind his question, but Erin didn't hear it. She heard only the harsh punishing voice that relentlessly stripped her.

"The baby is mine. I want to keep it. I need to give this child the love I never had."

Truth, bright and blazing as only truth could be, sharpened the rawness of her voice. And there was something else, a desperation that Mace tried to ignore. But before he could continue his interrogation, she spoke.

"I wanted to tell you. I was afraid. When you wrote back, enclosing the bank draft, I thought we would have time to know each other."

"Time to use every female trick created and passed down, you mean."

"No. That's not true. I was not going to marry you without telling you the truth."

"Then why the hell did you!" he shouted, closing the distance between them until he planted his fists on either side of her, towering above her. But fury had taken hold and all he could see, all he could think of, was the seductive promise of her mouth parting for him, her sleek hot body pressed against his, the tiny sounds of wanting she made. He grabbed her shoulders, shaking her. "Why the hell didn't you tell me?"

"You wouldn't give me the chance."

Somewhere in his mind the words fell, but he wasn't hearing them. Rage still clouded his thinking, the desire that had instantly burned inside him for her, for this... Suddenly he realized he was touching her. He looked at his hands squeezing the quilt and her flesh beneath it so hard that he could feel her bones. Mace snatched his hands away and backed off the bed.

"Christ," he pleaded, throwing his head back. "What the devil should I do with you? I can't take a whore back to raise my children."

Whore? Erin felt a tiny spark of anger spring to life. She knew what a whore was. She could have become one. She tried not to answer him, bit her lip and told herself she deserved whatever he called her. But she found that she couldn't let it pass.

"I never took any gifts from him or any man. I never took money, Mr. Dalton."

Her whisper cut through him. "Lucky him. Unlucky me. You think that's what makes you a whore?"

"No, Mr. Dalton. I am sure you could explain each and every way a woman becomes one."

If there had been pride or sarcasm behind those words, Mace wasn't sure what he would have done. But there was only her deadened voice, filled with the certainty that he wasn't done with her.

"I need to think. Figure out a way—"

"No. I'll leave. You can say whatever you please to those who matter. I won't be here."

"And what the hell do I tell people who know I married you? Should I say you're as cold as the frozen river and I sent you back? Damn you! Don't you understand? I married you!"

She flinched, hearing the condemning sentence he made of that fact. All she wanted was peace and a place to raise her child. Somehow she had to find a way to make that possible.

"Is an annulment expensive?"

"Annulment? What are you muttering about?"

"I don't know when I would be able to pay you back for the trip," she continued as if he had never spoken. "I still have twenty dollars left. Please take it. As for an annulment, we didn't... I mean you didn't... There are grounds for one.''

"I wouldn't know about such things. I married my wife because I loved her. Unlike you."

Erin thought the knife thrusts were finished. Now she knew he had merely sharpened his blade on her. He had loved his wife and she hungered to have someone to love her. It didn't matter what more he said. The pain stopped hurting. All she cared about was giving this child life. Whatever the cost, she would pay it. She couldn't fight him with words; he had all the right on his side. She had deceived him. Whatever was to be done would be by his choice. The vow to survive grew.

Lacing her fingers tighter didn't stop their trembling. The waves of his savage masculine rage broke over her and nausea churned in her stomach. She wrapped her arms around her body to stop the cold sickness from spreading. But she couldn't warm her body, and she couldn't make the bitter bile recede.

Dragging herself off the bed took every bit of her physical strength and sapped the little determination she had left.

"What are you doing?"

Erin shook her head, swallowing repeatedly, refusing to be sick in front of him. He had humiliated her and she wouldn't add to it. She eyed the door on the other side of the bed, knowing she had to pass him to get to it.

"Where do you think you can run?"

Erin ignored him. She held tight to the edge of the high carved footboard with one hand and used the other to keep the quilt around her. Chills shook her body, but she had to get out of this room.

Mace repeated his demand. She couldn't have paled beyond the whiteness he had seen. But that's the message his eyes gave to him. Her unfocused gaze revealed eyes as terrified as a stalked fawn's. But his rage hadn't run its course. He reached out and grabbed hold of her arm.

"You're not escaping. I'm not done with you." He was shocked to feel the coldness of her flesh seeping through the cloth to the warmth of his hand. Now he saw the tiny beads of sweat on her skin.

Cursing, he let her go long enough to grab the washbowl and bring it to her.

Erin glanced from the bowl to his face, then away.

"I'm bigger, stronger and harder than you. I'll keep you here until you use it or choke. The choice is yours."

There was shame and then there was shame. Erin had known too much of the first, and now found it had another, deeper level. She couldn't be sick in front of him. She just couldn't.

She begged. Silently. With her eyes, with the tears that involuntarily came, blurring her vision. She found that Mace Dalton described himself perfectly. He was bigger, stronger, and filled with a hardness that she couldn't hope to match.

He lifted her, sat her on the bed, placing the bowl on her lap, then crowded her with the heat of his body.

"Go ahead. It won't be the first time. And as sure as the devil's laughing at me, it won't be the last."

Erin gagged. She stared at the bowl, then his face. Shame was stacked against the survival price of keeping her child. Her shame didn't matter, she told herself. Nothing he did to her would ever matter.

Chapter Seven

The morning had long since stolen the night when Erin finally awakened. She lay with her eyes closed, wishing she had been able to steal away, as well, but Mace Dalton had effectively put an end to the thought. He placed the overstuffed wing chair in front of the door and spent the remainder of the night sprawled in it. Erin had not wanted to sleep in the bed, but he didn't offer her a choice.

Maddie had been so wrong in thinking that once he had seen her, it wouldn't matter to him about the baby. And Erin was the bigger fool for wanting to believe Maddie.

Sunlight streaked across the bed, forcing her to feel its warmth and open her eyes. Erin fought it off a bit longer. It was frightening not to know what Mace would do. He had said nothing more once her sickness had passed, gave no indication of what his decision would be. Erin, however, was sure that whatever it was, she would willingly do it to keep her baby.

The sun's warmth beckoned her. She tried to shake off the stupor from last night's emotional storm. She opened her eyes and cautiously gazed around the room, realizing that she was free of his dark, overpowering presence.

Having no idea how long Mace had been gone, or when he would return, Erin forced herself out of bed.

Heated water was in the pitcher, the washbowl gleamed, and fresh linen towels were set in a neat pile on the washstand. She glanced at the door. Luck, if there was such a thing, didn't seem to be holding for her. She did not want him walking in on her.

But at the door, Erin stared down at the empty keyhole. Twisting the doorknob, she found she couldn't lock Mace out, for he had locked her in.

She had been soundly asleep when he had left. Other guests of the hotel, a maid, anyone could have entered the room. Common sense beat back the initial panic she felt. Mace had not imprisoned her, he had protected her privacy.

Erin didn't waste another moment. She would be dressed and composed by the time he returned. But for all her hurry to wash herself, brush out her travel suit, don it and pin her neatly braided hair into a thick twist, she found herself pacing the room waiting for him to come back.

Countless times she stopped by the window, watching as people below hurried about their business. The wind was strong; women were holding their hats with one hand, coats billowing out. A farm wagon pulled up across the street. Erin watched a lanky man step down, hurrying around the wagon to help the woman from the seat, before he lifted two chubby little girls from the back. She couldn't hear them, but the smiles they exchanged told their own story. The woman held each girl by the hand, close to her side, accepting the kiss the man pressed to her cheek.

They presented a charming picture. A family, and one Erin saw that shared a great deal of love. The man had stepped away, but at a gesture from one little girl he went back to give each of the children a kiss.

Erin let the curtain fall into place. She envied them. Was what she longed for never to be hers?

Footsteps sounded in the hall, and she spun around in expectation, staring at the door, but they continued on.

Where was Mace? What was he doing? She had tried to keep the questions buried. Was he buying her a return ticket to San Francisco? Had he taken the balance of the money?

Reaching for her reticule, Erin opened it, relieved to find the twenty-dollar gold piece still there.

She didn't understand why that reassured her, but it did. If she knew more about Mace Dalton, she could be prepared for his decision. But he had told her so little of himself and less of his children. His letters were in her valise, but she didn't want him finding her with those. And she had read them so many times she knew their contents.

It was simply futile to speculate about him.

But her thoughts strayed to last night when he brought her a fresh damp cloth to wash her face and hands. And a glass of water to rinse her mouth. When she was done, he had handed her the nightgown and turned his back while she put it on.

He never said another word about her or the child once he'd ordered her into bed.

She couldn't give up hoping. Hope was all she had to cling to.

Mace ignored the brisk wind, watching the last of his supplies being loaded into the back of the high-sided farm wagon. He wanted to lift the hundred-pound bags of grain and flour himself. He needed a physical outlet, but Harry Tobin, proud owner of his new store, wouldn't hear of it. He paid his sons to take care of customers. Two cases of canned fruits forced Mace back to the one subject he had avoided—Erin Dunmore.

These were to have been the last canned fruits ordered, the last of the jellies, and when he stopped at Otto Brechtel's bakery, the last of the store-bought bread. He had believed he would have a wife to take care of these things. Riding into Walla Walla, he had made vague plans to take her out and show her where the wild fruit grew. The seeds for a vegetable garden of their own were already packed beneath the other provisions. Thinking of Becky's excitement about a garden brought a frown to Mace's lips. What was he going to tell his children?

"That's the last of it, Mr. Dalton."

"Thanks, Charlie. Split this with your brother." Mace handed the boy a silver dollar, knowing Harry wouldn't take offense for the tip. He walked inside to settle his bill, the rich aroma of tobacco melding with the brine of pickles and pickled beef. He had to wait while two women dickered with Harry over the eggs they wished to trade for tea and spices.

Mace didn't see Flo Jamison until she placed her hand on his arm. "I hear congratulations are in order."

Her voice was as soft and sweet as her body. Lips a shade too wide offered him a smile that was reflected in the golden brown of her eyes. He thought about lying. God forgive him, but he thought hard about it. But he couldn't lie to Flo. They had shared too many years between them. "Right. Congratulate me, Flo. But if you'd've said yes—"

"Oh, Mace, you know if I ever considered marrying again, it would've been to you." Laughing with the same generous warmth she gave to everything and everyone, Flo glanced around the store. "Is your wife with you? I'd like to meet her. That is," she added, looking at him, "if you won't feel uncomfortable."

"I've never been ashamed of you. Don't see reason to start now." He curved his left hand over hers, holding it in place on his right arm. "She isn't with me. Tired from her trip and all."

Mischief danced in her eyes. "I'd bet it's more the 'and all' that's keeping your bride in bed." Her teasing, a natural part of their relationship, did not bring the satisfied smile she expected. His eyes darkened, his lips thinned beneath his silky mustache, and for a second his fingers tightened over her hand. "What's wrong?" She knew he wasn't going to answer her. But Mace Dalton was the most unbridled male she knew, in bed and out. There were shadows in his eyes and they weren't from lack of sleep.

"I hope we'll still remain friends. You know if you need to talk, Mace—"

"I know." He removed his hand, leaving her no choice but to release him, as well. "You're sweet as sunshine and twice as warm, Flo. But more, you're an honest woman."

"You're not happy. No, don't lie to me. But I'd hoped that you found someone to care for you and the children. Becky and Jake need a mother. Give her time, Mace. I don't know what woman would refuse kindness and time."

"Got your bill total, Mace," Harry called out, eyeing them.

Unwilling to have anyone gossip about Flo, Mace stepped forward, stopped and turned. "You'll always be welcome at the Diamond Bar D."

"I know." Her smile was forced, but she turned away, looking at the dry goods stacked on the table. Mace was a good man, hard and strong, but there was gentleness in him, too. It wasn't her place to tell his wife those things and a few more besides. But she did wish him to be happy.

"Now, Mace, you make sure to tell your missus that I can order anything she wants. Women up from the big city like Frisco's likely to have fancy tastes."

Mace nodded, ignoring the talk, paying his bill, wanting to escape.

Tipping his hat to Flo, he left the store. But there was no escape. The news of his hasty marriage had spread. He was angry that his pride kept telling him he had no choice but to take Erin home with him.

And do what? he asked himself. Keep her hidden away until she had the baby? Claim it as his own? She couldn't have more than five or so months to go. Dragged back to the memory of her face last night, he knew it was the first time she had felt the baby move. But he had no intention of letting that memory surface again. Rage had burned itself into a cold, hard knot in his gut and he meant to keep it there.

Feeling he was caught between a rock and a hard place, Mace drove the wagon to the hotel, steeling himself to face her again.

But first he had a stop to make.

Erin gave in to the overwhelming need to sleep. And that is how Mace found her when he unlocked the door, asleep in the wing chair. He set the small tray he carried on the dresser top, noting that her valises were packed, the bed linens folded and not a trace of her possessions was in sight.

Her head rested on one hand. The other was curled into her lap. Faint shadows were visible beneath her eyelashes and while her skin was still pale, there was color to the soft line of her mouth.

There was something childlike and innocent about her, something that begged for a response from him, but Mace turned away before he discovered what it was.

Unable to overcome his reluctance to touch her, he made unnecessary noise packing his bag, slamming each dresser drawer closed after he had emptied it.

Erin came to with a start, saw the uncompromising line of his profile against the light from the window and quickly sat up, lowering her feet to the floor. With hands laced together in her lap, she waited for him to notice her.

Mace tossed his shaving mug and brush on top of his clothes and closed the bag. He knew she was awake, he'd heard the catch in her breath. Even through his thickly lined sheepskin jacket, he felt her watching his back as he walked to the door to set the bag down.

"There's tea and a corn muffin on the tray for you," he stated without turning. "If you can eat more, I'll go down to the restaurant and get it."

Erin believed herself deadened to pain. He was so obviously ashamed of her that she couldn't help feeling hurt. But not enough to reveal that it mattered. "Thank you, Mr. Dalton. This will be enough."

Cold. Polite, but cold. Mace wasn't sure what he expected from her, but it wasn't this. He turned around and saw that her hand shook as she poured out a cup of the tea. The chair that left more of his body off than on it last night dwarfed her fragile frame. Her black hair, thick and tightly braided, almost seemed too much weight for her neck as she sat with head bowed, sipping repeatedly from the delicate china cup. She looked beaten. It was the only way he could describe her. Beaten and resigned.

He had sworn he wouldn't, *couldn't* feel pity for her. But even he wouldn't kick a dog when it was down.

"You'd better eat that muffin. It's a long ride out to the ranch."

It was a long ride, Erin decided, long, cold and lonely. The blanket that Mace had taken from beneath the seat and handed to her without a word kept her hips and legs warm, but the wind cut through the thin cloth of her coat at her back and whipped around her feet. Her lips felt chapped, and her ears had lost all feeling a few miles back.

Sneaking a look at Mace, she wondered how he could stand the cold. His jacket was open just as his first two shirt buttons were. The gloves he wore were of a supple thin leather as he sat with one booted foot resting on the lower edge of the wagon frame. Feeling brave, Erin lifted her gaze to his face. The brim of his hat curled up at the side, the crown low, the color as dark as his hair.

Before he could turn and catch her looking at him, Erin lowered her gaze to the floorboard.

But her movement drew his unwanted attention. "If you're shaking with cold, why didn't you say something?"

His voice was colder than the wind and harder to bear. He drew up, tying off the reins before she thought of a reply.

"Save me from useless women," he muttered, grabbing the blanket from her lap. "Get up," he then ordered.

Erin stood up, but there was nowhere to brace herself without touching him. That, she would not do.

With a few deft motions, Mace opened the blanket, spread it on the seat and impatiently ordered her to sit. Erin sat. She chewed on her lower lip as he tossed one end of the blanket to her and unwrapped the reins from the pole brake. The wagon lurched and she lunged forward, having nothing to grab hold of.

Erin fell against Mace's outstretched arm and jumped back as if burned. She dragged the two ends of the blanket together, instantly feeling warmer, and turned to thank him.

"Don't bother. You won't be much good if you're sick. It's bad enough we got a late start today. But come first light, I'll expect you to have breakfast ready for all of us." Since he was the one who broke the silence, he waited for an answer. Just let her say one word wrong. Just one.

But Erin merely nodded. "I understand."

He had to wonder if she did. And he didn't understand why he goaded her. "There's all the house chores, of course. And the chickens, milking and laundry. Just ours, not the hired hands'. There's four year-round men who get three meals a day 'cept on Sundays. Come branding time there's as many as sixteen." Again he paused, waited, and from the corner of his eye saw her nod.

"Did I forget to mention the hogs? You'll care for them, too."

"Yes," she answered in a tight little voice, bewildered by what he meant. How did one take care of hogs? Chickens laid eggs, and gathering those couldn't be too hard. And how difficult could it be to milk a cow?

"Sure relieves my mind to know you're not put off by a little hard, honest work. There's no room for a useless woman on a working ranch." For good measure, still trying to get a rise from her, he added, "I'm pleased to know you're not a nosy woman who's always asking stupid questions."

Erin heard the taunt in his voice and knew she would bite the tip off her tongue before she asked him anything. But the questions burned to be spoken. She longed to know what the names of the massive trees were that lined the dirt road and absorbed the sunlight at their towering tops. She wanted to ask the names of the birds she heard, and the mountains in the distance. She needed to know more about his children, the hired hands, his home. What would he tell them about her? She kept quiet.

Glancing again at his profile, Erin knew what Maddie would have called him after one look. Mace Dalton was a hard piece of business. Hard and business summed up her forthcoming relationship with the man.

But after last night, he was offering her more than she expected, if a bit less than she had hoped for.

The road angled around a bend and Erin's breath caught. High above the valley rose majestic mountain peaks. Clouds hid their tops, softening the line of ragged granite, and as the road declined she wondered if the Lord had scooped out the bowl where the ranch buildings sprawled below.

In his last letter to her, Mace had not elaborated about the size of his ranch. There was the house itself, two barns, outbuildings whose number she lost count of. Corral fences checkered the valley floor, cattle as black as her own hair in some, russet-coated animals in others. Horses filled a few, some alone, others with small herds. As they neared the house, details came to her, the sun slanting on the weathered gold of the logs, the grayish chinking between them. Smoke curled from two chimneys, lazily rising, for the wind had been left behind. Nothing spoke of neglect, but then, Mace Dalton was a man who demanded perfection.

The enormity of her deceit hit Erin. Everywhere she rested her gaze bespoke pride. Mace had every right to his pride. And every right to his anger. She vowed then that he would never have cause to regret his decision to bring her into his home.

Mace was already regretting his decision to bring her here. He guided the horse team around to the back of the house, perplexed why no one was around. Glancing at her as he tied off the reins, he had doubts she would survive until spring. The edge of the blanket hid all but her eyes, and those ridiculous little feathers on her hat drooped almost as much as she did.

"We're here," he said, hoping for a word of praise. He was proud, maybe too much so, of the home he had carved from this valley.

Erin, waiting in dread that someone would greet them, was afraid of what he would say and so remained quiet.

With the kind of swearing better suited to a muck pile, Mace jumped down and came around to her side of the wagon. He held out his arms, waiting for her to move.

Erin measured the distance to the ground. She released the blanket, gripped the side of the wagon and managed to get one leg over the side before he grabbed her by the waist and swung her out and down. She fought to recover her balance on legs cramped from sitting too long in the cold, but his standing there, dark and overpowering, made her back away. The smooth leather soles of her high-buttoned shoes were never meant to achieve purchase on river-smooth gravel. Erin slipped, then regained her balance as Mace came forward, reaching for her. Her arms wore the livid bruises from his punishing grip of the night before and she had no desire for more. She slipped again and he was faster than her move to dodge him.

Hauled up against his powerful body, Erin felt the chill leave her just as her breath did.

"Woman, you're gonna be useless if you're this clumsy."

"I'm not. I just—"

"Or was this a ploy to get me to put my hands on you again?"

"N-no. I wouldn't—" Erin stopped herself from saying another word. Her lips parted, quivering, as she looked up, directly into his eyes.

Mace felt heat explode through him. Every place he was hard, she was soft. Her eyes darkened to a green blaze that provoked in him every male instinct to conquer. The small unconscious sound she made sent need surging into his blood. But the force of will that he used to subdue it shocked him.

"Stop it," he demanded, knowing he was being unreasonable. He knew on some deep level that she was innocent of what she did to him. "Just stop pushing me."

Erin stared at his fierce expression with dismay. She was bewildered by his accusation. Suddenly dealing with Mace Dalton became too much. She yanked free of his grip, turning and running up the three steps to the door.

"Wait. I need to tell—"

Erin didn't hear him. She opened the door and froze on the threshold.

Chapter Eight

Flour. At first that was all Erin saw. There was tracks through the layer of it that covered the wooden floor. Her every inhaled breath drew flour dust into her lungs. And burnt offerings. The air was thick with smoke.

A coating of white had drifted over the large wooden table and chairs. Below the table were clumps of it, and a few decorated the wall. The cast iron stove threw off a heat that was stifling.

Erin's gaze moved with reluctance toward the window. Standing by the dry sink, one slender hand on the pump handle, was a child of startling beauty. Straight black hair was clumsily forced into a semblance of a braid. Delicate arched brows framed eyes nearly as dark as her hair, and her skin was the smooth color of caramel. The child's small pointed chin came up, but the movement was lost on Erin, for she saw the startled fright in the child's eyes. It was a look she had seen too many times when she was growing up in the orphanage. She was sure her own eyes often held the same look.

While the fear in the child's expression was enough to hold her silent, she turned and stared at Mace. Every feeling of having been fooled, of his failure to tell her

about his children, was there for him to see. The girl had
Indian blood.

Erin had witnessed the treatment Indians received on
her journey. It seemed to make no difference if it was a
man, woman or child. If they were Indian they were
treated with less care than animals. She was angry with
Mace for not warning her. How dare he take the chance
that she wouldn't do or say something to hurt his child?

He met her look with defiance, ready to do battle for his
children.

Erin never gave him the chance. She could not hurt a
child no matter what its heritage was. Ignoring the flour,
she stepped into the kitchen.

"You must be Rebecca."

"Becky. That's what everybody calls me."

"I'm Erin, Becky."

From beneath the dry sink's lopsided skirt came a faint
whisper. "Is she here, Becky?"

"Come on out, Jake. They've seen it all."

With barely a rustle of material, a little boy peered
around Becky's faded calico skirt, one grimy hand gripping the once white apron she wore. He was a miniature
replica of his sister, or so Erin judged from the little she
could see.

"Are you the new mommy?"

"If that's what you'd like me to be, Jake, then I am."
Erin began unpinning her hat, handing over pins and hat
to Mace, who still stood behind her. "Since my bags need
to be unpacked, Becky, do you think you could lend me
an apron so I can help you clean up?"

"Sure. You can have mine. Well, it's mine now, but it
belonged to my mother."

"Then I'll need to take extra special care of it for today." Erin stepped closer. Why hadn't Mace told her

about his children? Was this prideful man ashamed of them?

"Where's Ketch?" Mace asked, still tense, still waiting for Erin's anger. He was ready for it. Just let her say one word. He'd tell her what for and then some. Guilt wormed its way between the layers of tension and lingering betrayal. He should have told her about his children, not for her sake, but for theirs. He'd never thought how they would feel when she rejected them. No. He wouldn't let her. After what she had done to him, she owed him. And he was just the man to see the debt paid in full. No one was going to slight them.

Becky glanced from her father to the woman tying on the apron. Something was wrong. She wouldn't ask her father now, but she had to know. Dragging Jake out from behind her with one hand, she said, "This is my little brother, Jake. He's not one for talking."

"Becky, where's Ketch?" Mace didn't know how to halt the defensiveness in his voice. He didn't want Erin to judge his children or his home and find them wanting. No matter what anyone thought or said, he was proud of Becky and Jake and gave them all the love he had.

"Ketch is sleeping. His tooth starting hurting again and he tried to put just a bit of whiskey on it, but it wasn't enough."

Erin had held her tongue at Mace's harsh tone, but she couldn't be still now. "How could you leave your children with a drunkard?"

"He's no drunkard. Ketch can't drink or he passes out."

"Oh."

"Yeah, oh. Don't make snap judgments about any of us."

Erin looked at him, but did not reply. She had made a snap judgment. She let him have the last word. Feeling a tug on her gown, she hunkered down to Jake, so that their faces were level. The boy's eyes weren't as dark as his sister's, but they were definitely more wary. Anger that Mace didn't warn her was replaced by regret. She could easily have hurt these children by a wrong word, wrong move. Instinct was all she had to guide her. Offering her hand to Jake, Erin had to fight the urge to hug him. There was more than shyness at work here. She sensed it.

Jake glanced at his father, then at Becky. He touched his fingertips to Erin's. "Pretty."

"Thank you, Jake. And you're very handsome."

"Father?"

"What about him?" Erin asked, disconcerted to find that Becky's watchful eyes were pinned on her.

"Jake wants to know if he's as handsome as Papa."

"Oh." Erin smiled, buying herself a moment. What was she to say? A quick look over her shoulder showed Mace leaning against the doorjamb, arms folded across his chest, hip canted to the side, his eyes every bit as watchful as his daughter's. She looked at the slender little boy, finding the strong resemblance to his father now that she was looking for it.

"Yes, you're every bit as handsome as he is. But more important is the goodness you have here," she said softly, barely touching his chest. "What's in your heart is all that matters."

Her cramped leg muscles protested as Erin forced herself to remain still. Jake came closer, his legs touching her knees, the barest hint of a smile lifting the corners of his mouth. He brushed his fingertips across her cheek, bending to touch the flour and bringing those whitened fingertips back to her face. He stared for a few seconds and

Erin held her place, wondering if this were some Indian ritual.

"White. Soft."

"Now you got her dirty, Jake. Say you're sorry," Becky demanded, reaching to brush the flour off Erin's face.

"No, it's all right, Becky. I'm not dirty and if I was, a little soap and water would get rid of it." Erin rose to her feet awkwardly. "If you show me where you keep the broom, I can begin helping you by sweeping."

If Erin had any doubts that these were indeed Mace Dalton's children, she lost them. Becky faced her with her arms folded across her thin chest, hip canted out to one side. "Ain't you gonna ask us what we were doing?"

A glance around the room told its tale, but Erin found herself turning to Mace for guidance. He was gone. The coward.

"We baked," Jake said, tugging on the apron for her attention.

"That's right. We wanted to surprise you with a cake so that you'd like us and want to stay."

"Of course I want to stay, Becky. What ever gave you the idea that I wouldn't?" Erin felt uncomfortable questioning the child, but again she let instinct guide her.

"None of the others wanted to stay."

Given Mace's temperament and the disgraceful state of the kitchen, Erin couldn't blame any of the others, whoever they were. But she had married him, for better or for worse, and consoled herself with the thought that since the worse seemed behind her, perhaps it would get better.

"Becky, I'll depend on you to show me where everything is kept. We'll need a large pot to boil water." Erin trailed her fingers over the top of the stove. Grease thick enough to stick to her fingertips covered the surface. "A very big pot, Becky. We're going to need lots and lots of hot water.''

"Me?" Jake asked, once again tugging on the edge of the apron.

"Yes, you'll help, too." Erin tried the pump handle. She pushed and pushed down again. It wouldn't move.

"Sticks sometimes," Mace said, coming into the kitchen carrying her bags. "If you don't have any more strength than a pile of goose feathers, woman, how do you expect to get anything clean?"

Erin tried the handle again, going up on the tips of her toes, putting every bit of strength she had into yet another push. It groaned in protest but moved halfway down before it stuck.

With a snort of disgust, Mace set down the bags and came to stand behind her. "Watch. I don't want to show you twice."

Erin relinquished her hold, but he caged her with one hand on the handle and the other on the edge of the dry sink. The handle didn't dare groan when he pushed down. It didn't even stick a bit—not then, not as Mace pumped a steady stream of water.

With his breath whispering across her cheek and neck, Erin fought to control the shiver that began inside her. She longed to ask him why he didn't tell about his children, but didn't dare. She was here on sufferance, Mace Dalton's sufferance, and she must do nothing to provoke him.

But she couldn't stop looking down at his hands, those same hands that had touched her with passion before the anger erupted.

"Since you're pumping the water, Papa," Becky said, coming to stand beside them, "could you fill the pot?"

Startled, Erin tried to turn, only to find herself pressed up against Mace. The breadth of his shoulders was daunting. She refused to look at his face. With a pointed glance at the hand still barring her way, Erin waited until he lifted it so she could slip away from him.

At the stove, she fitted the handle to the large, pancake-like burner, lifting it to see if the fire was still burning hot. The heat was the reason she drew shallow breaths, she told herself. It had nothing to do with being near Mace.

The wood box was almost empty of split wood, but even as she turned to ask where she could replenish it, Jake came inside carrying an armful.

Hearing her thank his son so politely, Mace turned to look at Erin. Her cheeks were flushed as she fed wood to the fire. He found himself envying the smile she gave to Jake.

"Will you carry the pot to the stove, Papa?" Becky asked, anxious to show Erin how much they all would help her.

"Sure, Becky. Then you'll tell me what's been going on while I've been gone."

Erin had already turned away from the stove, and with Jake helping, began to sweep the floor. She listened to the murmur of Mace and Becky's voices, heard that someone named Cosi was hunting a wolf that attacked the calves. There was more, but as she moved away from them, she couldn't hear.

"I'd best see to Ketch," Mace said, leaving them alone with a twinge of reluctance. He was sure she'd start questioning Becky and Jake the moment he was gone, but it would happen sooner or later anyway, so maybe it was best to get it out of the way now.

The second his back was through the door, Erin felt the tension seep out of her. Becky disappeared with one of the valises, but Jake dogged her heels as she swept up the flour and tested the heat of the water on the stove.

True to Mace's belief, she did question the children when they were together again, but not as he had suspected. "We need to plan something for supper, Becky. You know what's in the pantry, so I'll depend on you to tell me what everyone likes to eat."

"Lots," Jake answered before his sister.

Erin brushed his hair from his forehead, unable to stop herself from smiling again at the little boy. "I'm sure you're right. I've never lived on a ranch, so I don't know how things are done. Will you both tell me?"

Erin wiped out a small pot and used it as a dipper to fill the wooden bucket Jake found for her from the slowly heating water. As Becky told her about the housekeepers they had over the years, Erin set the dirty dishes she had gathered up to soak in a pan in the sink. Giving Jake a damp cloth, she set him to wiping down the chairs, and wondered how a man like Mace lived like this. If he had hired women to keep house, he had apparently never asked one of them if they knew which end of a broom was up. All she could hope to accomplish today was to get rid of the flour. The kitchen, the only room of the house she had seen so far, needed a day of lye soap and boiling water to scrub it clean.

"'Course she didn't like milking the cow."

"Who, Becky?"

"That was Miss Nolie. She didn't much like the chickens, or slopping the hogs, either."

"Oh. Are they hard to do?"

Erin missed the look Becky shared with her brother. She was staring at the window over the dry sink. It was covered with greasy grime inside and splatters of dirt on the outside so that a bare gray light filtered into the room.

"Not so hard," Becky finally answered, adding, "if you know what you're about."

Erin thought of admitting that she didn't know what she was about when it came to milking, or slopping hogs, or whatever had to be done with chickens. But if she did, Becky was sure to tell her father, and Mace would have her packed and out of here before she had a chance to tell him that she would learn. No matter what it took, she *would* learn.

Back to sweeping out another corner of the kitchen, she asked Becky about a smokehouse.

"Sure we have one. And a well house near the spring."

Erin found herself smiling again to hear the pride in Becky's voice. She didn't know and wouldn't ask when their mother died, but Erin had a feeling that not only had Mace loved his wife, they had both loved their children.

"If there's bacon or ham, Becky—"

"Lots," Jake said, scooping up the flour and dirt Erin swept into a pile.

"That's good. Becky, would you please choose one so we can start supper?"

"Gosh, supper! Guess me and Jake really messed things up to forget about supper. We tried hard to make biscuits and the cake, but everything burned and we paid no mind to supper."

Erin stopped her sweeping to look at Becky. "It should not have been your responsibility to worry about it."

"But we made work for you—"

"Yes, you both did, but you're both helping me to clean it up. That's all that matters, Becky." Erin thought about the loaded wagon outside. She had no idea what Mace had bought, but surely there were foodstuffs. And the pantry... "We'll make do, Becky. You'll see. We'll do just fine together."

When Mace returned, he found the kitchen empty. Clean, too. He turned to Ketch, who was still mumbling apologies and rubbing his swollen jaw. "Guess she turned tail and ran out."

"Sorry this happened." Ketch winced as air hit the exposed nerve in his tooth. "Should've gone to town."

"See if you can find where they took themselves off to while I go change."

"Sure, boss."

Mace stopped at the doorway to his bedroom. Erin's valises were neatly piled in front of the bed. He swore at her daring to bring her things into his room, the room he had shared with Sky. Without giving himself time to think, he grabbed them up and strode down the hallway to the spare bedroom all the housekeepers had used. He set the valises on the bed so Erin would make no mistake about this being where she belonged.

Returning to his bedroom, he removed his jacket and shirt, spotting a jar filled with dried evergreens. He smiled, thinking of Becky trying to make the room a little prettier, wanting to please. With a weary sigh he sat on the edge of the bed, wondering if he had done wrong by bringing Erin here.

He had put his children at risk for a woman who stirred his blood with a need that wouldn't quit. He didn't want to admit it, not even silently to himself, but admit it he did. Sky had never caused this fierce craving to burn inside him.

And Erin was his wife. She wouldn't refuse him. She would... What was he thinking of? He didn't want a woman whose belly was filled with another man's child!

Kicking off his boots, he stood to strip off his pants. The image of Erin's face so close to Jake's came to mind. He heard again his son's longing that she be the new mommy. And he had to remember that Erin didn't scream or shrink away when Jake touched her. She had briefly closed her eyes, as if savoring the acceptance his child offered.

But if he were going to be truthful with himself, she had been furious when she first saw Becky and Jake. He had better keep in mind that she needed a home more than they needed her. If he remembered that, he wouldn't let his thoughts stray from her motives.

A worm of guilt wiggled its way into his thoughts. He had lied, just as Erin had. Lied by omission. The deed was done and they were all going to have to live with it.

Hearing a murmur of voices from the kitchen, he hurried into his work clothes, afraid to leave her alone with the children for too long.

Erin held a child at each side, and Ketch followed her into the kitchen carrying one large smoked ham. They fell silent seeing Mace in the doorway from the hall.

Jake broke free from Erin's hold and ran to his father. Swinging the boy up into his arms, Mace buried his face against his son's small shoulder. Jake squirmed, pulling his head back so he could look at his father's face. His smile went far to alleviate Mace's misgivings.

Holding his son easily with one hand, he used the other to tousle his hair. "Happy, little one?"

Instead of answering, Jake turned to look at Erin and, to her joy, held out his arms to her. She started toward him when she saw Mace's strange expression.

"You come here, Jake," she said, lifting up the sack of potatoes she had set by the door after Ketch showed her the root cellar. "If I put you up on a chair, you can scrub these."

"Bring me something?" Jake asked, drawing Becky's instant attention.

Eyes alight, Becky ran to her father. "Yes, please."

Wearing a teasing grin, Mace shook his head. "Don't know that two young 'uns like you should be expecting anything."

"Candy!" called Jake, while Becky snuggled closer. "And peppermint sticks for me, Papa."

"Might be. We'll see once the wagon's unloaded." Over the groans of the two of them, he added, "All right, there's a surprise or two."

Erin listened, feeling a warmth toward Mace that grew when his whispers brought the children's laughter. How lucky they were to know a parent's unconditional love. From her brief acquaintance with Mace, she had expected that his temper would flair upon seeing the mess Becky and Jake made. But she had been wrong, as wrong as she had been about the man Ketch. A fool could see that Mace adored his children. Maybe there was hope for her, too.

Setting his son down with a last tickle, Mace motioned to Ketch and left them.

With Becky eagerly showing her where things were stored, Erin managed to get supper started. Nearly two hours later Ketch returned, lending Erin support and a feeling that she had an ally.

"You'll do, Mrs. Dalton," he said with a decided twinkle in his eye, despite his painful tooth. "Do us all jus' fine."

Chapter Nine

Erin lingered over finishing the last of the kitchen chores. She had met Ray Heppner and Pete Malott, who everyone called Dishman because of his being chosen to wash dishes when they were between housekeepers. Their kind compliments went far to relieve the tension that Mace brought with him to supper. The talk was of ranch work, of Cosi Sawtell's hunting an elusive wolf that had attacked their calves, of several miners found camping out near one of the upper streambeds.

She had listened, passed dishes when asked and said little about herself, nor did Mace volunteer to enlighten anyone. She had to place that in his favor, but for how long could he hide her secret?

At least Ketch seemed to be resting comfortably tonight. She had found a small bottle of oil of cloves, which he had rubbed on his tooth, swearing he would go to town to see the dentist.

The children, under Mace's gentle insistence, had made do with a quick wash in their room, since it had been too late to heat another large kettle of water for baths in the wooden tub stored in the pantry. Erin thought of wishing them good-night while Mace went along to tuck them into bed. The sounds of their joined laughter once again reached her, making her feel lonely. Softly the sounds had stilled, but Mace never returned to the kitchen.

Lowering the coal-oil fixture over the table, Erin blew out each of the lights before raising it again so no one would hit his head. She had delayed her own bedtime as long as she could. As she made her way from the kitchen into the hallway, she realized that she didn't know which room was hers.

The darkened hallway offered no clue. To her right was another hall, farther along one door. To her left were two. Perplexed, she stood undecided. She couldn't very well begin opening doors to find the right one. Ketch slept in the house, and had, he let slip at supper, since Mace's wife had died.

Erin had no desire to wake anyone, but she was tired. She headed for the single door. The house was well made; no floorboards creaked beneath her weight. Standing before the closed door, she hesitated before calling herself a fool. Mace had not seen fit to inform her where she would be sleeping.

A fine sheen of sweat broke out on Mace's brow as he heard Erin stop before his door. He lay rigidly on his bed, annoyed that he held his breath for a moment, waiting for her to open it. The damn brazen... Well, Miss Erin Dunmore was in for a shock. He slept raw and made no apology for it.

But he grew impatient as the door latch remained firmly in place. He sensed she was out there. Knew it with every taut muscle of his body. Curiosity forced him to sit up, cursing the creak of the rope spring in the bed.

What was she up to? Mentally he prepared the blistering he would give her for daring to think they would share a bed. And if the blistering held the snap and sting of a whip due to his own sexual frustration, so much the better. Someone had to pay for what he was suffering. Who better than the woman who caused it?

Raking an impatient hand through his hair, he swung his legs off the bed. Did the fool intend to stand out there all night? Or was she waiting for an invitation from him?

Sidewinders could skate on a frozen pond first! He hadn't been blind to the shy smiles she gave Pete and Ray. They fell over themselves telling her how good supper was, when Mace knew it wasn't anything special. She'd opened a few cans, fried potatoes and onions and served ham heated in the peach syrup. Sure there had been plenty, he admitted, but it wasn't filling for hungry men.

A wrong thought to be having along about now, he warned himself, coming to his feet and padding silently to the door. The woman was going to drive him crazy. He could swear her scent came right through the thickness of the tongue-and-groove wood door. Had anyone told her where her room was? The question he asked himself surprised him. He couldn't remember. He had tucked the children to sleep. Ketch went to bed nursing his tooth, and Erin had been in the kitchen and only the kitchen, from the moment she arrived.

He wrenched open the door.

"I—"

"What—"

They both began at the same time, but Erin moved away until her back was against the wall. In more ways than one, she thought. The moonlight streamed through the bedroom windows, allowing her to see that he wore nothing. A choked sound escaped her and she turned to flee. She couldn't do it. She could not go into that room with him.

Mace grabbed the back of her skirt, all he could, and pulled her up short. Hand over hand, in a moment he had her against his chest. "What were you doing prowling out here?"

Bracing herself, Erin whispered, "I didn't know where to sleep. I guessed this was your room and—"

"You're not sharing it," he stated harshly against her ear. Mace knew he had made another mistake to add to the long list he was compiling. The air was filled with warm woman and it pierced him as he breathed it. "Damn you," he muttered, releasing her skirt only to take her arm. "I'll show you where. Far enough away from me."

Down the darkened hallway he strode, unmindful of his naked state, until at the end he threw open the door. "This is your room. Learn where it is so there's no mistake. I don't ever want to find you in my room again. You hear me?"

"Yes, Mr. Dalton. I hear you and I'm sure that Ketch and the children do, too."

He let her go and glared down at her shadowed features. "Won't matter, will it? They'll all know soon enough the reason why."

Erin walked into the room and stood with her back to him. She wasn't going to answer him. She was not going to allow him another victory over the hurt he dealt her.

Mace followed her inside, finding his way to the dresser and quickly lighting the lamp. Replacing the chimney, he saw for himself that the room was bare of warmth. A straight chair, washstand, dresser, wardrobe and single bed furnished the room. He thought about saying something, anything, but merely took the valises from the bed and set them near the wardrobe before he left her.

Erin waited a few moments before she closed the door and lit the fire already laid. Undressing quickly, she slipped into bed, fighting not to cry.

The tiny corner of hope that she had fought to keep alive folded in upon itself. The die was well and truly cast, and if it were to be changed, it would fall to her. She vowed then that nothing Mace Dalton did would surprise her. If she was prepared for rejection, it wouldn't hurt again.

Tiptoeing down the hall long before dawn, Erin lit the lamps in the kitchen. A few embers remained in the stove, enough so that kindling caught and soon spread heat into the large room. Praying that the pump wouldn't give her trouble, she filled the coffeepot and took stock of the pantry for breakfast.

In one earthenware jar she found sourdough starter, in others were barley, wheat and cornmeal. The sacks of flour and potatoes that Mace had bought in town were all neatly stacked on one side, and above them were jars of pickled corn relish, jellies, carrots and green beans. On top were stored dried beans and peas, along with jarred tomatoes.

Bread was the first priority. There were a few eggs left from the gathering yesterday and Erin used these to make pancake mix. She found the griddle, which fit over two of the burners, and thought of having bacon, but she was leery of going out in the dark to the smokehouse. She would need to decide on her meal plans the day before, either set her bread to rise at night or bake enough to have some left for the morning meal. She rushed, listening intently to see if anyone was awake, but it wasn't until she placed two loaf pans in the oven that she heard someone coming down the hall.

A sleepy-eyed Becky yawned her way into the kitchen sniffing and smiling when she realized bread was baking.

"Did I wake you, Becky?" Erin asked, anxious to know.

"I didn't want to sleep anymore. Can I help?"

Erin nodded, deciding she wouldn't say anything about Becky wearing the same soiled dress as yesterday. The child's hair was again untidily braided, so much so that Erin fairly itched to take a brush to it. Patience, she warned herself, taking up the basket.

"Could you show me where the henhouse is, Becky?"

"Oh, I'll gather eggs. I don't mind them. Guess Papa told you he always has eggs for breakfast."

"No, no, he didn't get around to mentioning it. How many will we need?"

Becky finished struggling into a coat that was too big for her. "Let's see...Papa has four, Ketch sometimes three, Jake eats one. I don't much like eggs. Dishman and Ray usually have three each. That's fourteen, not counting you. But don't worry, we have two dozen laying hens so there'll be plenty left for your egg money."

"My egg money?" Erin asked, moving the coffeepot to a back burner to keep it hot.

"You can sell the leftover eggs and keep the money. Mrs. McKenize told Papa she wouldn't feed the hens unless she got to keep the egg money."

"Mrs. McKenize was one of the—"

"Housekeepers," Becky finished for her and left.

A door opened and closed down the hall and Erin smoothed down her apron, but it was Ketch who came into the kitchen. His jaw was swollen and he held it cradled with one hand. Erin smiled at him, liking the warmth of his blue eyes and his face, which bore the webs and lines of a man who spent his years out in the open. His gray hair was neatly combed, but he had forgone shaving.

Erin fetched him a cup of coffee, setting it down at his place along with the bowl of sugar.

"You remembered," he mumbled.

"That you like your coffee hot and very sweet, Ketch? It won't take me long to know everyone's likes and dislikes if they tell me."

"Boss's, too?"

Erin cringed inwardly, but her voice betrayed nothing. "His likes and dislikes are the ones I'll learn first and the fastest." She busied herself checking the bread, then the heat of the griddle. Dribbling a few drops of cold water on the cast iron surface, she was satisfied to see them bounce and steam.

She debated with herself, knowing that it pained Ketch to talk, but needing information. "Becky is certainly a bright child. I was surprised when she said at supper that she's never been to school. Did the other housekeepers teach her and Jake?"

"Not the way you'd be meanin'. Miss Nolie set a store by her books. Weren't fit reading for a child, though, if you'd be knowin' what she liked."

Not having the vaguest idea, Erin stared at him. Before Ketch could enlighten her, Becky came back with the eggs. "Dishman's milking the cow for you. He'll be along soon."

"The cow! I forgot—"

"Don't matter," Ketch assured her, wondering why she looked stricken. "Ole Bessie's gentle enough an' don't mind waitin' a bit. It ain't like she just calved—then you'd hear her bawling clear to the mountains."

"But I was told that milking the cow, gathering eggs and slopping the hogs were my chores."

"Boss said that?" Ketch stared down at his half-empty cup. Shaking his head, cursing silently when the move caused pain to shoot from his tooth to his ear, Ketch pondered what was going on. Feeling as bad as he did, he'd left Mace alone last night, but he knew something was wrong between Mace and Erin. At his direction, Becky set the table.

Mace entered just as Erin turned the first batch of pancakes. The aroma of fresh bread filled the air and he sniffed in appreciation. His gaze caught Erin's and for a moment he swore she was daring him to say anything about her cooking. He took his seat just as she served him coffee.

With a small bit of bacon grease melting in the frying pan, Erin cracked four eggs, hoping she wouldn't break the yolks, feeling that Mace would want them as perfect as all else. It wasn't until a full platter of pancakes was on the table, eggs served all around and coffee refilled for those who wanted it that Erin took her place.

She fingered the tiny carved bird on her napkin ring and looked up to find that Mace was watching her. Without being told she knew this had belonged to his wife. Becky had told her that each of the napkin rings was carved with different signs of birds or animals. She wondered if they held any special significance for the Indian heritage that his wife brought to their marriage, but once again kept silent. She sipped at her coffee, enjoying the way the food was being eaten.

Spreading his third slice of bread with store-bought jelly, Mace glanced up at Erin, seated at the opposite end of the long table. "You're not eating."

His statement made her the focus of all eyes. Forks and cups stopped midway as Erin slowly shook her head in reply.

"Why not?"

Wishing Mace would leave it be, Erin knew she couldn't explain that she intended to wait until everyone was finished.

"Pete, pass her the last few pancakes." Mace waited until his order was carried out and Erin poured syrup over them. She looked as if she needed every bit she could eat just to put some weight on her, and never far from his memory was the additional reason it was necessary that she eat well. "Cosi, you've got the pitcher so pour out a glass of milk for her." The rebellious look Erin shot at him made Mace grin. No matter what else happened between them, he wouldn't have it said that he skimped on food for her. And he needed no reminder that ranch work was hard work for a woman.

With a curt nod that silently acceded this round to him, Erin ate, keeping her eyes firmly on the plate. She forced down each mouthful under Mace's watchful gaze, wishing he would leave.

First light made a feeble attempt to enter the room through the grimed window when Jake came in. He ran to his father, snuggling in his lap.

Erin returned the tousle-haired boy's smile. "What would you like, Jake, eggs or pancakes?" Like his sister, Jake was wearing the same soiled clothes as yesterday, making Erin think that laundry would loom as the first major chore of the day before cleaning the kitchen.

Biting into his father's slice of bread, Jake shook his head.

"You're growin' mighty fond of these clothes, boy," Mace said softly to his son. "You don't want Erin to be thinking you haven't got anything else to wear, do you?"

"Nope. Like them."

Once again, Erin felt put in her place and all without having said a word to Mace. But she didn't understand why he was not saying anything about Jake needing more to eat than bread and jelly when he wouldn't let her get away with it.

"Jake, would you like some milk?" she asked, watching the boy shake his head and reach out for his father's coffee cup. When Mace didn't stop him, Erin did. "You can't allow him to drink that. Coffee—"

"It's cool enough and he likes it," Mace answered, his cheek resting against the side of his son's head, both his arms holding the boy close.

Loving children was one thing, spoiling them without a thought to what was good for them was quite another matter. "Milk," she said, straining to be calm, "is better for a growing boy."

"You hear that, son? Milk is better for you." Mace took the pitcher from Cosi, poured out half a glass, then emptied the remainder of his coffee into it. "Will that satisfy you?"

Erin nodded, although it didn't. Yet she couldn't deny that Mace could have chosen to take her to task for questioning the way he raised his children. As she finished her breakfast, the talk around the table turned to chores. Jake began on another slice of bread and Mace lifted him into is own chair as he rose.

"Ketch, you take Heppner into town with you. Don't figure you'll be able to ride back alone when you get that tooth pulled."

"Ain't no weak-kneed—"

"Know that," Mace cut in. "But I want that butter churn and barrels from the cooper. I didn't have room for them."

"Lambert, boss?" Ray asked him.

"Yeah. Those kegs from Preston didn't hold up. Pete," he went on, "you stick close by the house today. Can't have Miz Dalton getting herself lost between here and the barn." He heard the edge in his voice, and knew that Ketch and the other men heard it, too. But Mace didn't care. Cosi had been making calf eyes at Erin while they ate and all she could do was smile at him. He didn't like it one bit. She had no right to smile at any man. She was his wife.

When he grabbed his jacket from the hook near the door Jake begged to go with him. Mace wanted nothing so much as to ride out alone, sort out his feelings and plan what he was going to tell everyone about Erin. But the boy looked so forlorn that he agreed.

Becky came to kiss him, and he glanced at Erin over her head. "Slice up some of the ham with what's left of the bread. I'll take that with me. Cosi and I should be back in time for supper."

She was moving before he finished, biting back the yes, sir, no, sir that burned her tongue. From the cupboard she took a clean napkin and wrapped the half loaf of bread that remained from the three she baked this morning. Thick slices of ham followed, and Erin walked to him with both bundles.

"See if you can make something filling for supper."

"Roast boar, perhaps?" she snapped.

"You touch one bristle on that boar's hide and I'll hang yours out to dry, woman. Stop shaking in your shoes and walk down to the smokehouse. There's sides of beef and venison. I warned you about how it would be."

"Yes, you warned me, Mr. Dalton," she returned in a whisper, feeling her cheeks heat. He hadn't bothered to lower his voice, so their rapt audience had heard it all.

With jelly smeared over a milky mustache, Jake grabbed his jacket and was out the door before his father. The men left as quickly. To her surprise, Becky went out, too.

Once the dishes were cleared away, Erin struggled with the large cast iron kettle, setting it on the stove, then, rolling up her sleeves, she snatched up the bucket and confronted the pump. This morning, the contrary handle worked smoothly. Once the wash water was heating, she filled another smaller kettle to heat water for cleaning the kitchen.

Woven basket in hand, she went first to the children's room, staring about in dismay. Assorted clothing rested where it fell. The sheets appeared to have been slept in for more weeks than she wanted to count and the quilt on one bed had mud smeared on it. All too quickly she filled the large basket with soiled linens, wishing it were possible to take the feather ticks outside and air them.

She hesitated before opening the door to Ketch's room, not at all surprised to find his bed neatly made, his soiled clothes piled in one corner and nothing out of place. His bundle of laundry joined her growing pile.

As she came out into the hallway, she spared a glance toward Mace's closed door. Remembering his warning of the night before, she shrugged and went into the kitchen. He told her not to enter that room and she wouldn't.

Rolling out the washtub from the pantry, she sorted out sheets from clothes, set them into the tub and added slivers of lye soap. Testing the water, she was disappointed that it was as cold as when she pumped it. The smaller kettle was having more success. Finding a scrub brush, Erin used another bucket to clean down the table. The smooth grain of golden oak emerged beneath her steady hand. Stopping every few minutes to test the wash water, she soon stood back and felt pleased that the trestle table needed only a light coat of lemon wax to make it gleam.

There was ample room for ten at the table, and sixteen could fit with a bit of squeezing.

She had not forgotten what Mace told her about the extra hands. Digging her fists into the small of her back, she rubbed away the small ache that started and washed out her cleaning bucket. The sideboard needed the same scrubbing.

Sunlight began to make patterns on the floor. But she didn't want to think about washing it until she finished the other chores. Frustrated that the wash water was still lukewarm, Erin finished the sideboard. Washing her hands, she once again took the sourdough starter and began to double the amount of dough she had made in the morning.

There was no sign of Becky, although she did stop several times to open the door and look for her. Erin had just emptied another bucket of water into the tub when Pete came in.

"Here, ma'am, don't be lifting that. I'm supposed to be helping you."

Erin thanked him, gladly handing over the bucket to be filled again. Pete was not much older than herself, nearly as tall as Mace but without his muscular build.

"I came in to see if the cream's up."

"If the cream's up?" Erin repeated, staring at him blankly. Honestly, these men were talking the same language but combining words in ways she had never heard used.

"When I strained the milk this morning I put it into the two milk cans in the pantry. The cream rises to the top, gets skimmed off, put into the churn and made into butter," he explained, figuring quickly that she didn't know how to make butter. "Bessie gives enough cream to make near a pound of butter a day. Most folks would be waiting two or three days to make some, but you heard the boss man."

Erin didn't attempt to stop her rueful laugh. "I heard him, and so did everyone else."

"Want me to leave some milk for you, or take it all down to the well house?" he asked from the doorway to the pantry.

"Whatever you think best, Pete. I need to get this wash done." Erin set the washboard into the tub and knelt before it.

"Ma'am, don't think I'm interfering. But why didn't you start the fire outside? 'Course it's chilly, but it'll save you having to bend and then carry the wash out to the lines."

"What are you talking about, Pete?"

"There's an old washtub stored under the back porch. I forgot which one it was of them ladies the boss had here to tend to the house, but she made him fix things so she wouldn't be carrying laundry up and down the stairs."

Erin stared at the clothes soaking. "Well, there's no help for it now."

"I can get the fire started and fill the wash kettle for you. Should be ready long about the time you're done here."

Once again she thanked him, venting her anger that Mace had not been the one to tell her on the clothes she scrubbed.

Rinsing out the clean clothes, Erin looked over her shoulder when Becky called out that she was back. Her nose wrinkled at the strong smell of lye soap, and without taking off her coat, she went to the stove and poked at the rising dough.

"You gonna work all morning?"

"There's lots of chores to do, Becky. Don't you have any?"

"Not really. Pa lets me and Jake do what we want long as we don't stray far from the house."

Uncertain what to say, Erin let it pass. Her limited experience in child rearing was learned at the orphanage, where every waking moment was accounted for by chores of some kind. The thought of giving Becky and Jake no direction at all didn't sit right with her. Nevertheless, she was not going to make the suggestion that Becky help her set the house to rights. Mace would likely misconstrue her motive and she needed no more confrontation with his biting tongue.

After watching Erin give the clothes a final rinse, Becky said, "Bet I could learn to do that."

"When you're grown with a home of your own you'll have time enough to learn how," Erin answered.

"I thought maybe you could teach me and all."

The underlying longing in the child's voice made Erin look at her. "If you're willing to learn, I'll teach you, Becky. But you must promise me something in return."

"Sure. What?"

"That you teach me what I don't know about the ranch and caring for animals."

"That's easy. You just—"

"Not right now, sweetie. Now, we need to punch down that dough or there'll be no bread for supper."

"Can I ask you something?" Becky saw Erin's nod. She followed her to the clean table where she sprinkled a bit of flour before turning the dough out of the bowl. "What do you want me and Jake to call you?"

"Erin, if you'd like." The dough received the punch Erin would have offered Mace Dalton if he was present.

Why didn't he spend any time telling his children about her?

"All right."

Erin had to ignore the note of disappointment. What could she possibly tell Becky? Imagining Mace's reaction if either of his children called her anything else sent goose bumps down her spine.

"Gee, the kitchen sure looks cleaner, Erin."

"We'll have it gleaming when I get a chance to put some lemon wax on the wood. I bet your mother kept it real nice-looking."

Hands locked together behind her back, Becky swung to and fro. "I don't remember her much. She died when Jake got born. Never even saw him, Papa said. I was three."

Folding the dough into a ball, Erin placed it in the bowl, covered it over with the clean cloth and set it on the stove to rise a final time. "You mustn't be sad, Becky, you have your father and anyone can see that he loves you and your brother."

"You really think so? Sometimes, well, he gets real busy and doesn't have much time for us. Do you have a family?"

"No, Becky."

"No one at all?"

"I grew up in an orphanage with other children who had no families, or if they did, the people weren't able to take care of them."

Becky's hand covered Erin's. "Now you have a family. You have me and Jake and Papa. And Ketch, of course. You'll like Cosi. He sure laughs lots and teases, too. Pete's real nice and Dishman makes the prettiest music you ever heard. None of them have families, either. So, you'll be happy here having all of us to be your family."

Erin wasn't sure who moved first, but they were hugging each other tight. The hope she had buried came rising up and she cherished the child who gave it back to her.

For minutes they stood, Erin with her dreams spread out before her—a home and family, hers to care about and be cared for, love freely given and returned.

Becky pulled back, smiling up at her. Erin closed her eyes against the image of Mace's forbidding expression that superimposed itself on his daughter's face. He would see to it that there would be no closeness, no family, no love. Before long it would be apparent that she had trapped him into marriage carrying another man's child. How kindly would anyone treat her then?

Chapter Ten

Ketch stopped in the shadow of the open barn doors and watched Erin come up from the springhouse, carrying a half wheel of cheese. He wiped off his brow, the corner of his mouth lifting with a smile as he saw that she was lingering to enjoy the warmth of the midday sun, although he had warned her a few days ago that the unseasonable February weather wouldn't hold.

She was pretty enough for even an old geezer like him to enjoy watching, however briefly. She was always rushing from one chore to another. In the six weeks since she had come here, Ketch realized he had never seen a woman so driven to set things to rights, but then, he'd never seen Mace ride anyone as hard as he did Erin.

With his bow-legged gait Ketch went toward her, intending to offer to carry the cheese for her.

"Mornin', Miz Erin. Carry that up to the house for you?"

"Oh, it's not that heavy, Ketch. But thank you. A right pretty day, isn't it?"

"Sure. An' you're as pretty." Ketch knew she would just turn aside his compliment as she had everyone else's. But on those rare occasions when he saw Mace catch her eye, Erin would color up like a straight heart flush.

"Are you busy, Ketch?" Erin asked, having made a decision last night that Ketch was the only one who might answer her questions about Mace.

"Got a few minutes. What's on your mind?"

Erin gnawed her bottom lip a moment, then looked directly at him. "I want to know about Mace. I heard you talking last week about being with Mace the longest. That you came up from Oklahoma with him."

"That's a fact." Erin was as jumpy as a cricket on a hot stove. Ketch wondered if Mace had been at her again. She was staring off at the mountains and he let her be for the moment. More than once he'd kept quiet when Mace had blistered her soft hide about something she did that didn't please him. Made a man wonder if Mace knew what the devil he wanted from Erin. The woman was pretty, sweet-natured and a hard worker. Seems like a body just mentioned what needed doing, and she tried to see it done. Clothes were cleaned, mended and folded, including the men's laundry, which she didn't have to do. Cosi made it known he was partial to buttermilk biscuits and they appeared at every supper. Mace, as far as Ketch could remember, was mighty partial to them himself, but you'd never tell by the way he tended to carry on.

Erin turned to Ketch to find him studying her. This was not an easy task, asking personal questions about Mace, but one that needed doing. "Was Mace married when he came up here?"

"Sure was. Didn't he tell you?" Erin's quick shake of her head told Ketch that wasn't all Mace didn't tell her. Well, he wasn't going to volunteer, but he wouldn't refuse to answer her. The matter of Mace and Erin sleeping apart came to mind. He had heard them in the hall that first night, and while he never figured Mace for a fool, Ketch was revising his opinion of the man he liked and respected. All a man needed was eyes to see that Mace wanted her. And the sweet lady in front of him was no better, with her sneaky looks when she thought nobody was watching her.

Erin set the muslin-wrapped cheese down on the porch. "This admission is painful for me to make, but it must be said, Ketch. I know that Mace cared deeply for his wife, but I don't understand why he married her."

"Loved her," he answered without hesitation. "Loved her enough to turn his back on his folks, who wouldn't accept her. She was Cherokee, full-blooded. Her folks farmed the place next to Mace's. Natural they'd get together. Saw it happening. Saw that no one believed he'd marry her. You know for yourself what a stubborn cuss he is."

"Yes," Erin whispered, finding the mountains in the far-off distance drawing her gaze once more.

Ketch shifted his stance, patient now that he saw the direction of her questions. Sometimes he believed she was no better than Mace, taking everything he dished out without fighting back. Wasn't natural for a body not to have a line that, once crossed, spelled out temper. Except when it came to Becky and Jake, he reminded himself. Then she lit into Mace for all her slender body was worth. She wasn't one to raise her voice, but he'd never met a woman who could put so much in a look from those green eyes the way Erin did.

Nodding to himself, he figured she was filled with plenty of sass and fight, all right, but something held her back from loosing it on Mace. He'd taken about all he could of these goings-on. The men mumbled about Mace's temper, but none wanted to confront him. Yet he couldn't shake off a feeling that if Mace took another slice out of Erin tonight in front of them, one of them would likely take the boss out behind the barn.

"Miz Erin, I'm likely steppin' out of place to be tellin' you this, but can't be holdin' it back no more. Mace cut himself off from everyone after his wife died. There's reasons only he can tell you, but he blames himself for her dying."

"What do you mean, Ketch? How could he blame himself?"

"Tol' you. Ain't for me to say." He glanced behind her toward the springhouse and saw that Owhi, a Yakima Indian who sometimes worked for them, had dropped to a crouch as if he was studying the earth. He couldn't figure what the man was looking for, hunkered down and touching the ground. Owhi was the best tracker to be found in these parts, and if he had found animal tracks near the springhouse, Ketch didn't want Erin to get upset. Her being a city woman, like Mace often called her, she wouldn't have noticed them. He made an abrupt excuse to leave her.

Unsatisfied, Erin hefted the cheese and climbed the back steps. There was a cool wind blowing down from the mountains and she longed to linger outside, to think about what Ketch told her, but Mace had been working close by repairing corral fences these last two days and took all his meals at home.

There was no sign of Becky or Jake, but she kept her worry to herself. The children were often gone for hours at a time. When she voiced a protest to Mace, braving his anger, he always reminded her that they were his and he would raise them his way. Jake was often still shy with her, and Becky, when she was bored, would help with whatever chore Erin was doing.

Learning that Mace blamed himself for his wife's death reinforced her feeling that he tended to spoil Jake and Becky beyond a man loving his children, although, secretly, she craved a bit of that love for herself.

"Find something, Owhi?" Ketch asked as he approached the Indian near the springhouse.

"The new woman of Mace carries her child low in her belly."

"The new woman... Oh, you mean Erin," Ketch began, then he stopped. His mouth was open and stayed that way when Owhi pointed to the prints in the muddy ground.

"See how she steps? Four moons will see the birth of the child."

"There's no child! You're wrong, Owhi. I know there can't be a child, and for sure not one coming in four moons."

"Four moons the child comes," Owhi insisted, rising to his full height.

"I've never had cause to doubt you, but I'm telling you you're wrong this time." Ketch shook his head, but couldn't help staring down at Erin's footprints. For all that he told Owhi he was wrong, he had never known the man to be anything but right. But what he was saying was impossible. Wasn't he just thinking about Mace and Erin sleeping apart? Even if... No! This wasn't true.

"You wanted work?" Ketch asked him, deciding to let the matter drop. He wasn't going to fight with him.

"I bring king salmon from the early run."

Ketch licked his lips. Owhi had a way of smoking salmon that he and Mace loved. "Went dip netting?"

Owhi smiled. "This is way to take as many salmon as needed."

"Dangerous, too," Ketch muttered, thinking of the one time he and Mace went along with Owhi. The Yakima had led them down to the river where the waters were forced through narrow channels and over low falls. Ketch had taken one look at the crashing, tumbling waters falling from one pool to another and felt his stomach heave. But Owhi stood on a wooden platform precariously tied to basalt cliff, extended over the whirlpools and eddies, sweeping his long-handled dip net from the upper to the lower pool. It had amazed Ketch that the fish couldn't be seen, only felt coming into the net and hauled up to the platform. The fishing station was highly prized among the Yakima, often passed down from one generation to the next.

"The salmon will be good for the woman. Give her much strength but no make fat."

Ketch stared at Owhi's moccasins and the small footprints near his feet. If Owhi was right, and he wasn't admitting that he was, but if it were so, the child wasn't Mace's. That might explain a lot. Heck, he told himself, it would explain everything.

"I bring fish to smokehouse."

"Yeah. You do that, Owhi, then come up to the barn. I've something for you."

Mace found Erin alone in the kitchen when he came in to eat. The table was set for the midday meal, steam rising from the platter of venison steaks. Bowls of hot green beans flavored with bacon, pickled corn relish and stewed tomatoes lined the center of the large trestle table. Erin had her back toward him, taking pans of golden brown biscuits from the oven.

Her hair was rolled tight and pinned to her head, but he remembered his one sight of it long and freely curling down her back. His reaction to her had changed in the six weeks she had been there. He woke hot, stayed hot, and slept hot as a firecracker lit at both ends and popping in the middle. Since she'd taken to wearing a long apron over her gown he couldn't tell if she was showing yet.

"Brown and perfect as could be," she said, using the linen towel to plop the biscuits into a basket.

He knew she didn't realize she wasn't alone, but he made no noise to correct her. She finished and dug two small-fisted hands into the small of her back, moaning and stretching while he watched.

He was so engrossed in watching Erin that he didn't hear Pete coming down the hall.

"Miz Erin . . . Oh, hiya, boss."

Erin spun around, not toward Pete but to Mace. The hot pan from the oven clattered to the floor and she cried out as it seared across the back of her hands. Before Pete moved, Mace closed the distance between them and grabbed Erin away from the stove. Pulling her arms to the side, he held her wrists apart, turning them over and staring at the already blistering skin.

He reached behind him to the top of the table, tossing off the glass cover of the butter dish without thought to its breaking. Taking the rounded ball in one hand, he used it to soothe the burns.

Erin bit her lip, trying not to cry out. She steeled herself for another sort of blistering, the type only Mace could deliver, which never seemed to heal.

"Stop standing there useless as a milk pail under a bull, Pete. Get two clean cloths." Mace resisted Erin's attempt to pull free of his grip. He stared down at her bent head as she stilled, refusing to look at him or talk. Mace realized it had been like this since the first morning. Only where Becky or Jake were concerned did Erin open her mouth. He knew she was trying damn hard to please him, but it remained unexplained why the more she tried, the angrier he became. He took the napkins Pete handed him.

Despite his anger, he was gentle wrapping her hands with the cloth. But when he was done, he held her in place and looked at Pete.

"You wanna explain to me what you're doing in the house during the day? I told you to ride fence, didn't I?"

"The window was stuck in Miz Erin's room and she asked me to fix it when I had time. The fence is checked, and I told Ketch what repairs are needed up in the high meadow."

"You had to rise mighty early to get it done and be back here so soon."

Both Erin and Pete shared a look that was not lost on Mace. Simmering anger began to bubble as it hit a low boil. She asked Pete to fix her window. She allowed him in her bedroom. She didn't think he noticed all those sweet smiles that passed between the two of them. She still thought him a fool.

"If there's repairs to be made you'd better get to it," Mace said, giving Pete a cold stare.

Pete didn't bother to point out that food was already on the table and he hadn't eaten since five this morning, putting in a full day's work so he could come back to help Erin with the heavier chores. He stepped around Mace and the table, grabbing his hat off the rack near the door.

"Pete, wait," Erin said, yanking her hands from Mace's grip. Placing her elbow against his waist, Erin shoved Mace aside and slipped around him to the table. "Take some biscuits and steaks with you." Her hands were clumsy trying to cut the still steaming biscuits and fill them with the venison.

Mace took the knife from her and with a few deft cuts opened four, filled them and had them wrapped in a napkin handed over to Pete before the man got close to the table.

"Get going or you'll miss supper," he ordered the younger man. Admitting to himself that what he felt was jealousy, Mace turned on Erin. "If you need fixing in my house, you ask me. Or were you looking for an excuse to get Pete alone here?"

"No. You're wrong, Mr. Dalton." Erin closed her eyes and her mouth. It was senseless to defend herself. When she opened her eyes to look at Mace, his expression relayed that he, not Erin, was the wronged party. She didn't understand and said as much.

"I'm trying to hold to your terms, Mr. Dalton. I've cleaned *your* house, cooked *your* food and tried to care for *your* children." Erin had to stop. He was standing so close to her that the heat from his body was something she couldn't ignore. This was the first time since the day she arrived here that he had been this close to her. She took a shaky breath, trying to control the shiver at the touch of his hands on her arms.

"Figured you'd be too soft for ranch life. I warned you how it would be, didn't I?"

"You warned me about the hard work, Mr. Dalton. You never said a word about stripping my hide at every turn."

"Stripping your..." Mace stopped himself from saying another word.

With a look, Erin begged him for a little understanding, but Mace had closed his eyes, drawing her closer to him without conscious thought.

The back door slammed and Mace jerked away from Erin.

Ray and Cosi came in, plunking their hats on the rack, sniffing appreciatively.

"Pete said food was on," Cosi announced, pulling out his chair.

"Couldn't find Jake or Becky, boss," Ray added, taking his place next to Cosi. "What happened to your hands, Miz Erin?"

"I was careless with the biscuit pan. Not to worry, I finished mending your good shirt for the meeting tonight."

Mace sat down, too, his anger at full boil. "What meeting?" he asked Ray.

"Grange," he said, passing along the platter of venison and helping himself to the corn relish. "You coming?"

"Guess I will. Where's Ketch?"

"Down at the barn. Owhi brought us salmon from the first run," Cosi answered, looking around and not finding the butter. Shoving his chair back, he snatched up a biscuit and headed for the door.

"Now what?" Mace demanded.

"We need butter."

"I'm sorry, Cosi, I used—"

"Not to worry, Miz Erin. I'll get it in two shakes."

He'd no sooner left than Ketch came in, each hand filled with a child's ear. "You'll never guess where I found these two, boss. Down by that damn bull again. Warned them, I did, just like you, but these two are ornery 'bout listenin' to what's good for them."

Mace's fork hit his plate with a clatter. He glared at Ketch. Since Erin had come here, Ketch appeared set on siding with her about Jake and Becky's needing a firmer hand. Most times he ignored him, but that bull had an uncertain temper at the best of times, and their disre-

garding his own orders to stay away from him demanded
Mace do something harsh to bring the lesson home. With
a hard gaze he looked at his two mud-strewn children.

"Wash up and sit. I'll deal with you two when we're
done."

Becky's mouth set in a mutinous line. She tried to get
Erin's attention, but she was staring down at her empty
plate. Dragging Jake over to the dry sink, she pulled the
stool into place. If Erin wouldn't interfere, they were sure
in for it this time.

As it turned out, Mace let them off with another stern
warning and chased them outside once the meal was done.
The men left to return to work, but he sat lingering over
a last cup of coffee. Erin hadn't eaten.

"Your hands still smarting?"

With a startled look her head came up. She shook her
head.

"Don't like what you cooked?"

Without answering, she rose, carefully holding her plate
between her wrapped palms. Mace stopped her by standing and blocking her way.

"You can't wash the dishes."

"Yes, I can."

"It's foolish to be this stubborn," he said, taking the
plate away. "I'll do them."

His offer was as unexpected as the gentleness in his
voice. But Erin had learned quite a bit about Mace in the
last weeks. Everything came with a price tag. "Thank
you, but I'll manage."

"Your hands'll sting in hot water and soap."

"They're my hands."

"You'll be useless tomorrow if you don't give them a
chance to heal," he stated flatly, trying to control his anger with her continued refusal of his offer. Why hadn't he

noticed the faint shadows beneath her eyes? Or had he in fact seen them and ignored them? Since he didn't sleep soundly, he often heard her pacing the kitchen at night and stopped himself more than once from getting out of bed to find out what was wrong.

Those dark green eyes of hers met his with a directness that he found disconcerting. His gaze drifted down to her mouth. He found himself angling his head downward to close the distance between them.

"I'm not asking you, I'm telling you, Erin."

The words were breathed over her lips. Erin felt the intimate heat of his breath. Snared in place by this abrupt change in him, she didn't attempt to move away. Erin licked her suddenly dry lips. He was watching her with a heavy-lidded intensity that should have frightened her. It didn't. Her heartbeat increased. His mouth brushed over hers, the touch so light, so soft, she thought she imagined it. Her eyes closed and once again his mouth barely touched hers. She swayed toward the warmth of his body. How could she desire his kiss? The question remained unanswered. Mace settled his mouth over hers.

The tiny sound she made from the back of her throat aroused him. The warmth he could sense stealing over her skin, the fine tremor of her lips, all heightened his arousal. He pulled back, staring down at her. The eyes she opened to his were luminous, but questioning. She lowered dark lashes, hiding her expression from him.

Rubbing his hands up and down her slender arms, he drew her closer to his body. He wanted her, now, even as he damned his body for its betrayal. But how could he resist lips that warmed and parted at his insistence? A man had to be crazy to stop exploring the sweet honey taste of her.

Driven by the heavy beat of his blood, Mace drew the tip of his tongue over the sensitive peak of her upper lip and was rewarded with the tilt of her face more fully to his. With a gliding caress, he traced her lower lip from corner to corner, drinking in a small sound of surprise when his teeth gently closed over her bottom lip, holding it captive. He released her in seconds, only to begin all over again.

His hand eased up, cupping her face, hunger replacing tenderness.

The beguiling warmth and gentleness of his mouth was gone, but Erin found she wanted the velvet excitement of his tongue gliding against hers. She brought up her injured hands, needing to touch him but afraid to do more than rest them lightly against his upper arms.

Once again the texture of his kisses changed, and her breath was stolen, her mouth his. Tension that had nothing to do with fear and all to do with passionate need filled her. She hungered for closeness, yearned for acceptance and longed to put the bitterness of the last weeks behind her. ·

His hand slid down her back, kneading the ache that was constantly with her, creating a deeper ache inside her, drawing her against his chest. With his other hand he cupped her hip, leaving her no doubt about the strength of his own need. She forgot where they were, losing herself in the increased demand of his touch and his kisses.

Erin tried to capture his textures. The silky brush of his mustache, the softness of his lips, the velvet glide of his tongue entwining with hers. Mace had strength but tempered it with a gentleness. That gentleness coaxed her to forget caution, to forget that she was here on his sufferance. The caressing splay of his hand on her back eased her loneliness only to replace it with a building fever.

The total surrender of her response to him drove Mace wild. He wanted to lose himself in her, but he wasn't so lost that he didn't hear the kitchen door open. He jerked his head back, turning to shield Erin with his body.

For a long moment there were no sounds but their harsh breaths, then he heard the closing of the door. He let Erin go, willing his body's demand to cease as he headed for the door.

"Mace?"

"Don't touch those dishes. I'll be right back."

Erin's rioting senses took a few minutes to absorb what he said. "Dishes?" she whispered, shaking her head. "The man kisses me senseless and all he can say is don't touch the dishes?"

Outside, Mace confronted Ketch. "Why didn't you say something?" he asked the man.

"You didn't look like you was wanting an audience or interruption, boss."

"Well, I got both, didn't I? So tell me what you wanted."

Ketch looked off toward the mountains. He was hemming and hawing now that he had Mace's attention, but he wasn't sure how to word what Owhi told him.

"Owhi brought plenty of smoked salmon. Said he'd be by when this first run is over to see if you have work for him. Funny thing about Owhi, the man's losing his trackin' ability."

Leaning against the porch post, Mace waited for the rest. Ketch was once again staring off at the mountains. He cleared his throat and dug his boot into the earth. Mace grew concerned. Ketch was never one to hesitate to say what was on his mind. This had to be serious.

"Owhi have trouble?"

"Not like you'd be meanin'."

Gifts of Love   147

"How's that, Ketch?"

"Told you, he's losing his tracking ability. Has some dumb fool notion."

"Never knew Owhi—"

"Well, this time he's a fool," Ketch cut in, his stand belligerent. He turned toward Mace with hands on slim hips, legs apart, and glared at him.

"You wanna spit out what's bothering you, Ketch, or are we gonna stand here and dance around it all day?"

"Think you're so damn smart? Iffen you'd heard what I did, you wouldn't be actin' so smug. Owhi was down by the springhouse. He said he seen something there that made me wanna get on him like a south Texas wind."

"That bad, huh?" Mace nodded, wondering if Ketch had lost his mind. He was blabbering. No two ways about it. And that was not Ketch's way. Moving closer, Mace flung an arm around his shoulders. "Maybe I can help if I know what you're talking about?"

"It's Erin."

"Erin?" Mace repeated, dropping his arm, instantly on alert. "What about Erin? What does she have to do with Owhi?"

"It was her tracks that he was looking at down at the springhouse."

Mace turned his back on Ketch and slid his hands into his pants pockets.

"Ain't got nothin' to say, boss?"

"What's to say? She's always down there. Can't imagine what got Owhi excited. Ain't many who don't know that I married."

"Yeah. That's true enough. But ain't many know why you got yourself hitched. Ain't many who know you're sleeping apart from your bride. And there ain't many who'd dare say what needs saying."

Ketch was satisfied to see Mace spin around. "Got your attention now, ain't I? Well, boy, we've been together a long trail. Guess I'm 'bout the only one to do this."

"Then do it, or say it, or whatever the hell you've got in mind," Mace grated from between clenched teeth. He braced himself, knowing what was coming.

"Owhi says four moons will see us with a new little one."

"Guess that's about right."

Ketch hid is surprise that Mace didn't deny it. But he started this and had to finish it. "Can't be yours."

"Ain't mine."

"Boss, I'm sorry. It's my fault, ain't it? Ridin' you to get hitched. Can't say it enough, but I'm sorry."

"Not as sorry as I am."

Ketch watched him walk away, his shoulders slumped, and felt again the hurt of seeing the pain in Mace's eyes. He glanced at the kitchen door and thought of Erin. Figuring he'd barely managed to confront Mace about this, and muddled it, there was no way he could talk to Erin. Not now, no how. But that little gal needed someone. He would bet his best boots and saddle on that. At best, he had his answer to why Mace rode her so hard. Mighty rough for a man to swallow what she done. And for a prideful man like Mace it had to be doubly so.

Ketch walked to the barn to finish his chores, but he found himself feeling tense, just the way he did before a storm broke.

"Only the one that's comin' ain't gettin' blown away by no wind," he muttered.

Chapter Eleven

Leaning over the dry sink, soaking her blistered hands in a fresh pan of icy well water, Erin closed her eyes and wondered why Mace never returned.

After she had waited a while, she had opened the back door but there was no sign of him. If something happened to his horses or cattle, he would have told her. It was a strange quirk of his, now that she recalled it, to always let her know where on the ranch he was working.

Having removed the linen cloths, she ignored the pain in her hands and cleaned the kitchen. Washing the dishes caused the blisters to break but she managed to block out the pain. For like a sore tooth the tip of a tongue couldn't leave alone, her thoughts skidded and returned to the way Mace had kissed her.

She hadn't sensed a bit of anger in him. But then, she chided herself, who was she to judge? They shared the same house and meals, and little else. Mace had made no attempt to breach the wall between them.

Until today.

Why? The question plagued her. A longing to talk to Maddie filled her. Maddie knew about men. What Erin knew would just about fill a thimble.

Which reminded her that she still had to finish the seams on the new shirt she was making for Jake. Taking her hands from the water, she dried them carefully and saw that all the blisters were weeping. There were herbs and salves in small clay pots on a shelf in the pantry, likely belonging to Mace's wife, but no one had bothered to tell her what they were for.

Mary Blue Sky. That was her name. And for Erin she held the place of wife even in death. Mace Dalton had seen to that.

But her need for something soothing to ease her hands sent her into the pantry. She opened and sniffed the contents of the pots, a few filling her with the scent of flowers, others pungent enough to make her wrinkle her nose. How harmful could any of them be?

She stuck her fingers into one and lifted out a bit of greasy salve. Bracing herself, on the chance she was wrong, Erin chose a blister, held her breath and dabbed the salve on. No sting. She quickly soothed it over the backs of her hands, deciding to take this one to her room. Quickly rearranging the others on the shelf, she stood back, sure that no one would notice this one missing. With Mace, she never knew what his reaction would be to her touching what had belonged to his wife.

With a rueful curve of her lips, she made her way to her room and amended her thought. Mace had no objection to her handling the dishes or cleaning the furnishings that he had built for Sky, it was the personal belongings that seemed to grab hold of his temper.

She had nearly an hour before supper had to be started and for once there were no other chores waiting. Erin closed her door behind her, breathing deeply to ease the tension that was always present when she left this room.

Afternoon light filtered softly through the lace curtains on the window. Sky's sewing basket, one of the items Mace had handed over with reluctance, sat on the floor near the straight chair where she had left it the night before.

As she lifted it to her lap, the twinge of envy that never seemed to leave her when she touched the personal items that belonged to Mace's wife was somewhat stronger today. Perhaps, Erin told herself, it was because she had been the one Mace had kissed and held as if he wanted her.

There were times, like now, when she was ashamed of her feelings of jealousy. She consoled herself with the knowledge that no one knew about them. And it wasn't as if she was trying to steal the memories of the woman away from anyone. She wasn't. Becky liked to talk about her mother, recounting things that Mace had told her. Since it made the child feel good, Erin merely listened. Jake had no memories of Sky, since she died giving birth to him. Erin still didn't understand why Mace blamed himself for his wife's death. She sensed it pained him to talk about Sky to the children, but he often did, which made her admiration for him grow. It was so hard not to envy the woman he loved. If a wish could be granted, she wanted a tiny part of that love from him.

She knew she was dreaming a fool's dream, for Mace's teasing and gentleness were reserved for his children. How could she make him care?

Smoothing the thick blue flannel of Jake's shirt, Erin knew that she would not ask Mace for anything for her child. How could she remind him that she was less than the perfection of his wife? Sky hadn't been afraid of the cow, and she had known how to gather eggs without the hens pecking her. Sky had gardened and canned and made cheese. She had traded what they didn't use. Sky had no qualms about wringing a chicken's neck the way Erin did. Sky would never forget to latch the pigs' pen, and if she did, the woman wouldn't have spent four hours to round them up.

And Sky could ride. She had often helped with the ranch work. Erin never could decide which of her crimes were the worst. But Mace compiled a long list for her.

If she had another choice, there were times in the past six weeks when she had thought about leaving here. But there was no denying that she had come to love the children. And in their own way she knew they cared for her, too.

Honesty compelled her to admit that Mace had shown her some consideration along with his barbs. He always asked if she needed anything whenever someone had to go to town. He certainly never balked about paying for the few items she requested. He had refused to take back the money she had left from her travel expenses, but in turn, she couldn't ask him to buy flannel for her to make a few baby clothes. And she couldn't ask Ketch or the other men to get it, since they didn't know about her child.

Setting aside the basket and shirt, Erin rose and untied her apron. She pressed the faded material of her skirt to either side and studied the slight swell and the thickening waist revealed in the mirror.

She would need to let out the seams again. The thought made her smile. Cosi teased that she was already putting on weight from all the good cooking she did. And there was a decided appreciative male look in his eyes when he said it. For a moment she lost herself, basking in the man's approval. When she realized what she was doing, Erin stopped. She was Mace Dalton's wife, even if he seemed intent on forgetting it at times.

Somewhere inside the man was goodness. She knew it as well as she knew that she would never be the woman to draw it from him.

But she couldn't ignore his seeking her out. She just couldn't forget the sweet heat of his kisses.

"Kissing her," Mace muttered, leaning over the corral fence but not really seeing the sleek coats of his cattle.

What had possessed him? And what was he going to do about it? She likely figured she had him where she wanted him now. Well, Erin would be wrong. He was a man, not a boy to be controlled by his body. Wasn't he?

Pounding his fist against the wood post, he swore at himself. Touching her again had been a mistake. But damn, she had felt so good in his arms. Warm and sweet, soft and responsive. If Ketch hadn't come in and left, he could have had her. Damn Ketch, too! Now he knew the truth. Mace wasn't worried that Ketch would tell anyone. He wouldn't. But then it wouldn't be long before they'd all know. How would they treat her? Cosi, Ray and Pete liked her, respected her and went out of their way to help her. He had kept quiet about the chores they did for her, since they never once left their own undone.

How could he want Erin, knowing what would happen?

He had sealed off his own need for love, his need to love a woman of his own when he had buried Sky. Gentle, loving Sky. The memory of her haunted him.

With a groan born of deep inner torment, Mace stared blindly ahead. Guilt pounded at him. His desire had killed Sky.

Just the thought opened the floodgates to hell.

Sweet Sky, who knew with a look that he wanted her and would stop whatever she was doing to come to him.

Sky, the girl whose love had grown as they had until there was no choice to be made; they had to be together.

His eyes squeezed tight, but his mind brought him the sight of Sky's joy when she told him she carried his child. And because he had cut them off from everyone they knew, he believed her reassurances that no harm would come to the child if they made love. As the months went on, their shared joy over her steadily growing belly seemed to increase their desire, as if they had both known they would need this to carry them past the time they couldn't make love.

Sky was a strong woman. He had never realized her strength until he came home and found that, alone, she had given birth to their daughter.

Memories came, faster and faster until his head ached.

He remembered Sky's fierce need to give him a son. Her arms and the gentle healing he found within her body when his letter home to his parents telling of their grand-daughter's birth went unanswered.

The winter storms they battled together with Ketch to save the cattle. Becky's first smile, first step.

The agony of the child they lost before Sky's third month. His own vow, sworn and held to, that he wouldn't touch her once she conceived again.

Sky. Doe dark eyes pleading with him. Soft hands that stroked him until fire burned. Sky, whispering that nothing would hurt the child. Nothing had hurt Becky. Sky... needing him as badly as he needed her.

Sky, smiling that she had given him his son. Sky, dying as he begged her forgiveness.

Mace lost track of the time he stood there, but slowly the cut of the wind made itself felt and he reached up to rub his eyes only to find his own tears.

With a deep cleansing breath he threw back his head and stared at the fast-moving clouds. He couldn't give in to the desire he had for Erin. He wouldn't relive the past again.

He could never do it, for his need burned stronger for her than it ever had for Sky. He wouldn't put Erin at risk no matter how he wanted her. And the wanting he held for Erin after what she had done to him still confused him.

What he needed was distance from the woman, more than the separation of rooms. He didn't trust himself to stay away from her tonight. The knowledge was simply there and he didn't bother to question it.

There was a Grange meeting in town. He'd ride in early, have dinner and a few drinks and be with people who didn't remind him of Erin at every turn.

Nothing to stop him, he told himself, heading for the house. Ketch could handle whatever came up. Rubbing his cheek, Mace decided he needed a bath and shave.

Once in the kitchen, seeing everything neat as a pin, he felt guilty that he had forgotten he was going to clean up. He didn't hear Erin moving around and guessed she was out of the house. She slipped outside at every chance. He'd seen her more than once, just walking and looking up at the mountains. Sky had also loved the mountains. From their bedroom windows part of the range could be seen, and she had loved to view them in every light, often calling him to join her.

It was Mace's nature to move quietly, and he brought the big wooden tub out from the pantry, set the big kettle on the stove and filled it in a matter of minutes. He shrugged out of his shirt and tossed it in the basket Erin set aside for dirty laundry. He had found out after a week that if he didn't put his clothes in it, she wouldn't go into his room and take them. The same held true for the linens. And he found that he enjoyed the sun smell of freshly washed sheets on his bed. Kicking off his boots, Mace set them aside and took the linen towels from the stack on a shelf in the pantry. Erin kept them there since everyone used the kitchen for baths.

Filling the tub partway with water from the pump, Mace found himself wondering when Erin bathed. The tub was heavy, something she shouldn't be lifting or dragging in her condition. It wasn't often that he let himself remember the baby she carried, but now that he opened his mind to it, thoughts of other chores she did came to mind.

For all that he deliberately looked to find fault with her, he knew she had fulfilled her part of the bargain. She cooked mouth-watering meals that made the men fight to be doing home chores rather than eat away. She kept the house clean, spoiled them all in small ways, and he had to admit that she loved the children.

Most men would be counting themselves lucky to have a woman like Erin. He knew Cosi teased her, and at first when Erin smiled in return, he had felt jealous, but she didn't make any attempt to single Cosi out.

Mace opened his belt buckle and slowly drew it out from the pant loops. Setting it on the chair, he unbuttoned his pants, unable to stop himself from thinking about Erin.

Absently, he tested the heat of the water and singed his fingers. Barefoot, with his fly half-open, Mace padded down the hall to his bedroom to get his razor and shaving brush.

He couldn't find the razor anywhere. Erin! She had disobeyed his order and come into his room. Slamming the bedroom door closed he strode down the hall to the kitchen, stopping when she rushed out of her room. Her hair was unbound. A thick, black silky cloud just settling around her. Mace felt his hands curl at his sides. Her eyes seemed to widen, and he realized that he was half-dressed but made no move to retreat to his room.

"You frightened me," she whispered, one hand at her throat.

"You disregarded my orders."

"I couldn't leave the kitchen—"

"Not that," he said, cutting her off, closing the distance between them until she backed toward her room. "You went into my room and took my razor."

"Your razor? Why? Why would I need your—"

"What the hell do I know why you needed it! I want—"

"And I wasn't in your room, Mr. Dalton," she protested, wishing he would have stopped at the doorway, but he was following her inside.

Mace forgot about his razor. He snatched up the remains of her nightgown. "What's this? Didn't you cut this up?" he yelled, shaking the cloth he held in one fist in front of her.

"I used a scissor," she returned, trying to snatch the cloth from his hand.

Her hair swung free, covering his hand, and before Erin could stop him, he dropped the cloth and caught a handful of her hair.

"Erin, I—"

"Please don't—"

They both began at once, then stopped and stared.

Erin's lips were slightly parted over her unvoiced protest. Mace remembered the fleeting taste of her mouth. A taste that he still craved to have. His gaze fell from her mouth to the pulse beating wildly in the hollow of her throat, down to the creamy skin revealed by the two undone buttons. He moved without thought, driven by need, crowding her against the dresser, sliding his hand through the thickness of her hair to cup the back of her head and hold her still.

"What is it that you don't want, Erin," he whispered against her mouth. "Don't want me to touch you? Not to kiss you? Tell me," he insisted, already sealing her lips with his.

There was no gentle coaxing this time. The sensations spilled through her, more forceful this time. She couldn't breathe, couldn't think, couldn't stop him. All she managed was a trembling that started deep inside her and spread so that she knew he could feel it. She clung to the strength of his bare arms, drawing his warmth into herself.

Mace's hands shifted when he felt her trembling and the giving softness of her body against his. Erin was not going to refuse him; the desire that had already claimed him was making its claim on her. He picked her up and carried her to the single bed, lowering her to the soft feather mattress and following her down.

His tongue thrust deeply into her mouth, filling her until she arched up to him, her hands clenched in his hair to hold his mouth to hers. The kiss deepened even more, and she felt his harsh groan as much as she heard it when he flattened her beneath him, letting her know every bit of his muscular weight.

The need to draw breath forced Mace to lift his head. He gazed down at her lashes, which fluttered but never quite settled. "Am I too heavy for you?" he asked, his voice rough with passion.

Erin shook her head, flexing her fingers in his hair.

Mace brushed aside her hair, lowering his head again, but his gaze fell on the cloth above her head. There was no mistaking the shape and size of the small gown. That's what she had cut out from her own nightgown. Clothes for her baby.

With a groan that was torn from deep inside him, he rolled off her, stunned for a moment and unable to order his body to move.

Bewildered, Erin turned on her side, raising herself by leaning on her elbow, and saw the gown. With effort, she managed to get up. There was no need to ask him what was wrong. She knew. What she wished for was the courage to demand that he leave her room and never come into it again.

The words remained unspoken.

Her body ached for the second time today. With jerky moves she began to gather her hair, blindly finding the discarded pins on the dresser, managing to coil and pin it in place. With fingers that shook, she buttoned her gown, trying to ignore the sound of his harsh breathing behind her. Snatching up her apron, she tied it and without looking at him left her room.

Mace went to the Grange meeting in town and with him went the tension that had made supper a silent meal. Ketch had lit the fire in the parlor, lingering as if he wanted to talk, but Erin was in no mood for anyone but the children.

She had a copybook of her own that she intended to share with them.

Erin knew she did not want them to learn as she had, without praise and with swift punishment for failure. She thought of a way to make this a game, one in which she could learn as much as Becky and Jake.

Stretched out on the floor, Erin placed the inkwell and pen she had borrowed from Mace's desk in front of the copybook.

"Now, as I explained to you both, we will think of as many things that are used or on the ranch that begin with the letter *a*. If a word comes up that I don't know, I'll depend on you to help me understand what it is."

"Do we get a prize for getting the most words?" Becky asked.

"Hands will hurt," Jake whispered from the other side.

"No, Jake. They're much better now. I can manage to use the pen." Twisting to look at Becky, who was on her stomach, legs swinging in the air, chin propped up on both hands, Erin admitted that she hadn't thought of a prize. "It really wouldn't be fair, Becky. I don't know as much as you."

"But Jake does. Anyway, you're not little like us so you'd have to know lots more. Papa said grown-ups are the smartest—"

"I'm sure he believes he's right," Erin said quickly, unwilling to get into a discussion of Mace. She needed to put him out of mind, just as he was out of sight.

"Me first," Jake said.

"All right," Erin answered, pen dipped and poised to write.

"Airtights."

"That's two words. No fair, Jake," Becky protested.

"Ketch says one," the boy answered, looking at Erin to settle the matter.

"Maybe if you explained to me what airtights means—"

"Don't know. It's what Ketch calls canned goods."

"Oh. Well, I'll guess it's one word. That all right with you, Becky?"

"I'll allow it."

"And have you thought of one of your own?"

"Apples, I guess. No, wait, apron."

Erin wrote both words in her neat hand.

"Will you show me how to make letters?"

"Me, too," Jake added, not to be outdone by his sister.

"I'll do better than that. I'll teach you how to read. I saw a bookstore in town and when Ketch goes in, I'll have him buy us a book."

"With pictures?"

Erin reached over and tousled Jake's hair. "We'll tell him to make sure and look for one with them."

Later, when they were ready to be tucked into bed, Erin hugged and kissed each child, surprised when Becky moved aside for her to sit on the bed.

"I want to tell you that I'm glad you came here. You bring lots of smiles and good things, Erin." With slender arms she hugged Erin and then snuggled beneath her quilt.

Pressing another kiss on her brow, Erin cherished the words in her heart. If only Mace could see her with his daughter's eyes. She stopped herself from thinking about him yet again and made her way to her room. With the lamp lit and the fire in the small wood stove banked for the night, she settled herself to finish Jake's shirt and begin work on her baby's gown.

She was still awake when Mace finally came home, his unsteady footsteps alarming her that he might be hurt. Before she could get her wrapper on, she heard Ketch's door open, listened as he called out softly to Mace and received a slightly slurred reply.

Had she caused him to drink? Despair filled her. She wanted a man who didn't want her. Erin returned to bed, vowing to redouble her efforts to stay out of his way.

Mace had other ideas.

Chapter Twelve

Dousing his head with cold water to clear the liquor-induced pounding of his head this morning, Mace was forced to come to a few decisions. They all concerned Erin.

After the Grange meeting last night, he had stayed to share a few rounds of drinks with his fellow ranchers. In silence, he had suffered their congratulations about his marriage. But what stirred his anger and jealousy so close to the surface these days was Cosi. Cosi and his bragging about Erin. She was a wonderful cook. Her pies were to be sure winners at the next fair. Pies? What pies? Mace had never tasted a pie she made. Then Cosi had showed off the tiny neat stitches with which she had mended the tear in his best shirt. The man talked about her smile and how pretty she was, and what a sweet voice she had when she sang. That last irked Mace as much as the pies did. He had never heard Erin sing. When had Cosi? Then the teasing began from the other men. Mace had better watch out or Cosi was likely to steal his bride.

For a moment or two he was tempted to tell Cosi to try. He could have her and her child. But the words never came. What did come was the decision that he had better keep Cosi away from her. He didn't want to fire Cosi any more than he wanted to get rid of Pete. Ray, to his credit, hadn't said much about her, but Mace didn't doubt for a minute that the man would praise her if asked.

The little lady would have to stop trying to work her wiles on his hired help. He'd be the only one around. So if she needed help, she'd just have to come to him.

She was his responsibility. He couldn't forget that air of innocence about her. Didn't she admit that the bank clerk had seduced her without trying? Somehow, much as he hated to admit it, he believed her. Cosi was a hard worker, but he fancied himself a real ladies' man. Erin wouldn't understand how a man might feel she was leading him on with her smiles and the thoughtful things she did for him.

Wiping the water from his face, Mace stared at himself in the mirror. He had enough to contend with. He was not going to have his wife gossiped about. So, he hadn't been the soul of kindness—that didn't excuse her for looking for a bit of comfort from any other man who was handy.

She was his wife. For better or worse. She owed it to him to be respectful and obedient.

And what about what you owe her? a small voice nagged as he turned away from his reflection and donned his shirt.

He'd done his share. She had a home. Plenty of food. He would never beat her, as some men treated their wives, though he had more reason than most. His ranch was thriving. He let her do things her way.

And never made her feel as if she were an intruder? the same little voice of conscience asked.

Well, he hadn't known how difficult it would be to see another woman using Sky's things. It would take time to make that adjustment.

But he didn't have too much time left, he warned himself.

Ketch knew about her child. Mace couldn't keep the fact buried too much longer. If he didn't bring it out into the open, the choice of how he handled it would be lost to him.

Hearing the voices and clatter from the kitchen, he hurried to tuck his shirt into his pants and join them for breakfast.

"Well, you think about it, Miz Erin," Cosi was saying as Mace took his place at the head of the table. "You tell me how many rows you want an' I'll make sure that garden land gets plowed."

"But I don't know, Cosi," she admitted, pouring out coffee for Mace without looking at him. "I never had a garden. There's time yet, isn't there?"

"My ma always figured two rows of everything for the table and two for canning," Ray volunteered, reaching for the platter of pancakes.

Seeing there were only two stacks left, Erin rose and went to the stove to start another batch.

"Since when did you two become farmers?" Mace asked in a cold, hard voice.

Erin shot a look over her shoulder at Ray and Cosi. She steeled herself, knowing that Mace would find a way to blame this talk of a garden on her.

"They ain't," Ketch put in, having caught Erin's pleading look. "I'm the one that mentioned it." He lifted his cup, sipped some coffee and carefully set it down. "I figured with the stalls needin' cleanin' again, some of that muck could start goin' to the garden. Been haulin' wood ash out there for the past week myself. Straw, ash and manure make the best fertilizer. Land that ain't been worked is gonna need all the help it can get to produce. You can't be findin' no objection to that, boss."

Mace glared at Ketch. He returned his glare, then grinned.

Erin held her breath, only releasing it a moment later when Mace asked Pete to pass the ham. She flipped the pancakes, willing them to brown quickly so Mace could eat and leave. She had promised the children that if all the chores were finished early, she would fix a cold lunch and leave it for the men so the three of them could pack a picnic and take it up to a special spot that Becky offered to show her.

Erin piled up the finished cakes on the platter, lost in her thoughts. She turned, only to have Mace reach out for the coffeepot on the stove at the same time. His hand smacked the plate, upsetting the pancakes, which fell to the floor. Erin's startled reaction caused the platter to slip from her hands, so that crockery broke among the mess.

"Of all the damn clumsy useless women!" Mace swore. "Can't you do anything right? I didn't hire you to waste food!"

There was more. Erin stopped herself from listening to him. She scooped up the mess with her apron, turning aside Cosi's offer to help, and dumped it all into the dry sink. Returning to the stove, she began again.

Hired? Had Mace really said that in front of all of them? Heat flamed her cheeks as anger took hold. Never once, not one time could that man find a kind word to say to her. The griddle, she saw, was too hot, for she was almost burning this batch. She didn't care. After the pancakes had cooked to the accompaniment of the heavy silence behind her, she slid the plate on the table in front of Mace and fled the room before she did something like use the griddle on his thick head.

"Boss, you didn't have to lace into her like—"

"Cosi, if you wanna keep your job, shut up!" Mace heaped pancakes he no longer wanted on his plate. He buttered them and poured too much syrup over the stack, realizing that the men were all staring at him. "What's wrong?" he demanded, refusing to back down and apologize for what he had done. "Well? Is someone gonna answer me?"

"You made Erin sad again," Becky accused, pushing back her chair and standing. Jake followed his sister's action.

"Sit down. Both of you," Mace commanded. "I'll not be judged by my children in my house. And not at my table." With a look that dared any to dispute him, he glanced at those around the table, nodding when no one answered him.

"Seems more than a few of you forget that. And there's changes in the day's work. Ketch, you and Ray haul feed and hay to the cattle in the upper pastures. Cosi, you can cut out those cows for breeding. Maybe it'll take some of that sass outta that bull. Dishman, you—"

"Pete, Mace. That's my name. I don't do the dishes anymore since Miz Erin's been here."

"That so?"

"That's so," the younger man returned, matching Mace's glare for glare.

"All right," he conceded roughly. "Guess a man's got a right to be called whatever he wants. You'll finish riding fence. There was talk last night at the meeting about miners cutting some fences and letting cattle out. That's all we need."

"That and the Nez Percé getting riled over their land being claimed," Cosi added, hoping that this talk would channel Mace's thoughts away from Erin.

"Yeah, that, too." Giving a pointed look to each of the men's empty plates, he added, "Since you're all done eating, I can't figure why you're all still sitting here. That's not what I pay you for."

Chairs scraped back and with telling shared looks, the men grabbed for hats and jackets.

"One more thing," Mace said before they left. "There's no need for any of you to ride back for midday. Becky'll ride out with your food." Mace grinned at his daughter, feeling satisfied that he solved the problem of keeping the men away and at the same time pacified Becky by giving her something special to do.

Only Becky wasn't smiling at him. Her straight brows had come together in a thundercloud. But before Mace could ask her what was wrong, Jake came round to his side.

"Me, too?"

"You'll stay around here and help me today. That find favor with you, Jake?"

Jake smiled and nodded. When his father turned his attention back to Becky, he stuck his tongue out at his sister.

Shamefaced when her father caught her doing the same, Becky mumbled that she was sorry.

Mace hid his surprise when Becky began to clear off the table without being asked. And Jake, to his added surprise, hurried to help her.

When Becky came to take his plate, Mace gently cupped her shoulder and stopped her. "You want to tell me why you're not pleased about taking the meals out to the men? I can recall a little girl who begged to be allowed to do that not so long ago."

"You spoiled our day."

"Spoiled your day? How?"

"Erin and Jake and me were going to have a picnic."

"Oh," was all Mace could think to say.

"She was gonna finish the story 'bout a puppy," Jake said, wiggling his way between father and sister. "Can I have a puppy like the boy?"

"Oh, say yes, Papa! A puppy would be so much fun."

Mace smoothed Becky's hair, noting the neatly made braid and the sparkle in her eyes. He moved his other hand to Jake's head, realizing that the boy's hair wasn't brushing his shoulders. He supposed he had Erin to thank for getting him to sit still long enough to cut his hair.

He wanted to deny the softening he was beginning to feel toward Erin, but the crack in his veneer had been made. She really cared about his children. She had not rejected them.

Never once had she accused him of tricking her into marriage by lying about his children being half-breeds.

Resting her head on her father's shoulder, Becky stroked his cheek. "Papa," she whispered, "will you go find Erin? I'm sorry I made you mad. But you shouldn't make her cry so much."

"Do I do that a lot, Becky?" Mace asked with a voice that was suddenly choked.

"Every time you yell at her. I hear her crying in her room at night. She doesn't know I know. Promise you won't yell at her again."

"Promise?" Jake added, climbing up into his father's lap.

"You like Erin, don't you?"

"Lots, Papa," Becky answered. "She's funny when she tells us stories, and she can sing so pretty. And she never yells at us. Not even when Jake broke a jar of jelly and she had to wash the floor again."

"Made me a new shirt," Jake added.

"And she promised to make me a new dress," Becky said, not to be outdone.

"Seems I married myself a real paragon."

"What's that?" Becky asked. "Is it someone nice as Erin?"

"Yeah, Becky," Mace answered, trying to rid himself of a hard core of resentment. "Tell you what, I'll go look for Erin and you two finish the dishes."

But Mace never had a chance to move, for Erin walked in and saw him seated with Jake on his lap and one arm holding Becky at his side.

He could see for himself that she had been crying, but the words of apology stuck in his throat.

Jake saved the awkward moment. "Erin, Papa's gettin' me a puppy."

"Not just for you," Becky was quick to say. "We'll share it, just like in the story."

"No. Mine."

"Hold it, you two," Mace said, stopping Jake from pushing his sister away. "I didn't say I would get—"

"Yes. Yes, please," Jake begged, then turned to where Erin still stood near the door. "Tell him yes, Erin."

"I can't, Jake. Your father will make his own decision about getting you a puppy." She had seen the men ride out and hoped that Mace was gone, too. Unwilling to look at him, Erin busied herself with clearing the table. Becky came to help her.

But when she saw the remains of smashed pancakes and broken crockery in the dry sink, Erin realized she wasn't strong. Tears sprang to her eyes, spilling down her cheeks.

"Papa," Becky whispered, jerking her head toward Erin's back.

He saw her shoulders shake, her head bowed over the sink and for a moment thought she was sick, but Becky was drawing one of her fingers from the corner of her eye down her cheek, miming tears. He set Jake on his feet, and pressing his finger to his lips motioned them to go outside.

As silently as his children had left, Mace rose and went to stand behind her. "Erin, I..."

Wildly she shook her head, brushing frantically at the tears that wouldn't stop. Without touching her, he placed a hand on either side of the edge of the sink so she could not move.

"Look, I had a few drinks last night and wasn't in the best of moods this morning."

"You never are," she blurted, stricken once the words were out.

"Guess not," he admitted, clamping his hands tight so he wouldn't touch her. "But all this crying of yours is upsetting Becky."

"I can't help it." His accusing tone forced the admission, but Erin realized it was true. She did seem to cry over the slightest thing.

The memory of Sky's voice making the same admission when she carried Becky hit Mace. Sky never cried, not so that he would see her. Likely that's what was bothering Erin.

"Listen to me, Erin. You can't let every little thing upset you. It's not good for... it's just not good," he finished lamely, unable to mention her child.

Her head came up and, between sniffles, she answered him. "You are by no means a little thing, Mr. Dalton. But you sure can pick on little things—"

"Dropping my damn breakfast—"

"I didn't do it on purpose! If you hadn't reached for the coffeepot just when I turned I wouldn't have dropped the platter. But you couldn't ask for it, could you? Oh, no.

And if I wanted to drop the platter on purpose, I would have used your lap not the floor!"

"And if you put the coffeepot on the table by my place where it belongs, just like Sky did, I wouldn't have had to reach out for the damn pot!"

"Don't yell at me. I'm not Sky!" she screamed. "I can't be Sky. I don't want to be Sky." Poking her finger into his chest, she shook with anger finally free. "I can't be Sky. I'm me. Erin. And that's all I want to be, Mr. Dalton, just myself."

"Who the hell do you think you are, yelling and poking me?"

"I'm your wife! I'm alive, not dead. I resent your not caring, not being given any respect, never having a kind word from you. I'm not an animal. I'm a woman. I made a mistake and paid for it. But you'll never let me forget, will you?" Erin couldn't see. She was blinded by the tears in her eyes. The fight seeped out of her. She hated being compared to Sky. But it would always be Sky who held first place in his heart and mind. First place, and only place. "Stand aside," she demanded, "I need to blow my nose."

"Your nose can wait. This can't. I told you all this crying isn't good. You can't want to keep Becky upset, can you?"

The mention of Becky distracted her. Shaking her head, Erin admitted, "I didn't think she heard me."

"Well, now you know she did." Wrapping his arms around her, Mace leaned his cheek against her hair, ignoring her struggle, his chest pressed to her back.

Erin tilted her head to the side, unable to bear his touching her like this. All the gentleness she longed for was here, now, but Erin braved his wrath again.

"You must realize this is a mistake. You don't know me, and what's more," she added, still sniffing, "you don't want to. You should have left me in Walla Walla when I asked you to do so."

"No!" Mace spun her around, grabbing her by the shoulders. He hated the way she flinched at his touch. Ignoring her hands as they futilely tried to push him away, he cupped one cheek and lifted her face to him. "Don't close your eyes and hide from me, Erin. Things can't go on as they are. I meant what I said. This isn't good for you, my children or me."

"I d-don't know what you want from me. I'm not as perfect as Sky was. I can't be her. You snap at me all you want and dare me to answer you. Then you dare to..." *Kiss me till my insides melt.* Erin's eyes flew open, one hand covering her mouth. Had she said those words aloud?

Mace's eyes darkened, meeting her startled gaze, and she saw that the sensual line of his mouth seemed softer below the dark brush of his mustache. Spoken aloud or not, she was sure he knew the words. She was simply too vulnerable to him.

"Do you know," he whispered, brushing his thumb across her cheek to wipe up the still-flowing tears, "that this is the first time you've fought back?"

His touch, filled with gentleness she longed for, made her tremble. Erin had to lean over the edge of the sink. She couldn't take a breath that wasn't filled with his scent. And she didn't trust him. She had to remind herself of that, but no sooner was the warning silently sounded than it seemed to disappear.

"Is that all you want from me, Mr. Dalton? You want me to fight?"

"Stop calling me Mr. Dalton."

"Yes, Mr. Dalton. I'll remember that."

"Such a sassy little mouth, Erin. Say my name." There it was, happening all over again. He got close to her and raw need dictated his words and actions, making him forget her deceit. His fingers traced the delicate arch of her brows, watching as her green eyes darkened. He felt the uneven lift and fall of her breasts against his chest as he bent over her. The small sound she made, the way her fingers dug into his shoulders made him ease his big, hard hands beneath her, arching her up to his hungry mouth.

But Erin covered his descending lips with her hand to stop him. She denied her own desire for his kiss, refusing to forget as easily as he did the harsh words so recently said.

His lips opened on her palm, his breath hot, the tip of his tongue making tiny circles on the only bit of her flesh she allowed him access to. She closed her eyes, fighting not to give in to the seductive coaxing, and felt the baby stir. Quickly she worked her other hand down between their bodies, trying to prevent him from feeling the same.

But it was too late. Mace did feel the child move, pressed as he was against her. He pulled back, releasing her, fighting to still the heat of his blood.

Erin followed his gaze to where her hand curved protectively over the slight swell of her belly. "You'll never forget. Never let me forget." She looked up at him, once again fighting tears. "Please, if you won't let me go, then stay away from me. You don't want me as a wife, Mace. You don't even like wanting me at all."

This time Mace was the one who left, for he couldn't deny the truth she spoke.

Chapter Thirteen

An uneasy truce developed between Mace and Erin from that morning. The following week, the children got their wished-for puppy.

Jake, flushed with excitement, carried the squirming pup into the kitchen to be presented to Erin. The cream and brown marked dog was the runt of the neighbor's litter.

"I don't care that he's tiny," Jake told Erin. "He licked me first and let me pick him up."

"He's a pretty little thing," Erin murmured, petting what she could reach of the dog still held tight in Jake's arms.

"He's a boy. Boys can't be pretty."

"Handsome, then. I'm sure you made a good choice, Jake."

"Becky said no. She said he's too small, but I like him."

Erin knelt on the floor as Jake set the puppy down between them. She laughed with the boy as the puppy scrambled for purchase on chubby legs, darted around the kitchen chairs, jumped up to lick Jake's chin, yipped and then ran off to repeat the cycle again.

"You should've come. The mama didn't bark or try to bite us when we went near her babies. So many, Erin."

Jake presented his small fingers for her to see, frowning and then tucked his thumbs into his palms. "That many of them."

Erin tousled his hair, wishing that she could have gone with them. It would have been nice to visit with the other woman, but she was, to her eyes, beginning to show. Mace never tried to discuss what she would say about her child and she was uncertain how to approach him about it. There was an uneasy truce between them, and she was loath to break it. She made the decision that the less anyone saw of her, the less chance she had to cause him embarrassment.

"Perhaps another time, I can, Jake."

"Can what?" Mace asked, coming in with Becky. He pushed his hat back, watching Jake play with the pup, but his gaze targeted Erin's flushed face. The lingering smile on her lips did not reach her eyes to dispel the sadness he saw there.

"Told Erin she should've come," the boy answered.

"All she had to do was ask. Why didn't you come, Erin?"

"Yeah." Becky echoed her father. "Why didn't you come? The puppies were so cute. They were all bigger than this one. Can't understand why Jake had to have that little thing."

"Becky, that's unkind," Erin chided gently, stroking the pup's belly as he flopped over on his back by her side. "And the puppy is for both of you to share."

"I'm gonna call him Scrap 'cause he's so little," Jake announced.

"That's a dumb name," Becky countered.

Scooping up the puppy between her hands, Erin studied the small face. "Scrap seems to fit him." She was rewarded with several chin licks before she placed him in her lap. The little dog circled several times before he curled into a ball and nestled his head on tiny paws.

"He likes you!" Shyly, Jake smiled at Erin. "I like you lots, too."

Mace stood there, watching as Erin's head angled closer to that of his son's, a smile curving her lips before she pressed a kiss to his forehead. He couldn't hear what she whispered to Jake, but his son was giggling as he took the pup from her lap. The moment seemed to freeze inside him. The warmth of the kitchen, the scent of spices, Erin glowing with a softer beauty, his son, the smiles . . . Mace shook his head.

He wanted to help Erin stand up, but remembered his promise to keep away from her. He could see the telltale thickening of her waist along with the darker line along the seams of her faded gown that showed she had let them out. There were lengths of calico and other dress goods stored in the blanket chest, material that Sky would have used. He knew Erin wouldn't ask him to buy any for her, but surely she would not refuse the goods if he gave them to her.

Conscious of Mace watching her, Erin ignored the twinge in her back as she stood. "We'll need to find a bed for him, Jake, and make a place in the pantry for his food and water."

Cuddling the pup, Jake turned his head and looked up at his father. "He's gonna sleep with me."

"No! I don't want that silly little dog in my room. Tell him no, Papa. He'll chew up everything."

"Will not, Becky!"

"Will too!" Becky yelled back.

"Stop it, both of you," Erin scolded, forgetting Mace. But it was only for a second. With her fingers pressed to her lips, she glanced at him, waiting for him to tell her not to interfere with his children. But he merely nodded, his expression unreadable, and she turned to Becky. "If we find him a bone or a rag to chew on, he won't ruin any of your things. And to make sure of it, you'll need to keep your room picked up. No more leaving socks or shoes on the floor. Jake promised to take care of the dog and as long as he does, the pup can sleep in your room."

"He'll smell."

"He'll be scared outside," Jake countered, pressing close to Erin. "Tell her how he's too little to be alone."

But Erin didn't have to, she met the understanding in Becky's eyes and nodded. "You remember the story, don't you?"

"Well, it's not fair. The puppy was for both of us. Now Jake thinks he's all his."

Erin hid her smile at Becky's stubbornness. She tried to find a way to placate the girl and suddenly had an idea. "But you treat the pony as if he was all yours, don't you, Becky? When Jake wants to ride by himself, he must ask you first. If Jake has the dog to care for—"

"I know, Erin," Becky said with a sigh. "He'll be like the boy in the story you told us and learn how to be responsible for someone 'sides himself."

Erin didn't bother to correct her mispronunciation of responsible. It was enough that Becky remembered the lesson in the story.

"Now that this is settled, will you help Jake find a basket and some rags to make Scrap here a bed?" Holding out her hand to Becky, she waited for the child to make her own decision. Pouting, Becky walked over to them. "If you hurry and get Scrap settled, there'll be time for oatmeal cookies for both of you."

"I'll have five 'cause I'm bigger," Becky declared.

"Me, too, 'cause I'm a boy."

"Three each and no arguing," Erin said.

"Three now and three after supper."

Throwing up her hands, Erin laughed. "I give, Becky. All right, three now and three after supper, but only if all chores are done without being asked."

"Come on, squirt," Becky said to her brother, "I'll get the cookies for both of us and we'll go to the barn to find him a bed."

While Jake battled his puppy for possession of the cookie he insisted on having, Becky led the way outside.

And Erin realized that Mace was still there. She pleated the sides of her apron nervously. "Did you want something?" she asked, uncertain of his mood.

"This go on all the time?"

"Pardon?"

"Becky and Jake. They fight like this all the time?"

"Oh, they're not fighting, not really. It's natural for children to test themselves and each other over who will be leader. But Jake," she added with a smile to herself, "is learning to hold his own with her."

"And where did you learn to be so tolerant of children's squabbling?"

Erin raised a stricken gaze to his face. She felt as if she were on trial, judged and found wanting. But she answered him. "In the orphanage where I grew up, Mr. Dalton. The older children had to look after the little ones. There wasn't anyone else to do it."

The moment she replied, he regretted asking. Her eyes instantly took on a distant look, her smile disappeared and she seemed to become smaller, less sure of herself than she had been a minute ago with the children.

Realizing that she was still standing there, idle as could be, Erin searched the kitchen for some chore to do. But it was too early to start supper, her baking was done, wash and ironing complete, and everywhere she looked all was neatly in its place.

Mace took off his hat and jacket, hanging them on the hooks near the door. It appeared as if he had every intention of staying inside. Erin turned to leave. She could not stay in the kitchen with him.

"I wouldn't mind having some of those oatmeal cookies myself."

Erin almost tripped over her skirt hem in her hurry to get the crock from the sideboard. "Please, help yourself."

He did, to a large handful, watching her start to retreat from the room, from him. "Coffee would be nice, too. That is, if you're not in the middle of something that needs doing."

Erin stared at him. What was he saying? Asking her polite as could be, as if he hadn't stated time and again that this was his home and she was merely there on sufferance. As if she would refuse to make him coffee even if she was in the middle of something!

"It's no trouble to make a fresh pot," she said. But Erin felt his eyes watching her every move, so she was extra careful not to spill the coffee grounds once she filled the pot. What was he up to, sitting in the kitchen in the middle of the afternoon?

"You handled that business about the pup real well. Did you have a dog at the . . . the place you grew up?" He couldn't say orphanage. He didn't want to scare her off.

Erin, standing with her back toward him at the stove, merely shook her head. A dog? She was lucky to have enough hot porridge to eat.

"Didn't you ever hear that a watched pot will never boil?" Mace asked, determined to have her turn around.

Was that truly a note of teasing in his voice? Erin was curious, and glanced over her shoulder to where he sat. He was grinning at her.

"It's true, Erin. Sit down until the coffee's done."

"Oh, I can't. I still need to...to—"

"It can wait." Mace closed his eyes, hearing his harsh command. He looked at her and decided there was no sense in delaying what he was determined to say. "We need to talk, Erin. No one's around now, and this can't be put off any longer."

Without a word, she chose a chair two places down from his and saw that it annoyed him. Clasping her hands in her lap where he couldn't see them, she steeled herself for whatever blow he intended.

"Must you look like a scared rabbit?"

"Pardon?"

"You, Erin. You're sitting there, scrunching up, ready to jump and run."

"Well, Mr. Dalton, if I was looking at you the way you are staring at me, I'd like to see how you'd be sitting."

"That bad, huh?"

"Likely more," she returned in a prim voice.

Mace threw back his head, laughing.

Stunned, Erin merely stared, but in moments, his laughter became infectious and she joined in. His droll expressions brought a fresh burst from her, for she had never heard him like this, or knew that he could mock himself with comments that made her laugh until her sides ached. As suddenly as the laughter had started, it stopped. Erin wiped her eyes.

"Foolish woman," he teased, "how can you cry when you laugh?"

"It's your fault. I don't remember ever laughing so hard."

The smile she offered warmed his insides. Laughter was a good sound to hear, even better to share, and Mace was well aware that it had been missing from his home since Sky died.

But his expression was so sober that Erin rose from her place.

"Don't leave. We haven't talked."

"I'll get your coffee, first." Anything to put off what she sensed was coming. Taking his favorite large cup from the corner cupboard, she filled it near the brim. Mace took no milk; he liked his coffee black and strong.

"Aren't you having any?" he asked when she set the cup in front of him.

"No. I find it . . . no."

"Finish what you were going to say."

She cringed at his demand, hating herself for it. "The coffee," she said softly, "upsets me, so I haven't been drinking it."

"Oh." Well, Mace, there's your opening and all you can say is "oh." He sipped from his cup and set it down. "It's what I wanted to talk about. Your baby." She nodded, her gaze firmly focused on the table. She was back to sitting like a scared rabbit, he bitterly noted. "A decision needs to be made about what to say."

"Yes," she whispered through dry lips, once again clutching her hands together in her lap.

"The children need to be told," he continued in a neutral voice.

"Whatever you want."

"So kindly accommodating? Thank you." But Mace was disappointed to see that his sarcasm did not revive the spark of spirit he had been witness to earlier. She seemed determined to make this as difficult as possible for him. "Ketch already knows."

Well, that got her attention. Her skin paled and her head rose slowly as her gaze locked with his. Mace nodded to make sure she understood. He again lifted his cup and swallowed a mouthful, watching her over the rim, as if by will he could keep her attention on him.

"Ketch has known about it for a few weeks. That day Owhi came with the salmon, he told him that you'd be having a child in four moons. Ketch can add as well as any man."

"But how..." She swallowed, trying again. "How did this Owhi know?"

"He's the best tracker around here. No one's his equal. I've seen him. He can tell the height and weight of a man, whether he's right or left-handed, even his age, just by his footprint. Owhi, as I said, is the best."

Erin was too upset to question him, but she wished she knew if this Owhi had mentioned it to anyone else. The thought of the men knowing made her head begin to pound. Absently rubbing her forehead with one hand, she understood why Ketch had been distant with her recently. More pressing was the question of what Mace intended to do.

She was at a loss as to how to act with Mace. He made her feel vulnerable, like a cornered animal, whenever he came close. Now, he was watching her every breath with those dark eyes that hid his own thoughts. His features were set in a stern expression and his overwhelming sense of raw power rested comfortably on his broad shoulders.

Mace was almost sorry he had confronted her with this. But, much as it bothered him to see her upset, he knew they had to talk about it.

"You could," he finally said, breaking the stretching silence, "say that you had been recently widowed and needed to marry quickly because you lost your home."

"If that's what you want." Even as Erin murmured assent, she thought of Maddie suggesting the very same thing and her own refusal.

"You don't like what I said, Erin."

"It doesn't matter."

"It sure does. You came up with a good enough tale to hook me, so you can put some effort into helping me with this one." Immediately, he wished he could take back the words. Her face whitened until he thought she would faint. "Erin, I—"

"Don't say you're sorry. You spoke the truth as you see it." She stared beyond him, trying to wrap the pain inside her and keep it in a small enough place to deal with later. She swallowed, her mouth so dry that it hurt her to talk to him. "Are you finished with me?"

His gaze tracked the soft trembling of her mouth and, despite his will to the contrary, his thoughts answered her question in another way. Just as his body did. He knew he would not be finished with her until the ache inside him eased. His own vow came back to taunt him. He was a man of pride and honor, and he couldn't forget that he had given his word to stay away from her. But did he have to be put on a rack for it?

"No, I'm not finished. We can't let this wait, Erin."

"Then we... I shall say that. Anything you want. That I lied. That I..." She couldn't say more. The pounding in her head increased and her stomach churned. She tried to fight both, knowing that further upset was not good for her child. That meant getting away from Mace. But one look at the scowl he wore told her he wasn't done. A chill shivered over her skin. Erin knew her body was warning her it had reached its limits.

She jumped when he suddenly shoved back his chair so hard it fell over, but he was up and around the table before she could move.

"Is that what you thought I wanted? That you should lie?"

His voice was soft, making it all the more chilling to her. Knowing she was going to be sick if she didn't get away from him quickly, she answered without thought.

"I don't know. What's more, I don't care." She braced her hands on the edge of the table and started to push her chair back, but he stood directly behind her, stopping the motion.

"If you want to say I trapped you, say it. If you want to say I lied, do so! If you want...if you want to go to hell, do that, too!" she yelled, feeling the hysteria rise along with her lack of control.

"Move away, Mr. Dalton, else you'll find yourself the unwilling recipient of the result of your talk."

"Again?"

In mute misery, Erin nodded, waving one hand to motion him away.

Guilt for upsetting her, Mace told himself, was the only reason he stayed.

When Cosi walked in and saw Mace holding Erin while she heaved over the dry sink, he asked what was wrong.

It was the same guilt that made Mace snap, "Fool, she's having a baby!"

A lone lantern lit the bunkhouse where Cosi, Ray, Pete and Ketch sat around the battered table. The silence since Cosi had told them what Mace said and Ketch verified that baby wasn't Mace's was stretching to the point of becoming uncomfortable.

Ketch knew they were waiting for him to speak, and he kept them waiting. He had not reconciled himself to the fact that Erin had lied to Mace. And he felt guilty that his nagging pushed Mace to marry again, pushed him right into Erin's arms. He gazed down the long narrow interior, lined with single wooden bunks against the walls, pinning his stare on the potbellied wood stove in the center of the room that threw off its heat to where they all sat.

Yet, as much as he wanted to feel angry with Erin, he couldn't. He liked her. Liked what she had done for Jake and Becky. She hadn't changed from the caring woman he knew her to be. His feelings toward Erin warred with his loyalty to Mace. Ketch shook his head. He didn't know what to say or do.

The call for supper would be coming soon, and Pete, the youngest and the most impatient, broke the silence. "Like Cosi said, we can count as well as the next man. The baby she's having ain't the boss's. But Miz Erin don't seem like no soiled dove to me. Can't figure how a lady like her got short-skirted. The think is, what're we gonna do about it?"

"Don't see," Ray drawled, "that's our place. We ain't got to do a damn thing. Boss married her. She's his responsibility."

"Aw, Ray, you know what I meant," Pete insisted. "How you figure on acting? Ketch, you understand. What d'ya say?"

"Don't reckon this is one of the times I've got a sure answer for you, boy." Ketch sat forward, hunching his shoulders, forearms resting flat on the table. "I'm the one that pushed Mace to get married. Didn't think he got the short end when I first saw Erin. Pretty she was, and still is, now that she got some weight on her. Seein' her gus-

sied up like a lady made me figure she was one. Manners
sure fit the picture.

"Don't mind confessin' I'm proud of the way she took
to Jake and Becky. Those kids needed themselves a ma
and Erin took to them right off. But this business's thrown
me." He didn't want to tell them he had known about her
baby long before. The men weren't blood, but they'd been
together for almost three years, Pete being the last to join
them, Ray five years before and Cosi seven. Cosi was the
only one who had known Sky, and he'd feel right put out
that Ketch didn't tell him. Shaking his head again, he
muttered, "Don't know what more to say."

"Well, I know," Cosi stated, shoving his chair back.
"Miz Erin's done fine by me. I figure to treat her just like
I always do. She ain't no light skirt chasing after men. I'd
know," he said with a glare at the others that dared them
to remark about his reputation with women. "The way I
see it, whatever's happened to her don't change what she
is. This kinda talk ain't getting us nowhere. What we need
to figure on now is how to help her."

The nods of agreement pleased Ketch, both for Erin
and for Mace. He knew Mace's pride would not allow him
to take a slight to his wife quietly. Mace would try taking
on each one of these men, and then fire him.

"Cosi's got the right idea," Ketch said. "But don't go
all fired up and get the boss mad, either. He's been makin'
sure we're all workin' away while he's been keepin' tight
to the place. They got some problems of their own that
need workin' out. Too many of us hangin' round after
hearing 'bout this baby would light up his temper."

"Only if he catches us." With a wide grin Pete looked
at each of the others. "Guess I can get by with less shut-

eye. Won't take much with four of us doin' her outside chores. An' we won't say anything to the boss so his pride don't get bruised. When he's ready to say what needs saying he will."

Ray stood up, drawing their attention. "Why're you all figurin' that she needs our help? She ain't no puny thing. Proved that already. Hell, my ma had seven of us an' never lost more'n a day between them."

"I'm keeping the woodpile full and you can do as you want, Ray." Pete pushed back his chair and rose.

The clang of the supper bell came, yet no one ran for the door as they usually did, for Ketch stopped them.

"Listen up, you three. Don't act different. Mace ain't gonna like that. Take my word, the man's strung tighter than skin set to dry."

Once more came their nods of agreement as the bell pealed again.

"Last thing," Ketch warned. "Remember they's wed lawful. Ain't a one of you got the job to be offerin' comfort to another man's woman."

"Hear you," Pete and Ray said together.

Only Cosi remained silent and Ketch eyed him. "Yeah, Ketch, I hear you."

"Know that. Thing is, do you understand me?"

Cosi was out the door and never answered.

Erin watched the men file into the kitchen for supper. She prayed that the Lord would help her get through the next few hours. Mace had insisted, as long as she felt well, that she not go off and hide herself. Erin wanted to do nothing else. Two heaping bowls of stewed chicken and dumplings were quickly passed along. Biscuits and butter followed peas. Erin took her seat without looking at anyone. She knew her prayer had been answered when Cosi started talking about the cows he had selected for breeding. One of the knots in her stomach unfurled, easing the tension that held her in its grip.

When that subject lagged, Jake bragged about the doings of Scrap, and Becky was quick to tease him. Another of the knots opened and Erin took a deep breath, releasing it when she realized that this was going to be a supper like on any other night.

No, she corrected herself, glancing up to find Mace's eyes on her. Not quite the same. His scowl was gone. When she heard him say the stew was good, and agreement came quickly from the others, Erin thought her ears deceived her.

Long before the men were finished, Jake began to squirm in his chair when Scrap started whining near the door.

"Can I let him out, Erin?"

"Go on, Jake, and Becky, you go with him," Mace said. Before Becky had a chance to answer, he added, "And check on Tariko's colt for me. Make sure he's got water."

The moment the door closed, Mace set his fork down and cleared his throat. "I've got an announcement to make." He avoided Erin's panicked look. He was having trouble trying to think of exactly what to say. They had to be told, just as his children did, and that, too, had to come from him.

"Boss?" Ketch said, nudging him from his thoughts. "You were saying."

"Yeah, so I was. I was saying that me and Erin are having a baby."

Chapter Fourteen

Erin heard him, but she felt as if someone had used a broom handle on her middle. The breath seemed to leave her in a rush and she couldn't get it back fast enough. She dug up the courage to glance around and see how this startling announcement was taken. Cosi smiled, and Pete and Ray both were grinning, murmuring their well wishes. She was stunned. And Mace's words, those precious words that they were going to have a baby... why, it sounded as if... as if he was claiming this child as his own.

"Settle down, all of you," Mace said, feeling uncomfortable with the attention. "There's more I need to tell."

Eyes wide with disbelief, Erin stared at him. "There is?" she whispered, unaware that she had spoken. But Mace nodded, and surely she was mistaken that his eyes appeared somewhat kinder than ever before.

A warmth stole through Mace to see Erin, even if she appeared stunned by what he was saying. He hadn't been sure that he would claim her child as his, but the glitter of tears in her eyes convinced him what he was doing was right. He now knew exactly what to say. Erin was, as she claimed this day, his wife. By his words and actions she would be respected or not. He could not throw her on his men's mercy and tell the truth. The truth would have not only his men but decent folks hereabouts shun her. Those, he amended to himself, who had not already condemned her for marrying a man with two half-breed children. In the long moments that passed, Mace found himself remembering how Erin accepted his children and showed her love for them. He wasn't only doing this to salvage his own pride, but Jake's and Becky's as well.

"A time back," Mace began, "when I was trying to find that breeding bull, I was down in San Francisco way. I met Erin then. It wasn't time for us to talk about marriage, but when she wrote and told me about the little one on the way we made our plans in a hurry."

Mace sat back, one arm bent over the chair back, a very satisfied smile curving his lips. Ketch caught his gaze, and Mace could feel the slight flush that crept up the back of his neck. Ketch knew he was lying. Mace wouldn't back down, though. Thankfully, Ketch was the only one who knew about his answering Erin's advertisement in the newspapers. While he held Ketch's gaze, Mace remembered, as he was sure Ketch also was, what he told his men about his forthcoming marriage. It had been little enough so no one could point a finger and say he was lying now.

"Well, Ketch," Pete was the first to say, "guess the boss had you hornswoggled but good."

But Ketch didn't look at Pete or acknowledge his remark. He was still staring at Mace. There was a silent plea in Mace's eyes that he refused to deny. Just like the time he had stood by when Mace told his folks that he was going to marry Sky and nothing would stop him, not even them ordering him to leave their home. Mace had not asked him to go with him. Ketch had made his own decision, for he loved Mace like a son. Slowly, then, he nodded, a smile breaking over his lips. He turned to face Erin.

"Boy's right. I got hornswoggled but good this time."

Erin searched his face for a sign of heat, but his gaze remained steady and calm. There was no anger underlying his words. And the nodding continued as she responded with a shy smile that silently thanked him while her eyes flooded with relief.

Later, when Mace asked her to allow him to tell his children alone, she agreed. But as she waited in the kitchen to learn their reactions, she found herself pacing before the hallway entrance. She was so tempted to listen at the bedroom door, but something held her back. This was a private time for Mace and his children. And she had enough to sort through on her own.

The big rocker easily held Mace's powerful frame along with Becky and Jake. With an arm around each of them, he knew he had done the right thing in assuming responsibility for the telling as well as for the child. The glow in Erin's eyes, the flush of her cheeks, the shy smile that never quite left her lips as he helped her with the dishes, all brought him a warmth that seemed to increase as he held his children.

He couldn't deny the feeling of a terrible weight being lifted from him. And when she tried to thank him, he allowed her to have her say, because he understood how her own pride demanded that she give voice to her feelings.

Jake and Becky each rested their head on one of his broad shoulders, content for the moment to share this silence. But Mace knew he had to tell them, and use words that would insure that they wouldn't feel hurt. Where did the wisdom come from, he wondered, to guide a child's life? A strange mood seemed to be creeping up on him, a mood that lent weight to the responsibility of raising these children. Had he somehow cheated them by not waiting to find a woman to love? A foolish thought to be having, when he had just admitted less than an hour ago that he married Erin for that very reason. Sure, he reminded himself, he hadn't used the word love, but he implied it strongly by saying that her child was his.

"Papa," Jake murmured sleepily, "Scrap's waitin' for me to sleep."

"In a minute, son. I've got something very special to tell you and Becky."

"A secret, Papa?" Becky wanted to know. One of her hands rested on his chest, the other around his neck. This was the best time of day, when they were together and told him something nice that had happened to them, or about something extra special they had seen. Sometimes, she wished that Erin could share this time with them, but she had never asked.

"Well, it was, but not anymore. How would you two feel about having a baby around here?"

"To play with? A boy, Papa. A boy like me."

"No, silly. A baby can't be played with. They're too little. Right, Papa?" Becky rubbed her head against his cheek, then suddenly sat up. "Is Erin having a baby?"

"Erin?" Jake said with wonder, sitting up, too.

"First, Jake, I don't know if it's a boy or a girl. And yes, Becky, you're right. They are too little to be played with. And yes, it is Erin who'll have the baby."

"I'll help take care of it. I'm the oldest and a girl."

"So what, Becky. I'm takin' good care of Scrap. Erin said so."

"Puppies aren't babies! Tell him, Papa, tell him I'm right again."

"Whoa, both of you. Erin will need you both."

"Babies cry a lot," Becky said.

With eyes filled with remembrance, Mace rubbed his hand over his daughter's head. He walked the floors a few nights with Becky when she was cutting her first teeth, and couldn't help but agree. As for Jake, well, Mace had walked more nights than he cared to think about, since there had been no one else to do it.

"Papa," Jake said, straightening up so that he could look at his father's face. "What if we don't like it? Can we send it away?"

"No, silly, you can't. Brothers are dumb. You can't send a baby back. You're stuck with what you get. They cry and everyone runs around to make the baby stop."

"Is what Becky said true, Papa?"

"Before I answer that, son, I'd like to know where you learned so much about babies, Becky."

"Oh, Miss Nolie told me. She said she would never have a baby 'cause it ruins your figure. Men won't like you anymore when you're all fat and ugly. Or was it Miss Jessica who said that?" With a shrug, Becky lifted her head away from her father's shoulder. "It was one of them. Anyway, when new babies come, no one wants to be bothered with the other children. Everyone gets to just fussing over the baby and makes you be quiet so they can sleep. And she said big people are cranky."

Mace couldn't hold back his smile, but he tried to answer and explain to them all that wasn't the truth.

"Babies come from love—"

"Oh, Papa, that's silly," Becky cut in. "Babies come from mamas."

"Yes, yes, they do, but the Lord blesses the love a man and woman share with giving them children. That makes a baby a gift of love. And a woman isn't ugly when she carries a child."

"Was my mama pretty?" Jake wanted to know, snuggling close.

"The prettiest ever. And to finish answering Becky's notions, it's true that babies cry a lot and need someone to look over them all the time. Guess I can't deny big folks get cranky when they don't sleep enough, but it's just for a little time. And babies are sweet smelling, soft and cuddlesome. Just like you two were," Mace whispered, hugging them both closer. "We didn't love Becky less when you were born, Jake. That's part of the Lord's gift, too. He makes sure that papas and mamas have plenty of room in their hearts to love lots of children."

"Erin didn't have a mama to love her. She didn't have a papa. She didn't have no one."

"How do you know, Becky?" The saddened note in his child's voice disturbed him.

"I asked her. Erin told me she didn't have anyone special to love until she had us."

Tugging on his shirt collar, Jake sought his attention. "Papa, will Erin still love us special when the baby comes?"

Mace didn't answer immediately. He thought about the cracks Erin had made in his own hard veneer. He felt torn over her entrapping him into marriage, yet he couldn't deny the conflicting feelings he had for her. Only a fool would doubt that she had opened her heart and given generously of her love to his children. But Jake had a point, a damn strong one. Would Erin turn away from Becky and Jake when her own child came? The hurt she could cause them made Mace harden his heart toward her. He would never allow her to slight his children. They had borne enough.

"Won't Erin like us anymore?" Becky asked, restless that her father wasn't quick to answer.

"Settle down, honey. Erin won't be like that. Nothing will change. I promise that to both of you." Only he knew how truly empty a promise that was. He couldn't force Erin to love Jake and Becky more than her own child; he couldn't force her to love them at all.

Long after the children were asleep, Mace still sat in the big rocking chair, thinking of what his announcement at supper had committed him to.

He had claimed Erin's child as his own.

From his memory came Erin's passionate declaration that she was his wife. And from the deeper recess of memory came her emotionless voice on their wedding night, telling him of her own dreams to have a home and a family of her own to love.

Wasn't it the same dream that he had once? Didn't he leave people he loved, a land that was part of his soul, and strike out on his own to make that dream come true with Sky?

With a bone-weary sigh he closed his eyes. When had he let his dream die? He still had Becky and Jake. And now, with his word, Erin and her coming child. Pride and honor still warred within him over Erin's lie. And yet, as he sat there and remembered all she had said, he began to question why he still held that against her. What other choice did she have? He winced inwardly, recalling his naming her a whore. Never once had Erin given him reason to believe it was true.

That she could easily have become one to earn money for herself and her child was not something he could deny. Yet she had not taken that path. No one could fault her manner. Erin worked hard to bring order to his home. Unbidden came the addition, as if it were truly her own.

His wife, Erin. That came unbidden, too. Was giving his word to claim her child as his such a terrible thing to have done? And how much more would be expected from him now?

Through half-lidded eyes he gazed at his son, curled on his side, the puppy cradled close to him as Jake slept. He stared at Becky sprawled on her stomach, arms flung to the sides as if even in sleep she wanted to grab hold of the world and hang on to it.

He had told them a child was a gift of love. Erin swore that her child was conceived in less than the wonder and beauty of a man making love to the woman he loved above all others. A child was born with innocence into the world. How could he hold anything against it? How could he deny it the home and love it would need to thrive?

He had never held Jake's birth responsible for Sky's death. His son's birth had brought her joy and, as much as he mourned Sky's death, he had not loved his son less. Jake was Sky's last loving gift to him.

There were no clear answers to be found. He heard Erin make her way to her room next door, and wondered if she waited for him.

Would she be taking down her hair? Brushing out the rich thickness of it until it spread down to her hips? He had told his children there was nothing ugly about a woman who carried a child, for he believed this was so. Certainly nothing about Erin ceased his body's need to find ease with her.

Mace came out of the chair in a controlled rush. Desire had no place in this room. He opened the door quietly and closed it behind him, standing in the hallway to stare at the thin edge of light that came from beneath Erin's door.

She'd be worried about how the children took the news, he told himself, still not moving.

He could just take those few steps, knock softly so as not to wake anyone, tell her and return to his room.

He wouldn't linger in the doorway, breathing in the scent of her, or finding with his gaze all the little touches she added from odds and ends to make her room her own. He most certainly wouldn't be thinking of the ache inside him, or of the need that beat in his blood to take her mouth with his and hear that soft cry of hers.

And since he was in a mood to lie to himself, he could believe that a few kisses wouldn't make sleep impossible again tonight.

A sensible man would go to his own room. Mace was a most sensible man.

Erin opened the door before he could bring his hand up to knock.

"I waited..."

"I knew..." Mace stopped, just as she had. "You first," he offered, unable to meet her eyes. She hadn't taken down her hair yet. The cover was undisturbed on the bed, but his gaze was drawn to the pristine nightgown that graced one corner of it.

"Why did you wait, Erin?"

"To know... the children... did they..." She stopped trying to talk past the lump in her throat. The desire to be in his arms, held against the heat and power of his body drove all sense from her mind. He had let her tell him how grateful she was for what he had done when they finished the dishes. But it was more than gratitude she felt—much, much more.

"Jake and Becky seemed more concerned over the noise a baby makes than anything else. They need the reassurance only you can give them that they won't be cut off from you once the child is born."

"Yes, yes, of course," she whispered, searching his face for a sign of what he was thinking. "I wish I knew the right words to thank you for what you did." Her head bowed, for she was unable to look at him. "I realize that what you said must have cost you a great deal of pride, and I just wanted you to know that I promise I won't do anything to make you sorry."

"You shouldn't make a man a blanket promise like that."

"Why?" she asked, turning away from him.

"A man could read whatever he wanted into it." Bracing his shoulder against the door frame as if he needed to remind himself not to step into the room, Mace crossed his arms in front of his chest and watched her.

Erin turned slowly, unwilling to take his words at face value. She stared as his hands. Strong and callused, and so capable of being gentle. With a quick little shake of her head, Erin sought to dispel such thoughts. But there was very little she could do to stop her body's awareness of him. Or stop her gaze from seeing the age-softened denim that hugged his hips and muscular legs.

It disconcerted her that Mace seemed to diminish her room with his purely masculine force although he had not entered it. Her gaze rose to his chin, shadowed by dark evening stubble, and stopped. What was she doing? Standing there and staring at him, while she struggled to remember what it was he said. The words escaped her. All she could recall was his acceptance of her child.

"Please," she said without thought, "why did you do it?"

For a moment Mace thought about hedging, but he knew what she was asking. A shrug came first, until she raised her eyes to his. He saw bewilderment in their green depths. "There wasn't much of a choice."

"I see." She nodded, having no more understanding than she did before she asked.

Mace confirmed that. "You couldn't. You're a woman, and women never figure things the way a man does." The moment the words were out, he wished them unsaid. The soft glow of the lamp behind her seemed to make her softer, smaller, and once again his desire flared. His skin felt too tight, his blood too hot running beneath its surface. A smart man would get out now. A smart man would remember the tossings and turnings of the nights past. A smart man would not be thinking of her rashly given promise of seconds ago.

He used the only defense he had left. "Don't be thinking that this will change much between us. We'll go on just like we are." The light in her eyes died. How could she appear to be fragile without moving? With a restless shift, he found himself in the room. "I'll see if you have enough wood. Ketch swears we'll have snow by morning."

She thought about stopping him, but he was already opening the wood box's lid, nodding to see that it was full. "Guess that's it, then," he said, straightening and turning toward where she stood by the bureau's edge. For a brief second Mace swore he saw regret in her gaze. Was she thinking what he was, that if this were a real marriage, he'd already be in bed, watching her take down her hair, waiting for her to come to him? But that wasn't true and he was the fool for even thinking about it. "You've got an extra quilt?"

"Top shelf of the wardrobe," she answered softly with a wave of her hand. Why didn't he leave? She had thought he diminished the space before. There didn't seem to be enough air for them both to breathe now. Regret and deep longing spilled through her. If they were really married, she could ask Mace to rub the ache from her back while they lay together beneath the quilt. He would hold her close and whisper his dreams for the child and maybe, just maybe, he wouldn't find her ugly, so that a good-night kiss might lead to more.

"That's it, then," he repeated, still not making a move to leave. What had brought that dreamy look into her eyes? And the slight flush that colored her cheeks? She couldn't have any idea of what he was thinking. But would Erin reject him if he... No, he couldn't risk touching her.

And only he knew that his skin felt near to bursting as he walked by and closed the door.

And Erin blamed the changes the baby was making in her body for the tears that fell.

The days of March slipped in with the sweetly offered promise of the coming spring. Erin knew something had changed between her and Mace from that night he claimed her child as his. She seemed ever aware of him. He didn't even need to be within her sight. Mace continued to work close by and, more often than not, she caught herself stopping her own chores to watch him at his.

This morning he was chopping wood. Again, she realized. Ketch's prediction about the weather not holding had partly come true. The wind was bitter cold, but the snow had not come.

Leaning as close as her rounded belly let her, Erin gazed through the window at Mace, admiring the masculine grace and power of his body as the sharp bite of the ax sank into the wood. Cold as it was, he was working without his jacket and the muscles of his back and arms strained the soft blue fabric of his shirt. He stopped for a minute or so, wiping the sweat from his brow, and she swore he looked right at her. Thank goodness he couldn't see her peeking through the curtain. Her body filled with these strange shimmering sensations that raced through her as if she had a fever. Even though she was soon to be a mother, all her thoughts directed themselves to Mace.

How he smiled a bit more, how he lost the biting edge when he spoke to her now, how he wasn't above offering a compliment for a meal he liked. She wanted so much to be a real wife to him. Sharing his pleasures, and his problems ...

"Miz Erin, horses got more sense than you two," Ketch said, coming up behind her.

"Don't know what you're talking about, Ketch. I was just straightening the corner of the curtain. Must have gotten wet and dried curled up."

"You know what I'm saying, all right," he insisted, helping himself to a cup of fresh coffee. "Boss's out there, jus' like a stud pawin' the fence, dancin' round to show off. He's been keepin' all the other males away, or ain't you noticed none of that?"

Erin faced him, knowing her cheeks were brightening. "I see you here. You're a male. So that makes what you're saying sheer foolishness."

"Don't count. Me, that is. I'm too old."

Erin had to smile at him. There was a teasing twinkle in his eyes. This wasn't the first time Ketch had caught her watching Mace. It wasn't the first time he said anything to her, either. It had taken a while for her to sass him back, for she didn't believe what he was saying. What possible reason would Mace have for holding back from her, besides the fact that she carried someone else's child?

"Never knew a body to get what they's awantin' by jus' wishin' for it." Draining his cup, Ketch set it down on the table and left her to ponder his words.

Willpower, Mace told himself, that's what he needed more of. He knew things had changed since that night he had put pride aside for Erin. Well, that wasn't exactly the whole truth of it. He had done it for himself and his children, as well. But damned if he could understand why his vow not to touch her had to be strengthened at every turn. And why she seemed bent on destroying him.

He caught her, far too often for his peace of mind, with her gaze pinned on him. Those green eyes held a meld of surprise, curiosity and desire. Didn't the fool woman know what she was doing to him?

Need savaged him until he felt as if he spent every second fighting the fever that raged.

He stopped to wipe the sweat from his brow, glancing at the back door. Ketch was coming down the steps. Likely, he was going to tell Mace that he should ease up. Well, he did intend to. There were less than three months to go, if Owhi's reckoning and his own memory served. No, nearly five, he reminded himself. Erin wasn't Sky, as she repeatedly told him, and so she would need a good number of weeks after giving birth to heal.

With a black scowl he gazed at the woodpile. At the rate he was chopping, he'd have another two fields cleared of trees and enough wood to burn through two winters.

"You look fit to take on a grizzly, boss," Ketch noted, glancing from Mace's face to the ax resting against the chopping block. "Better put an edge on that blade, you're wearin' it plumb out."

"Old man, ain't you got nothing to do but devil me?"

"Sure. I come to tell you there's fresh hot coffee an' a heapin' plate of oatmeal cookies waitin' in the kitchen."

"Ain't got time." But Mace threw a quick look toward the house, licking his lips.

"Figure you'd say that. Well, there's a mare penned up in there that needs the sass taking out of her. You figure that's somethin' you got time for?"

A grin cracked Mace's lips. "You go an' muddy up her floor again?"

"No way. An' Miz Erin don't never say a word 'bout that. Truth is, she don't say much 'bout what she's a-needin'. Man like me, who's been round a while, can figure it out all by himself."

Mace hefted the ax handle to his shoulder and turned for the barn. "Maybe I'm not as smart as you."

"For sure," Ketch agreed, shaking his head as Mace disappeared into the barn. He stood there, rubbing the back of his neck, wondering what it would take to bring these two together. First there were the weeks where Mace stripped her hide for no good reason. Now, they walked around each other like each carried a pile-high egg basket and didn't dare drop one.

Something had to come to him. Mace was still hurting, still believing that he caused Sky's death, and Ketch knew the why of it. Plumb foolish notion, to his way of thinking, but Mace didn't see it his way. He gazed at the house, grinning to see that the kitchen curtain was back in place, but his thoughts only turned to Erin. She was hurting, too. A man had to be blind not to see that she was trying hard to look pretty and hide her growing belly. If she raised her skirt and apron hems any higher, her knees would be showing. He guessed she was as blind as Mace. How could she not see the man's gaze lingering on her every move? If she was all that ugly to him, why would Mace be killing himself just so he could sleep?

"The two of 'em go beyond mules," he muttered, heading for his horse. "They go all the way to mountain hard rock, jus' as thick an' jus' as stubborn."

Once Mace saw Ketch amble out of sight, he headed for the house. Just for hot coffee, he told himself. A mean wind was blowing, forcing him to gaze at the building clouds in the far distance.

Maybe the temperature dropping to zero would help cool him off, he idly noted, longing for any kind of a distraction.

Chapter Fifteen

Mace lowered his gaze, spotting the lone rider coming into his range of vision. He knew the hammerhead roan was Ray's, and knew Ray wouldn't be riding the horse all out unless there was trouble. Serious trouble.

"Mace!" Ray yelled, unaware that he already had his attention. "The cows are drifting off by themselves," he informed Mace, sawing hard on the bit to control the horse. "The wind's whipping snow off the peaks and we can hardly see."

"Saddle Tariko. I'll be right with you." Mace asked no more, for cows drifted off alone only to calve. No matter when he bred them, they all seemed to give birth at the same time. He ran for the house, yelling back, "Find Ketch!"

Throwing open the kitchen door, he was assaulted by the heat of the room. "Erin! Erin!" he shouted, grabbing his heavy jacket and gloves from the hooks by the door.

Responding to the urgency in his voice, Erin ran into the kitchen. "What's wrong?"

"Cows are calving and there's a storm coming in. Keep the coffee hot and get Jake and Becky to go down to the barn. They'll know what to do."

He was worried, yet she was annoyed that all he wanted from her was to keep coffee hot. "There must be something else I can do to help?"

Mace finished tugging on his gloves, sparing her a quick look. "You can't ride, can you?" A quick shake of her head brought his sigh. "That's all the help I need now. Someone to ride and lift newborn calves up in front of them to bring them in. Tell Becky to use the front box stall."

He was at the door when Erin, for reasons she didn't question, ran to him. "You'll be careful?"

Mace gazed down at her anxious expression. "Sure. And you say a prayer."

"Yes," she whispered as the door closed behind him. A chill rode her spine, one that didn't come from the cold that slipped inside from the opening and closing of the door. Mace's eyes had been bleak. Could he lose the calves? She swore at herself for knowing so little, but he had given her little enough to do, and she set to it.

The men would be cold and hungry whenever they came in, so her first priority was food. She had intended to fry the chickens Ketch had brought her this morning, but soup would be better. Feeding the stove, she soon had water heating, the chickens cut up and herbs sprinkled on top. A trip to the root cellar provided her with onions, carrots and potatoes. She doubled what she would have normally put in.

Once the soup was simmering, she headed outside to find the children.

She wrapped the shawl tighter around her head, bending against the fierce power of the wind that cut through the cloth of her coat. Becky was found easily enough—she was in the barn with Tariko's unnamed colt—but there was no sign of Jake and Scrap.

"Becky," Erin said, "your father said you would know what to do and for you to use the front box stall. Tell it to me, so I can help."

"You can't," the child answered, carefully closing the door to the colt's stall and securing the latch. "I've got to get the hay bales down from the loft. You can't climb the ladder. The men'll bring in the calves as they find them, likely using the wagon, and then go out to find more until they can't see."

Erin was shocked that this was all delivered in an emotionless voice. But before she spoke, she realized that to Becky this was part of the life-and-death cycle of ranch life.

"Becky, wait until I find Jake. We'll do this together. I can and will help you."

"Last time I saw Jake with Scrap, they were down by the big woodpile. Jake's still trying to teach Scrap to hunt wood rats."

Closing her eyes with a shudder, Erin hoped the puppy didn't catch one. "Just wait for me."

"All right."

Braving the cut of the wind again, Erin wrapped her arms around herself to keep her body warm as long as she could. The woodpile behind the shed showed no sign of Jake, but Erin knew he loved to climb the cut lengths of logs waiting to be split into firewood. She had tried to tell Mace to stop him before he fell and got hurt, but her warnings had landed on deaf ears. Shouting against the rising wind, she made her way to the springhouse, but that, too, proved empty. The wagon shed, pigpen and henhouse left her with only the men's bunkhouse to check for Jake. She rarely stepped over the threshold, respecting the men's right to privacy, but she was growing anxious as time passed and she couldn't find the boy.

Erin spared a few minutes to feed the wood stove so the fire wouldn't die, but once more she didn't find Jake.

On her way back to the barn, she decided to check the soup and was flooded with relief when Jake was found at the table, munching cookies.

"Where were you?" she demanded, her own fear bringing an unaccustomed harshness to her voice.

"Playing."

"You didn't hear me calling you?"

"No, Erin. Me and Scrap—"

"Never mind. You're safe. But Jake, please, don't go off without telling me where you are. I worry about you getting hurt."

"I'm a boy, Erin. Boys don't get hurt. And I've got Scrap."

At the second mention of his name, the pup yipped and pawed Jake's leg for attention.

Stirring the soup, Erin closed her eyes and knew she would have to tackle Mace about this again. But not now. She didn't know when the men would begin coming in with the calves and she wanted to prove to Mace and to herself that she wasn't useless when he needed all the help she could give him.

"Bundle up. We need to go down to the barn. Your father is bringing in new calves that must be kept warm."

Jake nodded, grabbed two more cookies that she didn't have the heart to deny him, and followed her with Scrap.

Erin felt frustration build when she entered the barn and found Becky up in the loft, pushing hay bales down to the floor where the force of the fall had split a few of them. Taking up a pitchfork while Jake took hold of another one, she began pitching hay into the box stall.

"Erin," Becky called out, standing near the edge of the loft. "You shouldn't be doing that. Papa said you can't lift heavy things."

"But he's only got us here to do this, Becky." Erin knew all the hours of hard work had honed her muscles, and was careful not to lift too much hay at any one time. But with three bales still to go, she felt the ache begin in her lower back and paused a few minutes to rest. Becky was scrambling down the wooden ladder, rushing to her side as Erin gently stretched.

She had to open her coat, for despite the chill in the barn from the wind that penetrated every crack, she was sweating from her labor. Erin's eyes widened in surprise to find that both Jake and Becky were staring at her.

"Is the baby moving again?" Jake asked first, his gaze lowering from her face to her belly. "Will you let me feel it again?"

"You got to do it last time, Jake, and I missed it. I go first."

Erin felt her throat close and tears threaten. She couldn't speak, so she held open her arms to each child, hugging them close. The love they had brought into her life filled so many of the empty spaces she had lived with for far too long.

With one hand hovering close to her rounded stomach, Becky glanced up at Erin. "Can I touch? I promise I won't hurt her."

"You won't hurt—"

"What makes you think it's a her, smarty?" Jake demanded.

"She's gonna be a little girl for me to take care of and play with, so there!"

"Is not!"

"Is, too!"

"Hush, now, both of you," Erin scolded, but without heat. "The baby isn't moving now, 'cause it knows we still have plenty of work to do. But if it moves, I promise to let you know."

Rubbing his head against her, Jake sighed and asked, "Is it really gonna be a girl, Erin? I want a boy to play with."

"I don't know what it will be, Jake. I only pray that the baby is strong, with—"

"I know, I know," Becky sing-songed, "all the right number of fingers and toes, two eyes, two ears, one mouth and a nose!"

Their laughter was cut off abruptly as shouting was heard outside the barn doors.

The three of them ran forward, fighting the wind that threatened to tear the doors free from their grips. Erin pulled the children to her side as Pete drove the high-sided farm wagon right into the barn. He jumped down to lend his strength in closing the barn doors. Once they were secure, he lowered the tailgate of the wagon and began to lift the bleating calves down.

Jake stood by the stall door, making sure none of the calves that Pete placed inside could get out. Erin and Becky finished forking hay into the stall.

When the last calf was securely inside the stall, Pete stood with his head bowed for a breather. Erin touched his arm to gain his attention, for the frantic cries of the tiny animals made it almost impossible to speak in a normal voice.

"How bad is it, Pete?"

"This group was gathered before the snow hit us. I don't know how many we can save."

He was already turning, settling his hat, when Erin stopped him. "Take a few minutes and go up to the house.

There's hot soup and coffee on the stove. Becky, Jake and I will take care of the horses.'' She pushed and tugged at his arm and finally he left them.

Erin set to work with a vengeance, drying off the horses with burlap sacking. She watched Jake and Becky as the two of them entered the calves' stall and began piling hay up the thick wooden sides to keep the seeping cold away from the newborns. Their urgent bleating filled the air, the cries for their mothers and milk touching her deeply. Pete came back far too quickly to please her, but he nodded to show that he had helped himself to the warming liquids.

"You'd better get back up to the house," he warned her. "Boss ain't gonna like knowing you're down here. And it's too cold for you."

Shaking her head, Erin stood back as he climbed up on the wagon and pulled his bandanna up across the lower half of his face. With a curt nod to show that he was ready, she made her way to the doors, struggling again with their weight.

The darkness outside stunned her. It was barely early afternoon, yet it appeared to be already dusk. Once again, not knowing how long it would be before another wagon would come in, Erin decided to take the children up to the house and get them fed. The pitiful cries of the calves reminded her how helpless she was to help them, but she could care for the children's needs.

Ushering them before her, Erin entered the steamy warmth of the kitchen, and it wasn't until that warmth seeped through her clothing that she realized how cold she was.

The hot soup helped, but she kept thinking about Mace and the men, out there in the freezing weather. While Jake and Becky had second helpings of the soup, she started to fill every pot and kettle she found with water and set them on the stove. With the children's help she dragged the big wooden tub into the kitchen.

"Blankets," she said almost to herself. "We'll need plenty of those." With a stack of mixed blankets and quilts set on one chair, and bowls, bread and cheese along with cups placed on the table, Erin glanced around to see if she had forgotten anything.

"We should get fires started in the other rooms," Becky suggested, setting out spoons and knives.

"Good, Becky. And once we're done, we'll go down to the barn. There must be something we can do to help those calves."

"Ketch'll feed them when he comes," Jake told her.

"Feed them what?" Erin asked, already thinking that if they started it would be that much less for Ketch or anyone else to do.

"Bessie's milk. 'Course, she ain't got much to give now since she don't have a calf of her own, but that's what he uses."

"And thinned down with water, it'll still be rich enough to make do," Erin murmured to herself, slipping into her coat. She knew little enough about calves, but any animal newly born nursed. The thought stopped her. They couldn't drink the milk from a pail. How was she going to feed all those calves?

She needed something, she thought, scanning the kitchen, to make a teat for the calves to suck. "What does Ketch use to feed them?" she asked after a few minutes and coming up empty.

"His fingers," Jake supplied. "You get messed, but Ketch said it's best. Hand's warm, you know."

Erin glanced down at her work-roughened hands. Her smile was bright when she thought of being able to save time and work for Mace. And maybe save those calves, a tiny voice added.

Bessie, good-natured cow that she was, didn't mind having her milking time disrupted by a few hours. Erin stroked her behind the ears, scratching the taffy-colored sleek fur, and spoke softly to the cow. "You'll be good and not kick over the pail on me, won't you, girl?" Stroking her fatted side, Erin reached down and moved the three-legged stool into place. The tiny seat barely allowed her to balance her weight on it, but she set the wooden bucket beneath the cow and began to wash her before milking. All the while she coaxed the cow, who had turned her head in the stanchion as far as the wooden bar would allow to watch Erin.

"Such pretty brown eyes, Bessie," Erin murmured, spreading her legs and leaning forward to gently grasp two teats. "And you're going to keep that tail still and not swish it back and forth over my head, right?" With steady tugs, the warm milk hit the sides of the pail. She made sure that there was plenty of molasses-sweetened grain for the cow to munch on while she milked.

When done, praise and pets were given before she left the cow and with the children's help, fed the fifteen calves in the box stall.

It was messy, but she had expected that. What she wasn't prepared for was the butting of small heads against whatever part of her body the calves could reach, along with the difficulty of telling one from the other.

Latching the stall door, Erin set the empty pail down, collapsing against the side of the stall and sinking down, overcome for the moment.

She rested her head against the wood, Becky leaning her head against her chest, and closed her eyes. She knew she should get up and go to the house to warm herself and the children, but nothing could force her to move.

Nothing but the sound of the wagon once again approaching the doors. Cosi was driving this time, with almost twenty calves that he explained they had the devil's own time trying to round up.

"Can hardly see up there," he managed to whisper through lips numb with cold.

When he made no mention of Mace, Erin had to ask.

"Pete never said nothing about you being down here," Cosi said. "If he had, the boss would've come himself. The wind's stronger, making it hard to see. Don't know how much longer any of us can stay out," he added, rubbing his arms and stamping his feet.

Mixing water with the milk again, Erin gave a bucket to each child, warning them to try to find the new calves to feed. "I'll be back," she said, "after I feed Cosi."

Once the soup and coffee had done their work and warmed him, Cosi helped her fill the washtub and set fresh water to heat.

"Will Mace come in at all?" she asked him.

"Boss'll be last. He'll be dragged back by Ketch. Thing is, Miz Erin, if the calf has just been born, we gotta wait till mama licks her baby over so she'll know which is hers. But storms like this have happened before, and if need be we'll just grab them and hand raise them. Snow's blowing so that we're working blind."

"Cosi why are they all calving at the same time?"

"Happens that range cows no matter when they're bred tend to birth close together. No one ever said cows were smart. Ketch figures that one drifts off and the others just follow. But I've got to get back."

"Be careful, Cosi."

Erin no longer counted the hours. The next wagon load came a long while after Cosi's, the next longer still. When Ray and Pete came in together with their horses tied to the back of the wagon, Erin knew the others would soon follow. True dark had fallen along with a blinding snow and a rising wind that cut through to the bone.

She had fed and milked Bessie again, watering down the small amount of milk to share with the last ten calves. They had already made over another box stall for them. Shooing the men up to the house for hot baths and food, she asked them to take the children with them. Alone and aching, she managed to finish the evening chores, thinking about Mace and the loss this storm would bring. For the first time, Erin felt as if she, too, had a stake in the ranch. And that, although they were apart, she and Mace were working together to salvage what they could.

Cosi rode in with a calf thrown over the front of his saddle as she was struggling to make her way to the house. He motioned for her to go on, and this time Erin didn't stop to argue.

She was huddled in a heated blanket at the table, a half-finished bowl of soup in front of her, barely able to keep her eyes open, when Mace and Ketch returned.

Snow dusted their coats and hats, and she forced herself to stand, intending to get food for them.

"Sit right where you were, Erin," Mace ordered, stripping off his gloves. "We'll tend to ourselves."

With her hands braced against the edge of the table, she shrugged off the blanket, moving slowly to the stove, shaking her head to ward off the sleep that was threatening to overcome her.

Mace watched her, but his skin was stinging as the heat of the kitchen began to make itself felt. He was too tired to argue with her, too grateful for the soup and hot coffee she set in front of him to do more than nod his thanks.

"There's plenty of hot water for you and Ketch to take a bath and get warm," she whispered, swaying where she stood.

"We'll be fine. Go to bed."

"How many did you manage to save?" she asked, determined to drag up strength from somewhere, needing to prove that in her own way she was as strong as Sky had been. Maybe she could not ride out and gather calves with the men, but she'd seen to their being fed and warm.

"Don't know," Mace mumbled, longing to rest his head on his arms and sleep where he was.

Ketch refused the bath. "Can't stand straight as it is. Toes near frozen. Bed's the only place I wanna be."

Erin watched him go and turned expectantly to Mace. "Do you want help?"

"Gonna scrub my back?" he teased, fighting to keep his eyes open. He couldn't believe that she had waited up for all of them with hot food. He'd expected her to be snug in bed like Jake and Becky by the time he rode in. He eyed the steaming water in the tub and longed for nothing more than to sink into its heat and warm his bones, but there were hungry calves to be seen to. Pushing away from the table, he rose, surprised to find that Erin was by his side.

"Would you want me to scrub your back, Mace?" she asked, telling herself it was the lines of weariness on his face that made her offer.

"Can't. Like to, though. Calves needing to be fed."

She knew he didn't realize that he was stumbling over his words, nor did he know she had already seen to the feeding as far as she could. "Unless you know some magic way to get Bessie to give more milk when she's been drained dry, there's no sense in going back out there.''

Shaking off the sleeping fog that clouded his mind, beckoning him to succumb to its lure, he stared at Erin, trying to make sense of what she said. "Bessie's been milked dry?'

"Yes. The children told me what had to be done for the calves.''

"And *you* did it?''

She nodded, placing one hand on his arm. Through his shirt, she felt the cold of his skin, and she tugged him along, surprised to find that he followed her. "You're chilled to the bone, so don't argue." With hands that shook, she reached up to open the buttons on his shirt, refusing to meet his suddenly alert gaze.

"Think you're gonna boss me?''

"Tonight, yes.''

"Can't argue?''

"Not a word, Mace Dalton,'' she returned, sliding her hands inside the opened shirt to push it off his shoulders. His union suit was damp, attesting to the labor he'd been through. Erin murmured soothing sounds, ignoring her own tiredness, her hands entangling with his as they both made an effort to get him undressed.

Mace shivered as he sat down to kick off his boots and watched Erin add another kettle of boiling water to the tub. He was still trying to make sense of what she had said she did. Why? The question plagued him. She had exhausted herself to save the pitiful number of calves that they had managed to find. He knew he was not thinking straight, fighting as he was not only his own exhaustion, but the loss of untold animals because of the storm.

Rising, he started to open the buttons of his fly and stopped. "You don't have to stay, Erin. I can manage.''

At least he had the sense to stop and ask. She looked flustered, those expressive green eyes darting every which way but toward him.

Even in his weariness, Mace released a male power that she couldn't ignore. The dark curling mat of hair formed a wedge that narrowed to disappear below his waistband. The lamplight spread a golden glow over him, and Erin, although she had tried not to watch him, found her gaze was drawn to him. Perhaps it was the lingering sense that they had worked together to salvage what they could from the storm that made her stay. For once, Erin didn't want to question the why of it. She just knew she needed to be near him, wanted him to allow her to do for him as a wife would, as only a wife could.

When she finally shook her head, Mace snagged her gaze with his and held it while he finished stripping off his damp clothes. He expected her to flee before he stepped into the tub and sank down into its offered heat with his knees scrunched up to his chest.

Erin came to kneel behind him, taking up the cloth and soap.

"You really intend to wash my back?"

"You're tired."

"And you're not?" he asked, bracing himself for the first touch of her hand on his shoulder. Her touch was as bad as he thought it would be and twice as good. The bad brought a heat rising from deep inside him, a heat that made him grateful for the close confines of the tub. Like the first time he had seen Erin, he was full, aching and hard, but he had learned to control himself. The goodness of her rubbing hard on his shoulders and neck muscles, which were painful now that warmth seeped into his body, brought a pleasured groan from him.

His eyes drifted closed, but his body wouldn't let his mind rest. It kept coming up with these impossible images of Erin truly being his wife, of the hands not only kneading the ache from hours of work, but touching him with a woman's need set free. Pleasured sighs escaped his lips when she abandoned the soaped cloth and used the heels of her hands with surprising strength to ease the tension from his neck. He wanted to stop her when she began to wash his arm, but he had been a long, long time without a woman's care. For once his guard was down and he allowed himself to enjoy her tenderly given ministrations.

For Erin there was both joy and agony in touching Mace this intimately. She tried to tell herself he was merely a bigger version of Jake, but that became impossible when his low rumbling groans seemed to be whispered into her ear. Her own exhaustion had disappeared, or maybe retreated, when she saw the lines relax on his face as color returned with warmth to his skin. It was awkward for her to get close to the tub, so she had to stretch across his chest to reach his other arm. It took a few moments for her to realize that his breathing evened out. Pausing, Erin leaned back on her heels to look at him.

His head lolled to one side, his lips slightly parted. His chest rose and fell with regularity and Erin smiled. She reached to brush the hair from his forehead, unwilling to wake him, but knowing he couldn't stay as he was. The tub was much too small for him.

"Mace," she whispered, cupping his dark stubbled cheek. She couldn't resist touching his lips or lightly brushing across his mustache with one fingertip. She called his name again, this time gently shaking his shoulder.

He came to with a start, his eyes blinking until her face, so near to his, was firmly in focus. "So damn tired," he murmured, struggling to stand. Water dripped to the floor as Erin whipped a blanket off the chair and did some struggling of her own to stand and wrap it around him.

"So cold."

"I know you are, Mace. Help me get you into bed and you'll soon be warm." Sliding his arm around her shoulders, Erin managed to hang on to the two ends of the blanket, praying he wouldn't trip on it. She coaxed him to walk with her, again repeating her prayer for the strength to help him.

Fumbling with his door, she wished she had the foresight to have lit the lamp within the room, for she couldn't remember where his bed was. Erin didn't want to think about the one night she had dared enter this room. It was best forgotten.

Mace tumbled down on the bed, taking her with him. Erin tried to free herself of his arms, which instantly snuggled her close, his hands locking together so that she was caught.

"Wake up, Mace. You've got to let me go. I need to get you covered."

"Warm."

Erin wasn't sure what made her still. The sleepy murmur didn't sound . . . right. "Mace?" she queried just as his leg covered both of hers. "Mace, you're awake, aren't you? You can't be sleeping?" She held her breath, waiting for his answer.

Chapter Sixteen

Seconds went by and she tried to coax him into answering. "Mace, let me cover you. You'll get sick if you don't get warm."

"Can't leave. Dying."

"Dying? Who's dying?" she begged to know, frightened to hear defeat in his mumbling voice. Was he talking about Sky? The calves? "Mace, talk to me. Tell me."

"Can't save all. Tried."

"Oh, Mace, don't blame yourself. You did try to get them all to safety. You didn't fail. You didn't," she repeated, twisting within the confines of his arms to lay her hand against his chest.

"Not enough."

The need to comfort him made her tremble. He nestled his head on her breast and she knew he had to hear the increased beat of her heart. His skin was still chilled, the blanket she had wrapped around him tangled half beneath him. He didn't know what he was doing, she told herself. He's half-asleep, far too exhausted to know.

"Listen to me, Mace. You've got to let me cover you. You need to be warm and rest." Pushing at the arm that held her imprisoned, Erin managed to move it.

"So cold."

There was a plea in those two words that stilled her.

"Sleep. So warm."

The damp heat of his cheek, the warmth of his breath—both pierced the cloth covering her breast. Erin pulled and yanked whatever she could of the quilt beneath them and the blanket he had to cover them.

"You'll sleep. You'll rest and—"

"Hush, Erin," he whispered, gathering her into his arms. "Stay. Stay with me and hold me. I need you to."

I need you. Erin repeated the words to herself, words she had dreamed of hearing from him. The initial panic she felt subsided. He had called her name. Hers. Not Sky's.

And he couldn't have been asleep!

But Erin instantly lost the thought of making that accusation. The seconds passed and tension left her body as she welcomed the weight of his leg across hers. His hair brushed her cheek and she felt the angular jut of his masculine hip pressed against her side.

"Better," Mace murmured, filled with a peace he had longed to feel again. Sleep was trying to stake its claim on him, and he knew he should heed its call. But Erin lay beside him, still and wary. Her lower back rested on his arm, the knot of her apron tie pressing his skin. She couldn't be comfortable dressed as she was. He shifted so that she rolled toward him. Ignoring her whispered query, he untied the bow and began to rub her back.

"Better still?" he whispered against the soft, lush swell of her breast that cushioned his cheek. He was rewarded with a series of sighs, each sweeter sounding than the last. Sleep was forced to release its claim as another stole into its place.

The soothing touch of his strong hand brought meaningless sounds of pleasure that Erin had no thought to hide from him. It felt so good, so right, to be held within his arms, their bodies' natural warmth creating a haven from the cold outside. With her arm free, she cradled his cheek, her eyes drifting close as contentment unlike any she had known filled her. She prayed the baby would sleep, feeling cosseted, as she was, and not begin the vigorous kicking it was wont to do at night.

Mace lifted her a bit, sliding the apron out and tossing it aside. He drew the quilt up from the side, making a cocoon to keep their body heat contained. His body curved the fit of hers, one hand cupping her hip, the other gently pressing the extended swell of her stomach.

She was a woman who carried life within her, and never had he needed to touch all that meant life as he did tonight.

Even with his eyes open, his mind supplied him with the images of tiny russet-coated bodies lying stiff and frozen in the snow. Death. He had been surrounded by so much death. He fought not to remember wading through knee-high drifts of snow to find another dead calf. But as the hours had passed and it grew dark to see, that was all he was able to find.

He had rejected this life that Erin carried so many times, tiny little innocent that it was. Staking his claim with words was meaningless. He never asked Erin what she wished for. He never asked if she was well. If she needed a doctor to see her. Needed anything. And now he longed to touch this life she held safe within her, as if it would renew his beaten spirit.

And Erin? he asked himself. How would she feel? "What would she do if I curved my hand over her belly?"

"What did you say?" she whispered at his side.

Mace tensed. He didn't know he had spoken aloud. But now that he had, he refused to lie, to take the words back.

He said he needed her. He meant it. Needed her more than a man simply wanting a woman.

"Mace?" Erin queried sleepily.

Sliding his hand from her hip, he splayed his fingers over the swell of her belly. "Hush. I won't hurt you."

Rigid at his side, Erin tried to adjust to the strange sensation of his hand holding her. This wasn't the same as Becky or Jake wanting to feel the baby move. This was Mace, and a flush started inside her at the feel of his light caressing motion. Her thoughts were not of his touch to the child near birth, but of how babies were first conceived. The feelings she had were not those of tenderness and warmth, but of need and hunger. Bewildered by her body's reaction, Erin didn't move. She was almost afraid to breathe.

She tried to still her thoughts, to stop the tremor that passed over her skin. She was making an effort not to press closer to him. But when his cheek made the same circular caress on her breast as his hand on her belly, Erin gave up trying. She'd found the reason for what Mace was doing. He simply wasn't in his right mind. He was dreaming, most likely. He couldn't want to touch her.

His lips pressed a tiny string of kisses over her breast until the damp warmth of his mouth and breath flooded inward from the already achingly tight nipple. She couldn't hold back the small sound of pleasure. She excused this, too.

But when his mouth closed over the peak that seemed to rise to offer itself, she knew Mace was aware, and wanting. Wanting to touch her.

The steady, gentle suckling created in her a fierce hunger. Desire that had been tormented by remaining unsatisfied these months wouldn't be stilled. And she didn't want it to be.

Erin made no move to stop him from opening the cloth buttons of her gown; she was lost in the wash of pleasure his attention to the ache in her breast was bringing to her. There was the feeling of sharp loss when he lifted his head, his hand spreading open the top of her gown.

Tiny kisses followed the plain edge of her camisole up to the hollow in her throat. He murmured satisfaction and dipped to taste the rapid beat of her pulse.

Her fingers slid into his hair, wanting to bring his mouth to hers.

"Sweet, lovely Erin," he whispered against her skin, "always so giving, so damn soft."

His lips wouldn't be distracted from rimming the line of her chin, seeking the sensitive skin behind her ear. Her hand slid down to his shoulder, gently holding him, unwilling now to guide him to what she wanted.

She was melting from the inside out, lifting her shoulder at his urging, feeling the slide of cloth as her arm was freed from the sleeve. She savored his calling her lovely, savored and held the word against the times she had thought he found her ugly. And sweet, she added to herself. He found her sweet and soft and giving. She yearned to be all these things for him. She had longed to know the heated power of his touch, the passion she had tasted so briefly one night long ago. She needed to give Mace all that he wanted, all that he would take. For she loved him, loved him but would never offer those words to him, knowing her love would be rejected. She would give him ease for the devil that tormented him this night.

She felt fragile in his arms, as breakable as delicate bone china, and Mace tempered his desire. The sweet rising heat in his body sent insistent pressure to his loins when she sighed and shook against him. He cradled her head with his arm beneath her neck, the other hand smoothing her hair from her face. Lowering his mouth, he meant only to kiss her lightly, but Erin's lips, soft and lushly damp from her tongue's licking, turned his tender touch into possessive claim. This was where she belonged, in his arms, in his bed, with his lips stealing the taste and breath of her.

And she gave. Gave him her mouth without hesitancy, gave sweetness that burned though his body, gave to him with every curve that softened itself to the hard planes of his.

She fed him, too. Fed him urgency with the way her lips clung to his mouth, her fingers kneading his shoulder. She didn't know she tore him apart. He was hard and aching, but the pain was exquisite torment. He wanted more. More of the tiny moans she made, more of the trembling of her mouth.

He wanted her skin bared to his touch, as naked as he was. Hurting with the same intensity. He wanted Erin wanting him, and only him. He needed to hear her tell him that he alone could still the prowl of relentless hunger that held him within its grasp and was taking slow, far too slow possession of her.

Wild. That was the way his blood surged through him. Hers had to match. The frantic play of her hand on his arm, his shoulder, now his back, told him she was feeling the tiny claws of passion sink deeper into her.

But not enough. Not nearly enough to satisfy him.

He lifted his head, denying himself the taste of her mouth. She quickly brought his lips back to hers. The tentative touch of her tongue to his bottom lip brought a groan up from deep inside him. He gathered her closer to his body and gave her what she silently begged for.

Kisses that claimed. The possessive ones that left no doubt that she was his. Kisses that grew deeper and deeper still, until the rhythm of the mating that would come enmeshed them in passion's snare.

And he wanted more.

Just as Erin was wanting. She helped him ease her gown from her body. Blindly, she tried to undo the ties that held both petticoat and camisole together. Mace stopped her.

"Let me," he murmured, soothing the impatient moves of her hands with his. "I want to unwrap you like a present. For that's what you are, Erin. A gift. A precious gift I need to have."

She fought the well of tears that surged to her eyes. She couldn't fight Mace—she had possessed no strength to before he spoke. Now her body failed her with its boneless state, its tremors that grew as his hands slid cloth away to bare her to his touch. She crossed her arm protectively over her rounded belly and he stopped easing the drawers down over her thighs.

"Don't hide, Erin. You're beautiful to me."

"No. Don't lie now, Mace. I see myself. I—"

"Hush, woman. Here, I'll show you." With an effort that racked his body, he lowered his head, kissing her fingertips. Using the tip of his tongue, he slid between her fingers and touched the taut skin beneath that they sought to protect.

His nose nudged her thumb.

Stubbornly, she refused to yield. How could she, when she was caught up in the most exquisite loving homage paid to her?

She felt the shape of his smile curve his lips. He gently doubled his effort. Erin's lips broke into a smile, too. But her smile reflected the sweet glory his kisses offered her. She held her hand in place.

Mace was determined to have her offer all of herself to him, no barrier between them. His hand caressed the shivering length of her thigh, his thumb pressing the crease below the target of his mouth. He was rewarded by the shift of Erin's leg, but still her hand remained in place.

Stringing kisses along the skin her arm rested upon didn't get her to move. He tried his tongue and failed. His body pushed him to finish this charming game quickly, but his mind overruled this time. Erin needed this. She needed to believe he found her beautiful. He longed for words. And knew he didn't have them. Not the right ones. Not the ones that spoke of cherishing the life she carried, of cherishing her for being a woman. For becoming his.

Mace raised his upper body, stroking her thigh, each time lifting his hand higher until his fingers found a way beneath her arm. He walked his fingertips across her belly, lowering his head, so that kisses followed . . . and trailed lower. His smile deepened. Erin's hand quickly sought to protect her from this new assault.

Mace rested his cheek on her belly. His hand, fingers splayed wide, joined it. He waited for the tenseness to leave her.

Erin stared up in the darkness, seared by his touches. She was going to cry, fought the need, and thought she had won, but Mace seemed bent on wringing tears from her.

He kissed her. His hand shaped her. He murmured, but she didn't hear. She was feeling. Tenderness. A cherishing. And loved. Loved? Yes! No matter that the words were not spoken. Her fingertips found his mouth and traced the shape of his smile. She closed her eyes, letting the tears silently slip out, emotions tumbling forth until she was steeped in all that was good. All that she longed for. All that dreams had offered.

The passing of time held no meaning. Desire returned and strengthened. She lifted his head, whispered her need and waited, vulnerable, exposed, willing him to come to her.

Mace took her hand and held it against his chest, where his heart thundered with the well of need that filled him.

"Feel what you do to me, Erin. From the first moment I saw you."

She gasped softly as he slid her hand down to the washboard ridges of his stomach, along the powerful strength of his thighs.

Mace sensed her hesitancy, and longed for her to trust him not to hurt her. He brought her hand to his mouth. "I need you. I hurt for needing you."

The sensual strokes of his thumb over her mouth held her still. Mace stroked the drawers down her legs and pushed them free. "This is how I want you. Trembling. Aching. Wanting me."

Didn't he understand? Erin wanted him. She needed him, too. Sharpening its claws, passion flared inside her. She moved against him instinctively, pressing closer, feeling a recklessness take hold of her. She had to make him know how she ached. Petting him didn't work. True, he shuddered as she tangled her fingers in his chest hair and skimmed the angular jut of his hip. But it wasn't enough. Her stomach clenched. She teased his lips with her mouth. His jaw invited a kiss, two, then more. She was rewarded by his breathing becoming faster.

Encouraged, Erin found she wanted to explore the curve of his shoulder; kisses weren't enough. She tested the heat and strength of him with delicate bites and then soothed them with her tongue. Mace was finally beginning to understand. He cupped her hips with his hands and brought her against him.

He was impatient now. She felt the fierce twisting need that spiraled through her, through him. Kisses landed where they could, touches were fleeting as heat built and yearned for completion. He was so careful of her sensitive breasts that she moaned with frustration.

He kissed her long and hard. She was hot and sweet and yielding. He felt the shocked awareness she tried to hide when his hand touched her inner thigh, but he caressed her gently, denying the potent force of his body that drove him.

Easing her leg over his hip, Mace murmured against her lips. He sought a hotter, sweeter softness that would bring an end to the torment racking him.

She shivered and cried out. Her body tightened with the first true desire she had ever experienced. She wanted Mace inside her. Recklessly, she buried her hands in his hair, pressing tighter to his body, straining to understand what was happening to her. She felt as if she would die if he didn't take her. With a choked sound mirroring her body's distress, Erin arched her hips, deepening his touch. A fever built inside her, a fever that spread until she gasped with the breaking of shimmering sensations that left her shaking.

There was no breath to draw without his heated scent filling her. Erin cried out again and Mace answered with a slow joining of their bodies that left her stunned.

She felt vulnerable as never before and yet powerful at the same time. He was still, his whispered question of hurting her unanswered for the moment. She was trying to absorb all that his possession brought with it. He moved, a small thrust of his hips, and Erin shattered so that she clung to him.

As each gentle thrust brought him deeper into her body, so did love for him flow deeper into her heart.

Even as Mace cautioned her to trust him, he felt his own control breaking. The ply of her fingers down his back

startled a growl of excitement out of him. He tried to
temper his grip on her, but her melting softness beckoned
his flesh, beckoned and enticed him to drive deeply. There
had never been such pleasure rocking through him. Never.
Fueled by the fire they created together, Mace felt the
balm of passion sealing off old wounds, smothering all
sense of betrayal.

Every movement, every shiver he called from her, every
cry brought the aching need for release. He couldn't catch
his breath for a moment when he felt her quivering and
then tightening around him. Her soft moans of completion took him to the edge. He faltered in the rhythm of his
thrusts, shuddering as the hard heat inside him burst into
flames. All he could do against its force was cradle the
woman who brought such fierce desire to him in his arms,
riding out the storm that refused to release him.

Erin held him, held him tight. She was overcome by the
depth of emotions still surging through her body. The
empty places inside her had been filled, far beyond their
fiery coupling. She felt healed of old hurts as love
bloomed in the joy he had given to her.

Mace brought his lips to hers, the kiss fleeting as the
exhaustion of the hours past finally staked its claim on
him. With Erin's head pillowed on his shoulder, sleep
came, and with it a blissful peace.

That same blissful peace slowly came to Erin as her
heart quieted and her mind found refuge in the wonder of
loving.

Hours later, her little one revealed its impatience with
a stranger's touch and smothering warmth. Hard little
kicks brought Erin awake and Mace along with her.

She was embarrassed that his hand covered her belly,
gently massaging her, murmuring when his touch didn't

bring a cessation of the baby's movement. Erin swore she heard a soft chuckle escape him.

She expected him to turn aside, an expectation that disappeared with his kiss. She expected the same tender loving as before. She stopped thinking when a wildness seized hold of her and only Mace's will kept it tempered so not to harm her.

"Let's see if we can't rock this little one to sleep, Erin."

His desire no longer frightened her, for she knew what was coming. Passion flowered rapidly through her, making fierce demands that Mace willingly answered and satisfied.

Erin learned ecstasy came with power, no less glorious than that which went before. Heat, lightning and thunder rocked through her as they found completion together.

When Mace shifted, she thought he would leave her, but he helped her turn to her side so that her back rested against his chest. With one of his arms below and the other above, she felt safe cradled in his arms. Smiling to herself, her last thought was that dreams were coming true.

Morning brought back reality.

Chapter Seventeen

Mace's vicious swearing awakened Erin as he untangled himself from the covers. The room was cold, a weak gray light filtering through the curtains. Squeezing her eyes closed, Erin was afraid to look at him.

How could the generous lover of the night turn cruel with the morning's summons? She didn't know and feared to ask what she had done.

Grating his teeth together to silence himself, Mace knew that if he had been drunk he might forgive himself. How could he break his own vow? How could he put Erin at risk? He didn't have the excuse of drinking. He had needed Erin and reached out for her. And she didn't have the sense of a forest-wary animal to beware of a predator. His gut churned with the thought that he might have harmed her. If he had . . . The thought remained incomplete. He couldn't, not even in the silence of his own mind, allow the words to form.

Yanking on his shirt, he stuffed the tail into his pants, hating the betraying tremble of his hands as they tried to fasten his fly. He eyed his room, searching for his boots, wanting to run, knowing he was wrong, but running just the same. Where he had left them hit him as he was forced to look toward the bed and found Erin cringing.

Mace longed to tear the quilt she had raised to her chin away from her. He wanted to see if he had bruised her. *And what about the ones he couldn't see?* How could he forget what happened to Sky? How could he forget his sworn word not to touch her?

With a shake of his head, unable to stand there and wait for her eyes to look upon him with accusation, he stalked from the room.

For a moment Erin didn't move. What had happened? Had Mace been dreaming that he was with Sky last night? No. He called her name. Not once, but over and over. He had made love to her, not the ghost that haunted him. But why was he cursing? Why did he leave her alone without a word?

Suddenly she didn't want to be found in his bed, in his room. Tiny twinges reminded her that she had done more than sleep in his bed last night. Scrambling around to gather her clothes, she slipped her gown on, praying that Ketch and the children were still abed. She would die if they saw her creeping from Mace's room with her underwear wrapped in her apron, carrying her shoes.

Thankfully the kitchen was empty, but she knew it would not be for long. She reached the door to her room just as someone opened the back door. Mace called out that coffee wasn't ready and whoever was there mumbled a reply. Erin slipped inside her room, hurrying to get dressed. But where would she find the courage to go out there and face him?

Mace solved the problem by simply not being there when she entered to begin making breakfast. He saved her from being flustered by his presence when Ketch came in, poured himself coffee and mentioned that Mace asked him to bring him whatever she made down to the barn. He had calves to tend before he rode out to check his cattle.

"Worse of the storm passed by," Ketch informed her, eyeing her over the rim of his cup. "You did real fine, Miz Erin. Got the makings of a real ranch wife."

Coming from Ketch that was high praise indeed, and Erin thanked him. For a second, she wished that Mace had said the words. But Mace, she decided, had said enough last night. For, whatever devil rode his back, he was punishing her again. But not this time. She was not going to meekly let him use her as a whipping post. Damned if she would!

"You get enough sleep?" Ketch asked, his sharp eyesight picking up the faint shadows beneath her eyes and the careful way she was moving.

"Enough."

"Testy, ain't we?" he prodded, seeing fire in her green eyes.

"We are not testy, Ketch. We are just fine." The smile she offered was as brittle as china and not half as pretty.

"Bristled up like a porcupine, she did," Ketch told Mace less than an hour later when he brought his breakfast out to the barn. "You did remember your manners an' thank her for all the work she put in savin' them calves, didn't you?"

"She lives here, doesn't she?" Mace snapped, having bolted down hot porridge sweetened with syrup. "Eats and sleeps the same as the rest. What we lose on the range hurts her same as us."

"That ain't no answer, an' you know it, Mace."

"It's all the answer you're getting." With plate in hand Ketch left, and Mace wanted to call him back. He wanted to know if Erin was all right, but if he asked, Ketch would want to know why. Damned if he'd tell anyone how he lost control and took her to his bed.

Now why did he go and open that latched door? He didn't want to remember the sweetly heated welcome his body found in hers. He refused to.

Feed, stock, fences and bookwork needed his attention. There shouldn't have been room in his thoughts for Erin. But there was room. He'd acted the coward, a damn fool of a coward, bedding her, then running out like a green kid caught with his pants down.

Grabbing hold of the pitchfork leaning against a post, Mace went back to mucking out the stalls. How was he going to rid himself of the taste of her? His senses were swimming in deep water, water the same green as her eyes. He had known she'd be soft and giving. That didn't surprise him. What shook him was the blinding explosion of passion that had matched his. A passion Sky had never equalled. He froze even as the traitorous thought formed. What the hell was he doing comparing Erin to Sky?

But if Erin had known about Sky, known his vow and what happened, she wouldn't be feeling hurt this morning. Yet to tell her about Sky would expose too much of himself, too much that shamed him. It wasn't a matter of refusing, it was just impossible.

Erin could think what she liked. If she was angry, that anger would serve them both. The woman had pride, let her use it.

Pride, Erin. Remember that, she repeated to herself when Mace refused to come in at midday to eat. The children were filled with boisterous spirits, running in and out of the house, tracking mud and snow along with wet clothes. She refused to snap at them, unable to summon the energy.

She longed to go out and see for herself how the calves that survived were doing, but Mace was out in the barn, and she wouldn't give him the satisfaction of thinking she was seeking him out. How could he just run off without a word?

Shooing everyone out of the kitchen once they were done eating, she tended to straightening up, but her mind was free to think back on all that happened last night.

She didn't imagine his gentleness. He seemed pleased that he wrung cries from her. If she didn't please him as a lover what could she do? There wasn't another woman to talk to—no one but Maddie. And she couldn't very well write a letter asking her about something so personal.

This was all Mace's fault, she decided, scrubbing a pot with a vengeance. If he had talked to her about Sky maybe she would have a reason for why he was acting like a...like that darn bull of his! How dare he make her feel like this? Just how dare he! She didn't ask him to bed her. She didn't flirt with him. *You didn't refuse him, either,* a tiny voice supplied.

Well, she was angry. Hurt and angry. Mace Dalton could keep his distance or she'd let him have what for. He was wrong to make her feel that he cared and then treat her as if she wasn't worthy of one word.

By supper time, Ketch, having the advantage of being the first to understand that something was wrong, noted the battle line drawn between Mace and Erin.

When one thought the other wasn't watching, looks were given in a sneaky manner six ways to Sunday. Mace scowled and snapped, Erin smiled and served. The meal's end was a relief for Ketch.

Trying to be helpful, he asked Mace to join him and the others for a poker game. Mace refused. He had bookwork. Ketch shrugged. He had tried.

Erin had little trouble getting the children to bed, for they were exhausted from their play. The spill of light told her Mace was still in the front parlor, but she resisted the impulse to confront him.

Once in bed, Erin stared up at the ceiling, praying for sleep.

Mace sat and stared at numbers that wouldn't make sense and wished he could crawl into a hole somewhere and pull it in after him.

Morning found corn bread, muffins, pancakes, bacon, ham and eggs on the table. Erin had cooked and cooked, and she greeted everyone with a sweet smile, everyone but Mace.

For Mace, the sight of all that food set his stomach to rebelling. Small tension knots had formed and redoubled. He forced himself to eat, feeling that everyone was watching him, but it was hard going to get food past the lump in his throat.

When he pushed aside his plate, he announced, "I won't be back till supper. I'm riding out to check the herd."

With a speed that amazed herself, Erin was up, packing sliced corn bread and ham into a napkin, rounding the table to hand it to him. "Take this with you then, so you won't go hungry."

He gazed up at eyes that flared hot with temper and lowered his head. "Thanks," he mumbled.

"Don't bother to thank me," she returned with sweetness dripping off each word. "It's the very least a wife can do."

That brought his head up. "Yeah. It's the least!"

She watched him storm out and knew someone was bound to remark about it. "I can't imagine what's eating him," she said, twisting her apron with her hands. "The calves are all doing well, aren't they, Ketch?"

"Calves is fine," he answered, giving her a knowing look. "It's the mamas he's all fired up about."

"Well, he should be," she returned with heat and left it at that. Thankfully, so did Ketch.

But by the time supper was ready to be served, Erin had calmed enough to decide on another course of action. Mace Dalton was not going to get away with ignoring her.

Two cows had been lost to the storm. Cosi brought in the frozen carcasses and Erin went out with him and Pete to butcher and store the meat. She was grateful when they both insisted they could manage without her, allowing her time to clean up before supper.

Erin took extra special care to fix her hair in a softer upswept style, but when she examined the few gowns she had altered to accommodate her rounding figure, she wanted to weep with frustration. How could she hope to look pretty when she felt like one of Mace's ready-to-birth cows? The cloth of every dress was faded and she knew she would look foolish if she tried to flirt with Mace. The man needed a pounding with a fry pan, not a woman gussied up to attract his attention!

But the soft waves framing her flushed face brought a gleam of frankly male hunger to Mace's eyes when he came in for supper. With a caution so unlike him, he tested the heat of Erin's temper by sniffing appreciatively and asking what was for supper.

"Steaks and mashed potatoes," she answered without turning from the stove.

"Smells more like gravy and apple pie to me."

"You might be right, Mr. Dalton."

So she was back to calling him Mr. Dalton, was she? He had best not complain. At least she was talking civil to him.

Ketch proved to be her ally. Dragging out his chair, he remarked with a decided twinkle in his eyes, "You sure do my eyes good lookin' so pretty after the day's work you put in, Miz Erin."

"Why, thank you, Ketch. But the work wasn't all that hard. I had Cosi and Pete helping me every step of the way."

Mace felt his muscles clench seeing the sweet smiles she bestowed on Cosi and Pete. He glowered at each man in turn so that they quickly began cutting into the two-inch-thick steaks Erin served them.

She set a plate in front of Mace. "I hope you like your steak rare. That's how I made it for you. And you were right. There's gravy, too."

He swallowed and nodded. He hated rare meat of any kind. Slicing into his steak, he decided he'd stomach it. Somehow he'd manage. But he wasn't going to let her get away that easily.

After a pointed look down the table, he lifted his gaze to hers. "Don't see a buttermilk biscuit in sight."

"Oh," she sighed, "did you particularly want them tonight? I wish you would've asked me. Every time Cosi does, I make them for him."

His eyes snapped with fury, belying his careless shrug. "Guess I should've known better. I should know that if I ask you'll give me anything, right, Erin?"

It wasn't a question, not really. She didn't need to reply. But she itched to, and the itch needed scratching more than she needed to keep her dignity. "Try asking sometime, Mr. Dalton, and see what happens."

Feeling she had held her own, Erin took her seat and found that her own appetite hadn't suffered a bit. She ate more than she wanted, for every time she looked up from her plate, she found Mace's brooding gaze pinned on her. She smiled a lot. She asked about everyone's day, including the children's. She listened and laughed and ignored Mace. When Ketch took another steak and a second helping of potatoes she teased him and delighted in the steam rising from the man opposite her.

But sleep once more was a long time in coming for her that night and in the nights that followed. There were nights when she cried and others when she tossed and turned for the ache that went unrelieved. An ache that Mace had created, satisfied and now left unabated.

Erin tried to find him alone, hoping to talk to him. The toll of the tension between them was beginning to show on Mace as well as herself.

He made excuses to leave the house after supper. He rode out during the day to where she couldn't follow. He spent time with the children, often ending the night sleeping in the big rocking chair in their room.

Mace lost weight. Erin felt she had gained every pound. He went back to taunting her. She retreated meekly. Not even the first of the wildflowers that Becky brought to her managed to chase Erin's dark mood.

She stopped blaming Mace for staying away from her. Who wanted to be near a woman who waddled instead of walked? No man enjoyed the sight of hair so limp it could have passed for noodles. Strength came and went so that some days she had to drag herself from bed, and others she felt bursting with energy. Erin was miserable.

"Miz Erin shouldn't be left with jus' Jake and Becky close by," Ketch said to Mace as they rode in early one afternoon. He knew Mace saw her struggling to tame the sheets on the line that the fresh April breeze was play-fully trying to pull from her grasp.

"Go help her," Mace ordered, resisting the urge to do it himself.

"Ain't my place, boss. Ain't my wife. Ain't my child she's haulin' round big as can be."

"You're proddin' me, old man."

"Boss, if proddin' gets the job done..." Ketch let the words sink home before he reached down and took hold of Tariko's reins. "Go on. You're fair to wastin' away tryin' to avoid her."

Erin had spotted them riding in, but she kept her eyes fixed on the laundry that threatened to escape her grasp.

From nowhere Jake was suddenly running, entangling himself between the wind-whipped clothes, Scrap at his heels, barking.

"Jake!" she yelled. "Come away from there. You and that dog. Go on," she continued, anger in her voice, for yesterday, two of Mace's shirts ended up torn off the line and in the muck pile. And as much as she had been tempted to leave them there, she had been forced to wash them again.

"Aw, Erin, we're just playing."

"Not here. You and the dog cause me trouble and work." Seeing Scrap lift muddy paws to grab a sheet, Erin flapped Ketch's union suit at him. "See! Now take your-self and that dog out of my way. I don't want either of you around!"

The stunned look she chanced to see on Jake's face in-stantly cooled her anger. She raised her hand toward him, but the boy turned and fled, Scrap at his heels.

Lord, but she ached from the inside out today. She couldn't even bend over to hook all of her shoe buttons and her ankles were chafed where the leather rubbed. Now she had yelled at Jake and hurt him.

Mace heard her, every word. She wasn't wrong to chase Jake and the dog away from the laundry, even he could see what was bound to happen, but he resented her yelling in anger.

But the sight of those half-buttoned shoes revealed by a wind gust lifting her skirt hem and petticoat forced him to still his resentment and approach her. She was all stubborn and no sense. All she had to do was ask for help.

"Go inside," he said by way of greeting. "I'll get the laundry."

Worrying over the way she yelled at Jake, Erin knew she shouldn't answer Mace. Her temper seemed to need something to snap at and he was too perfect a target. When he elbowed her aside to take down the sheet without a bit of trouble, she knew she wasn't having one of her meek days.

"I'll see to this myself, Mr. Dalton. It's one of the chores you hired me for."

Mace glared at her profile. Where did that nonsense come from? Hired? He claimed her as his wife, claimed her child and slept with her. "Don't get your back up over an offer to help."

"And don't you start telling me what to do!" Erin managed to toss clothes into the large basket, knowing the struggle she would have to carry it once filled.

"Listen, woman. You've got no call to snap my head off. I just offered to help you."

"Snap your head off? I should be so lucky. We all would be grateful if I could."

"Erin," he declared in a warning voice.

"And when I want your help, I'll ask. Don't stand around waiting, Mr. Dalton. Those mountains of yours will come tumbling down first." Ignoring the flapping laundry still on the line, Erin reached for the basket. Her every move pointed to her ungainly appearance, but she wanted to be away from Mace. The basket was long and wide, big enough for Jake and Scrap to squeeze into when they wanted to hide from her. Carrying it with her protruding belly was at best awkward, at worst, dangerous, for she couldn't see where she stepped.

Mace realized that very thing and with a snort of disgust, meant for her continued stubbornness, he yanked the basket away.

Erin stood where he left her, hurt beyond anything that he had done before. Snort at her, would he? It proved her every suspicion that he had lied to her the night she followed him to his bed like one of his docile cows. Lovely? Beautiful? Ha! He had needed a woman and she was the only one there, more than willing. But he didn't have to lie about how she looked.

He climbed the back stairs and opened the kitchen door, but Erin knew nothing could drag her into the house while he was there. She had plenty of chores waiting—each day saw her further behind in them—but they could wait. Frustrated anger and swift tears seemed to be the extent of her moods these days and tears were threatening now that anger passed.

It didn't take Mace long to realize that Erin had not followed him into the house. Worried, he opened the back door just in time to see her awkward walk take her past the springhouse. That walk reminded him of... a waddle. All she needed was a covey of little ones at her heels. The thought of Erin surrounded by children brought a grin to his lips. Mothering was an instinct not all women possessed. Erin had it in droves. Sky had made him feel at times that she cared more for the land and himself than the children.

The reminder did not bring the swift feeling of betrayal it once would have. Since the night he had broken his vow and made love to Erin, he knew he was releasing more of Sky to the past. And hidden in that past was his own mother, a woman who had turned her back on her only son, her only grandchildren, because they were less than the perfection she had demanded. But that had no power to hurt him now.

Erin did. And that made him go after her.

He knew she couldn't have gone far. The newly curled spring grasses released their scent as his boots pressed them to the earth in his search for her. He tilted his hat back, scanning the open land, then concentrated on the edge of the woods, hoping for a glimpse of her gown. The darn faded cloth was the shade of winter-worn wood, making his search difficult.

Spotting Becky, he called out to her. "You see sign of Erin?"

"Ain't she here? I want to show her these pretty stones I found."

"Go on up to the house, Becky. I need to find her."

"Try the pond or the clearing up above. She likes those places best, Papa."

Mace took his daughter's advice and found Erin up in the clearing. The slight climb must have tired her out, he thought, for she was prone on the grass, arms flung wide at her sides, staring up at the sky. She didn't make a sound or move as Mace neared and called her name.

"You'll have trouble getting up," he noted softly, dropping to his knees beside her.

"I know," she answered in a woeful voice.

The pale curve of her cheek called for his touch and Mace gave in to the impulse, glad she didn't try to pull away. All that she was feeling, all the changes the baby was making as it readied itself for birth, rushed at him, and he found in himself a deep well of tenderness, which he offered her.

"It'll be over soon, Erin."

He sounded so sure that he knew what she was thinking and feeling that Erin didn't question his statement. He must know, she told herself. He lived through the birth of two children with Sky. He had likely rubbed her back every night, and held her when she cried for no reason. And she was tired of fighting, so tired of being alone and uncertain of what was happening to her. If Mace was another man, she could ask him how it was with Sky. But Mace was not another man, and he didn't want to talk about Sky, babies or his marriage. She was being torn on too many fronts to fight them all. A weary sigh slipped from her lips, and Mace's hand stilled.

"Erin, things can't go on as they are."

"You said that before and now they're worse."

"There are reasons." He made an effort to ease the edge of anger from his voice. "Believe me in this. There are good reasons. I shouldn't have..." His voice trailed off as he struggled to find the right words. Telling her that he shouldn't have made love to her didn't seem right. Yet those were the words that came to mind. They had made love. Love? Erin? He turned them over silently, finding the more he repeated them to himself, the less strangely they went together.

Erin turned to look up at him. He appeared lost in his thoughts. She fixed her gaze on his chin, wanting to sooth the nick his razor had made. She couldn't look at his lips without seeing them break with a smile, or remembering the cherished feel of them kissing her. Memory supplied the way his mustache glided softly against her skin, and her eyes traced the line of his nose that had teasingly nudged her hand aside.

She wanted to be the one, the only one who could ease the lines of worry that furrowed his brow. The instinct to offer him comfort when she was the one in need of the same came up so strongly that Erin closed her eyes to examine it silently by herself.

Moments like this brought back the hope that she and Mace could have a real marriage. But only if he accepted her as the woman in his life. Only if he opened the secrets of the past. More and more, as the days went by, she wondered why he blamed himself for Sky's death. She knew his temper, but words did not bring the physical hurt that could cause death. She knew that, even if some of his taunts made her think she'd die at that moment. He was not a violent man. She had sassed him back and been given the same in kind. Why did he think he caused Sky's death?

Mace was the first to set his thoughts aside. Pain pierced him to see the tears silently slip from Erin's closed eyes. Without thought, he leaned over, drinking each bitter tear with his lips. His hand curved unbidden over the high round of her belly, gently turning her toward him.

"Don't," he murmured, scattering kisses over her temple. "Nothing's worth crying over, Erin. I promise you, this will all be over soon. I'll help you. And you'll let me. We'll try again."

Erin chided herself for being selfish and refused to open her eyes, refused to answer him. But it felt so good to be touched, to be reassured that she wasn't going to carry this baby forever, that there was still hope for her dream to come true.

His voice had deepened to a rich liquid murmur that
caressed her all the way inside. The kisses grew softer,
trailing down to her mouth, and she wanted, needed this
tender homage from him. Every sound, each lengthening
kiss soothed the hurts of the last weeks. She let him gather
her up against his body, took his heat into her own as her
dream formed, stronger this time, healed by the rocking
of his body against hers.

"I never meant to hurt you, Erin," he whispered,
stroking the tangled silk of her hair. He knew if he repeated the words enough, she might believe him. She put
her arms around him, and he wanted the tears to stop.
Husky whispers followed, and he realized she was emo-
tionally spent. Resting on his heels, Mace lifted her up to
his lap, pressing kisses against her hair. He held and
hushed her as he would one of his own children, waiting
for the storm to pass.

As the need for tears eased, Erin knew she had to brave
his wrath. He was right to say that things could not go on
as they were. But she wanted honesty between them. Hope
alone would not survive without that.

Her fingers curled around his neck, threading the col-
lar-length dark hair. She lifted her head to look at him.

"Mace, I believe you when you tell me that you don't
mean to hurt me. I think there are other hurts inside you.
Hurts you won't share with me. I need to know about
them. I feel as if there are parts to you that you keep hidden away. How can I trust you not to hurt me again when
you refuse to tell me why you turned away from me?"

Angrily, she brushed the tears from her eyes, sniffing
but determined to have her say even as she saw the tight
set of his lips, the closed expression of his eyes.

"Don't ask me," he said, feeling his jaw and muscles
tense.

"I must. Can't you see that? You offer me promis‹ that this will all be over soon. Will the birth of a ch‹ bring us a miracle? Will you forget what eats at you? W you tell me about Sky and why you blame yourself for h‹ death?"

Every word was a knife thrust in Mace. He shook wi‹ rage, but gently set her down, rose and then lifted her her feet.

"Mace?"

"Do you need my help to walk back?"

Erin shivered at his cold tone. She shook her head, ‹ alized his back was already toward her and whispere "No."

"I'll see you at supper."

Chapter Eighteen

When Erin finally returned to the house, Becky waited for her. Setting aside her despair, Erin admired the pretty stones Becky had found in a stream in one of the upper pastures.

"Where's Jake? I want to show them to him, too. These are better than the ones he found."

"Becky," Erin scolded gently, "there's no need for you to try to outdo your brother at every turn."

"Yes, there is," the child stubbornly maintained. "He's a boy. Papa loves him best."

"Who dared to tell you such nonsense? Your papa doesn't love Jake more than you because he's a boy or for any other reason." Erin cradled the slender child in her arms.

"Are you gonna love us the same when your baby comes?"

Gently pushing Becky back a little, Erin slid her hands around to cup the girl's cheeks and raised her face upward.

"I will always love you and Jake as if your were my very own. There's enough love inside me, Becky, to share with each of you and my baby. Come sit in my room with me and we'll talk about this."

Once settled on her bed, Erin drew Becky close. "Whe I was a little girl, smaller than you, I used to dream all th time about having a family that loved me and one that could love back. Even when I was all grown-up, Becky that dream didn't leave me."

"But you've got us. We're all your family now. A when the baby comes I can help take care of it. Yo promised. An' I promise to love it a lot just like you sai babies need. I won't let Jake get his dirty hands on th baby or let Scrap lick its face, either."

Hugging her close, Erin felt the faith and warmth onl love could bring. "Becky, ah, child, you don't know ho you make me feel."

Wiggling free, Becky looked up at Erin. "Is it a goo feeling? You said loving someone always makes them fe real good."

"And you do."

"Then why're ya crying again, Erin?"

"I'm happy. You make me happy. And I don't eve want you to say that your father loves Jake more tha you. He doesn't. Who did he pick to take care of the tw orphaned calves? It wasn't Jake. It was you. Your pap trusts you and trust is a way of showing love, too."

"I never figured it that way, but you're right, Erin. H makes me watch out for Jake. All the time, before yo married him, he always said I had to take care of Jak 'cause he was littler than me. And I was the one wh helped Ketch with the cooking and washing."

"And now you'll be helping to break Tariko's colt, Erin added. "You see, don't you, Becky, how you hav special things that only you can do? When Jake gets hu he doesn't run to your father. He comes to me or you. Smoothing the child's hair, Erin leaned close to whispe

'Females are best at healing. We're best at lots of things that men and boys can't do.''

Eyes twinkling, a grin breaking her lips, Becky whispered back, ''Men can't have babies. They can't ever be mommies. And they can't tell stories like you do. They don't smell half as pretty as you, Erin,'' she finished, leaning her head against Erin's arm.

''See, we females are special. And there's something else you forgot. Your father doesn't try to stop you from doing anything that Jake could do. You ride better—''

''That's 'cause I'm bigger.''

''You're better at fishing and finding strays, too.''

''Jake just likes climbing rocks and finding caves. Boy has no sense at times,'' she added, shaking her head.

''Feel better now?'' At Becky's quick nod, Erin struggled to stand. She braced her back with her hands, rubbing hard, and caught sight of her reflection in the mirror. Was it her imagination that the baby seemed to have settled lower? With Becky here, she didn't want to linger and look, so she headed for the door. ''Coming, Becky?''

''Yeah. If I could have some cookies, I think I'll find Jake and show him my stones. But nicely,'' she amended, catching sight of Erin's look.

''You do that, honey, and make sure you're back in time for supper.''

Becky returned in late afternoon just as Erin began to fry chicken.

''Erin, I can't find Jake. I've looked and looked all over. I even went up to that cave he found and called him, but he didn't answer me.''

''Likely he's with Ketch or your father. Why don't you wash up and help me set the table?''

Erin wasn't worried about Jake. She intended to apologize for snapping at him and Scrap and knew he'd come

home in time to eat. He'd changed so much in the fou
months she had been here—from a shy boy to one wh
was silent only when eating.

Erin still didn't worry when she saw the men ride in wit
Ketch and no Jake. He was with his father, then. Bu
when Mace came inside and said he hadn't seen Jake sinc
she had yelled at him, Erin began to worry. When Beck
confided as soon as her father left them to go to his roor
that Jake wondered if Erin would still love him after sh
had her baby, Erin grabbed her shawl from the hook an
told Becky she was going to look for him.

He wasn't hiding up in the loft. Erin, after having calle
him enough times, braved the rickety ladder to climb u
and see for herself if he was there. She managed to ge
high enough to peer over the edge, demanding that Jak
come out, but there was only silence.

It seemed forever before she stood on the straw-littere
floor again, heading for the tack room. That prove
empty. So did the woodshed, the springhouse and th
lean-to built to shelter Mace's precious bull. With hand
on hips, Erin glanced toward the bunkhouse. She hated t
disturb the men as they washed and donned clean shir
for supper, but there really wasn't much choice. Jake ha
to be found.

Mace beat her there. He had just closed the door whe
Erin came around the corner. "Where is my son?"

"I don't know. I was going to ask you."

"He ran off when you yelled at him. Didn't he com
back?"

"If you disciplined him once in a while instead of le
ting him run wild, I wouldn't have had to yell at him!"

"Don't raise our voice, woman. Not to me."

Erin backed away. "I won't. I won't say another word to you. I just can't believe you're blaming me for Jake being gone."

"And who should I blame," he stated coldly, anger for her stirring up the past churning inside him, "if not you? You're my wife. You're—"

"Am I, Mace? Am I really?" Erin didn't wait for his answer. She retraced her steps, calling Jake's name and calling for the dog. The corrals showed no sign of the small boy, nor did his favorite tree, and darkness was rapidly falling.

She had reached the edge of the woods, hesitating to enter since the shadows were so deep, when Mace walked up behind her.

"This is foolish, Erin. You'll get hurt. Come back to the house and let me look for him."

"No. I caused him to run off and I'll find him."

"I didn't mean that. I—"

"It doesn't matter. Finding Jake does."

"Then wait right here for me, Erin. I'll get a lantern and something warmer for you."

Erin hadn't felt the chill until he mentioned it. Jake didn't have his jacket with him. He was likely cold and hungry. That made up her mind. She couldn't stay and wait for Mace.

But she used caution entering the woods, ever mindful of exposed tree roots that could trip her. Becky claimed that she had searched the cave Jake had found. But Becky didn't like caves and Erin had the feeling that the child had not gone in beyond the opening. Jake could have hidden far back. Jake could be hurt, too.

Worry intensified. It lent her the strength to make the climb up a short hill, where she stopped to get her bearings. Across the field was another strip of woods and beyond that were the tumbled rocks that led to a path up the mountain.

Erin looked behind her but didn't see a light to indicate that Mace had followed her. She couldn't wait. As fast as she could, with an inner sense of need hurrying her now, she made her way across the field. Thankful that the branches were just beginning to leaf she was able to find her way through the woods with little difficulty.

Urged on by the litany that Jake needed her replaying in her mind, Erin began finding her way up through the massive rocks. The path was steep and she strained her arms pulling herself up. The smaller, loose rocks below her feet made every step treacherous, but she wouldn't stop.

From far below she heard Mace calling her, but she didn't have breath to answer him. Her hand slipped, the palm scraped raw, just as she lost her footing. Erin managed to get her hand to her hip, coming down hard on it. For a moment she was stunned. Pain, sharp and fast brought a moan from her as she struggled to push herself upright.

She could barely make out the shapes of boulders that surrounded her. Glancing upward, she thought there was a darker blackness that could be the cave's opening. Using extreme care, she started her climb again.

Her hip throbbed and her lower back ached as she found small handholds in the face of the rock and pulled herself by inches closer to where the cave should be.

"Jake," she called, surprised that her voice croaked, pain in her throat forcing her to realize that she had been shouting his name for a long time before. "Answer me, please. Are you up there?"

Erin touched the edge of a narrow ledge. There was no way for her to pull herself up and over to it. Knots of ten sion churned in her stomach as she rested her forehead against the cool rock.

"Jake? Jake, just answer me. Let me know you're all right."

The plea went unheeded. Strength was in short supply, yet Erin demanded all she had from her weary body. By touch alone, she secured a place for her hands, then her feet. At a crawl, she worked her way up a rock until she could brace her arms on the ledge.

Her heart was pounding with exertion, sweat trickled down her back and she was panting. Once again she strained to call the boy, sure she was directly at the cave's opening.

Erin didn't dare rest long. The yearning for more than a minute's stop was a demand she beat back. She had to find Jake and know that he was all right.

Driven now, she prayed no harm would come to her or her child as she wriggled her way onto the ledge. She could hear other voices calling her name, but they were too far away to hear her weak reply.

Blackness loomed in front of her. She inched along on her side, ignoring the rocks that pinched through her clothes. Trembling by the time she stood, Erin stared at the opening. It appeared a large black mouth just waiting to swallow her up. If only the moon would rise, she thought, glancing up at the night sky.

Her hand rested against the stone edge and she stepped forward. Think of Jake inside, think of him alone, maybe hurt, she urged herself, taking another step inside. A few steps more and she couldn't breathe. It felt as if the mountain was coming down on her shoulders, crushing her, crushing her unborn child.

With her palm protectively held over her belly, the other extended forward, Erin blindly went forward, calling

Jake. It took minutes for her to realize she heard the echo of her own voice coming back at her. The cave had to be deep, and it was filled with a darkness unlike anything she had experienced before.

Each time she set her hand down on the rock wall that guided her, Erin hoped that she would reach the end, but the tunnel seemed to go on and on.

Her throat was raw and parched, but she finally noticed that the air was as clean as outside. Somewhere up ahead there might be another opening. She could feel a light whisper of moving air across her face and bravely quickened her pace.

Once more she began calling out to Jake.

This time she was rewarded.

"Erin. I'm here. Down here."

The echo rebounded from the walls and Erin couldn't place where he had called from. She had to wait until all sound died away before she spoke.

"Listen to me," she said softly, keeping the echoed response down. "Am I close?"

"I'm down a hole."

"Dear Lord! Jake, are you hurt?" She had spoken too loudly, and too fast. Again she waited until the silence returned, afraid now to move for fear of falling to wherever Jake was. She should return to the opening and try to attract Mace or the men's attention. Erin knew it was the sensible thing to do, but she hesitated and then was glad she did.

"Erin."

"Yes."

"I'm scared."

"I'm coming."

Pressing her back against the rough wall, Erin lowered herself to sit. By rocking gently, side to side, she managed to work her way along. Keeping one hand extended on the floor of the cave, she guided herself until the ground gave way to nothing.

"Jake?"

Scrap started barking. The sound filled her ears and she couldn't hear if the boy answered her. "Hush him!" she yelled.

But long before quiet descended, Erin was trying to figure a way to get Jake out. Without a light, she couldn't see how far down he was. She didn't know how wide the hole was. And she became afraid to move farther. She needed something to lower down to him. But, foolishly, she had come with nothing but her shawl.

"Are you hurt?" Let him say no. Lord, let him say no. Please, she prayed, I'll not ask for another thing.

"My arm's hurtin'."

Seconds passed before Erin found enough moisture in her throat to talk. "If I let something down, could you manage to climb?" She was already stripping off her shawl, testing the wool's strength with feeble pulls. Would it hold his weight? But more, could she pull him up?

Turning to her side, Erin stretched out and let the shawl fall. She wrapped one end around her wrist and held it in a death grip with both her hands. She nearly doubled up when a sharp pain seared her lower back. "Don't let me choose between them," she whispered to herself, feeling the pain ease.

"Do you see the shawl, Jake?"

"I can't see at all."

"Find it," she commanded, knowing something was wrong. The ache returned, and she could feel it turn again to pain. It was stronger than before. "Hurry."

She tried to wave the shawl back and forth, hoping the movement would help Jake. When he tugged the end, she sighed with relief.

"Give me a few minutes, Jake." Erin forced herself onto her belly to better grip the shawl. She didn't know if she had the strength to pull him up, but she had to try.

"I can't leave Scrap," he pleaded.

"Just for now. Just until your father comes. I can't come get you. You have to try to climb." With her arms stretched out, Erin thought the first feel of Jake's full weight would tear them from her body. She didn't dare go forward to ease the strain, for she was afraid that Jake could pull her down.

Sweat dampened her palms and she squeezed the wool not to lose her grip. Once again pain built in her back, this time making her cry out. The cloth went slack.

When she could breathe, when she could whisper, she called down to Jake. "Why did you let go?"

"I thought I hurt you."

"No. No, it's not you, Jake. But hurry. Just hurry."

Pull, she ordered herself, bracing again for the pain. On and on, until she knew that Jake was nearing the edge by the labored sound of his breathing.

"A little more, Jake," she encouraged, taking the words into herself. She tasted blood where she had bitten through her lip to stifle the cries that wanted to wrench free. The pain wasn't receding at all. It built in intensity, lessened, but never left her. She couldn't abandon Jake. Just a few moments more. A few.

The touch of his hand on hers was the best of feelings. "You're safe, Jake. A tiny bit more and you're safe."

But Erin never had to lift him those last few feet, for other hands took hold of the shawl, strong hands that she relinquished her burden to. Erin crawled backward until she saw the lantern light and knew she was safely out of the way.

The soft glow of the lantern was a warm beacon in the dark cavern and revealed Mace, holding his son tight. She tried to summon a smile, so grateful that Jake was safe, but pain shot through her in agonizing waves. All Erin could do was curl on her side and draw her knees up. She didn't cry. Something was wrong with her baby; she couldn't deny it. She couldn't pray, either, for she had bargained that if Jake was all right, she wouldn't ask for more.

"Why didn't you wait for me?" Mace asked, lifting his head from Jake's shoulder. He found Erin quickly, lying on her side, ghostly pale and panting. She was covered with dirt and one hand was scraped raw. Setting Jake down, all the fear he had for his son turned to Erin.

Softly, he said, "Jake, go call out to Cosi and Ketch. They're real close. Tell them I need them here quick."

Kneeling by Erin's side, he placed his hand on her brow. Her skin was cold and clammy. "Why, Erin? Why did you do it? You put yourself at risk for Jake."

"Mace, I hurt. Something's wrong."

That raw sound of her voice slashed through him. He placed his hand on her distended belly and heard her moan. Her stomach was rock hard and he needed no more to know what was wrong.

"Erin, trust me. I'll get you home as fast as I can."

"It's the baby, isn't it? The baby's coming."

Mace couldn't answer her. The baby was coming, and far too early.

Chapter Nineteen

"Push, Erin," Mace demanded from his position at the foot of the bed.

Her shallowed, labored panting and a weak moan were his only reply.

"You want this baby, don't you? Try. Help me." His voice was gruff. His gaze slid quickly up her pale face, seeing the dark shadows bruising the skin beneath her eyes, her lips blood red in the late morning sunlight from where she had bitten them.

"How early is this baby, Mace?" Ketch asked, entering the room with fresh water.

"I'm not sure. By Owhi's reckoning, maybe four or five weeks."

Wringing out a cloth and coming to the bedside to wipe Erin's face, Ketch tried to speak calmly. "What do ya mean? By Owhi's reckoning? Ain't you ever asked her?"

"I never did."

The guilt-laden words silenced Ketch and he glanced from Erin's face to Mace's. He didn't know which one needed help more. He didn't have the heart left to berate Mace, for he could see, along with knowing, the torment the man was going through, and had been since that harrowing trip down the mountain with them and Jake.

"Help her sit up a bit, Ketch. She ain't got the fight of a weak kitten left in her."

Ketch did as he asked, sliding in behind Erin's head and gently lifting her exhausted body up so that he cradled her back against his chest. Her anguished cry sliced through him and Ketch began praying as he never had before. Mace would not survive losing another wife in childbirth. Ketch didn't have to ask him, he knew. And to help, he began to coax Erin just as Mace was.

Clawing pain gripped Erin, tearing her from the sweet place she floated toward. Mace's demanding voice began its litany again, and another's was added to it. She was tired. So tired. She struggled to do as they wanted, anything, just so they would leave her in peace. She felt the scream build inside her and opened her mouth, unaware that a pitiful whimper was the only sound she made.

"Want the baby, Erin," Mace pleaded, his eyes blurring with tears. "Help me. Dear Lord, let her fight." And in an anguished whisper, "Let her live." There was no room for shame that Ketch had heard him. He had no secrets from Ketch. He didn't have to hide the agony he felt at witnessing yet another woman, too weak to fight, too easily giving over to a call he felt powerless to overcome.

With his strong hands, he began at the upper slope of her belly, gently pressing downward. He could see the quiver of Erin's spread thighs, see the crown of the baby's head. Another weak cry tore from her lips and still he begged, pleaded and yelled, trying to reach through to her.

Pressure built, threatening to rip her apart. Erin was grateful for the hands that gripped her wrists, for the flow of strength that they imparted. She shook her head wildly, fighting to find the breath to scream.

"A little more. That's it, Erin. Just a little more."

Mace. That was his voice again. Praising her? Was she finally doing something to please him? Blinding pain seared her body. She couldn't do this. Couldn't stand . . . another moment. Again and again the pressure came, stretching her until she knew she was dying. The sudden flood of wetness brought the feeling of relief. Her life's blood was leaving her body. It was almost over. She knew it was almost over. Even Mace was telling her that. From far off, she heard him.

The baby slid free into Mace's waiting hands. His exultant shout roused Erin.

"Mace?"

"It's a girl, Erin. A little girl."

A half-formed smile teased her lips and Erin closed her eyes. A girl . . .

Ketch slipped out from behind Erin, lowering her down to the pillow, and came around to take the baby from Mace so that he could knead Erin's stomach and rid her of the afterbirth.

With the gentlest of touches, Ketch cleaned the baby, grinning at the squalling red face. "Fine lookin' little lady, Mace. A mite small, but she seems to have the right parts." The baby's lusty cry brought a whoop from Ketch. "Well, you hear for yourself how she's howlin' her way into the world."

But Mace didn't respond to Ketch. He was leaning over to whisper to Erin, stroking her brow. "It's going to be all right. I promise you. You're not going to die."

"Stop it, Mace. Look at her. She's gettin' a bit of color back. Erin's a fine, strong woman. She ain't dyin'. You've got to lay the past to rest."

Mace nodded, but Ketch wondered if he really heard him. After washing and wrapping the baby in a length of soft flannel, Ketch held her and crooned to her while

Mace cared for Erin. Once Mace had her in a clean night-gown, he lifted her into his arms.

"Gonna take her back to her room?" Ketch asked.

"No. Strip the bed and make it up fresh. She'll stay here with the baby."

"Well, then, set yourself down an' hold on to your la-dies, boss, while I tend to that bed. All they need is a good sleep. Best for all, to my way of thinkin'." Ketch caught Mace's absent nod and knew by the way he watched every breath Erin drew and released that he was still worried about her. Trying to distract him, Ketch said, "There's still that cradle you made up in the loft. Think I should send one of the boys to fetch it down an' clean it up?"

"Sure. Whatever you think, Ketch."

Smoothing the quilt on the bed, Ketch was satisfied and went to take the baby. "Get your woman in bed, an' then, 'us' to ease your mind, get in beside her."

Mace set Erin down, wishing he had thought to brush the tangled length of her hair. He brushed it aside with his fingers, moving over to allow Ketch to place the baby in the crook of her arm. Mace swallowed as he gazed down at the small red face sucking on its tiny fists as if the baby couldn't make up its mind which one it favored. Tiny and helpless . . . But you're gonna have your mama, little one, he silently promised. Come time to fight the devil him-self, I'll make sure of that.

He saw that Erin's breathing was deep and even and that Ketch was right about the color returning to her face. He lifted her hand and brought it to his lips, thanking the Lord that Erin and the baby had survived. He couldn't believe that she had risked her life and that of the child she wanted so much to save Jake. Just as he couldn't stop his mind from wandering back to the night Sky had given birth to Jake and the nightmare that followed as her life's

blood seeped from her no matter how he pleaded, how h
prayed or what he did.

Ketch rested his aged hand on Mace's shoulder. "Kno
what you're thinkin', son, an' this ain't the same. Eri
ain't Sky. You've got to stop lettin' the past haunt you.'

"I know. But something keeps pulling me back."

"The only thin' pulling you back is you. You won't l
go. I tol' you then an' I'm tellin' you now, weren't you
fault. The good Lord saw fit to take her an' nothin' yo
did was gonna stop it from happenin'. He left you a so
an' maybe, to the Lord's way of figurin', he's given you
second chance to make things right in your mind."

"Ketch, I—" Mace's voice broke and he lowered hi
head, unable to talk.

"Son, sometimes a woman's way of easin' hurt ain't s
bad for a man. I'll admit I did some cryin' myself when w
found Jake and Erin. I'll leave you now to see to you
own."

Dusk had forced Mace to light the lamp in the roor
and he led Becky and Jake in, his finger held to his lip
when he saw that Erin was once again asleep. She ha
been awake for a little while, long enough to nurse th
baby and count fingers and toes. Mace would never fo
get the shyness in her eyes, or the tenderness of her smil
when she looked at him and thanked him.

Becky and Jake stood near the cradle where the bab
slept. Her cheeks were still bright, her nose small as
button and tiny lips pale as a spring rose. There wasn'
much more of her to see, wrapped tight as she was. Wit
a hand on each of his children's shoulders, Mace waite
for Jake and Becky's reaction.

"She's tiny," Jake said, cradling his injured arm wit
the other. "I didn't think babies were so small."

"She's pretty and I'm gonna help take care of her," Becky announced in an important whisper, glancing over toward Erin to make sure they did not wake her. "Big sisters have to take care of little ones."

"So do brothers, right, Papa?"

Concerned that they would wake Erin with their talking, Mace ushered the children out, careful to leave the door ajar in case Erin called out.

Seated before the fire in the parlor, Mace gazed at the two of them. "You really feel like this baby is your sister?"

Becky chose to answer. "You married Erin, so what else is she? But Papa, what are we gonna call her? Erin never said."

Mace shook his head, not in answer to Becky's question, but in disbelief that they were so accepting of Erin's child. And he had to know if that was Erin's doing. Easier thought than said, for he never knew what turns Becky's mind would take and how much she would later reveal to Erin.

"Oh, so you don't know, Papa. I hoped Erin told you."

"No. We never talked about a name." *Or much else.*

"Now we're a bigger family," Jake supplied, basking in his father's sudden smile.

Mace was grateful for an opening. "Is that how you see it? I guess Erin told you that?"

"Erin didn't say it," Becky answered before her brother could. "She didn't have a family of her own. I told her we all loved her and would be her family. That was right, wasn't it?"

"Only if it's what you and Jake want."

"We do, don't we, Jake?" Without looking at Jake, Becky proceeded to tell her father about Erin's dream and when done, cuddled close to him. "It's going to be so nice to have a little sister. There's all sorts of things I can teach her. Erin said so."

"And me. Brothers can teach things, too. Even if she's only a girl."

"Well, one thing you won't be teaching her is to run off and not let anyone know where you are, Jake. There wasn't time to punish you because of Erin having the baby, but don't think I've forgotten."

"I ran off 'cause I was afraid that Erin didn't love me anymore. You can't spank me, Papa. I'm hurt." To make sure, Jake lifted his injured arm.

Hearing his son express his very fear softened Mace's thoughts about punishing him. But before he could speak, Becky interrupted.

"You're silly, Jake. I asked Erin and she said she had love for all of us. The baby won't take a bit away from you and me. If you asked instead of running off I could've told you so."

In the soft glow of the firelight, Jake's crestfallen expression moved Mace to hug him tight. "I think maybe we can forget a punishment this time. You learned your lesson."

"She yelled at me and Scrap. Erin never yelled at me like that."

Mace was caught between defending Erin and wanting to ease Jake's concern. He spent nearly an hour talking to them before he managed to get them to bed.

He felt as if a burden had lifted to know that his own fear of Erin turning from his children once she had her child had been groundless. To hear Becky speak of Erin's dream reminded him of her telling him that several times.

His own guilt for the way he had treated her these last months ate at him. He returned to the parlor, banking the fire, and found himself restless though tired. Pouring out a glass of whiskey, he stood with one arm resting on the mantel, staring into the dying flames.

He thought of the passion she had given to him, and wondered if Erin's love, lavished so freely on his children, could be his, too. A family, a real family...

Her dream was not an impossible one. The Lord knew that he was tired of burning with fever for her, tired of fighting himself and her. Jake and Becky needed Erin, and since it seemed a night for honesty, he needed her, too.

Need was not something he had shown her. Need and a host of other things. A quick swallow of whiskey eased some of the tension that was building inside him. But as he raised the glass to take another sip, the baby began crying.

With a rueful smile, he remembered other nights, but there was no bitterness to follow, for he wasn't alone to care for a helpless infant. Erin was here.

With a light step, Mace headed for the bedroom.

Erin was struggling to get out of bed. The soft swearing alerted her to Mace's presence and she fell back against the pillows. "The baby—"

"I'll get her for you."

Apprehensively, Erin watched as Mace turned the cover aside and gently lifted her swaddled child. Her eyes widened as he crooned meaningless sounds, his big hands cupping the baby's head and bottom. She couldn't help but wonder why the child had ceased its cry the moment he picked her up. Added to that was the time it was taking him to walk the short distance to the bed and give the baby over to her.

Her sleep had not been restful but filled with dreams of seeing herself fall over and over into a bottomless pit. She had called for Mace, screamed his name, but he never came, never answered her. With this fresh in mind, she reached for her baby, taking her from Mace with a possessive gleam in her eye. The baby's rosebud mouth worked frantically, searching for substance, but Erin was waiting for Mace to leave.

Apprehension turned to dismay when he seated himself at the edge of the bed, leaning over to catch a tiny fist and insert his finger. "She's strong, Erin."

"Yes."

Her reluctantly given agreement forced him to look into her eyes. Green eyes that were wary of him. Mace couldn't summon anger, for he felt she had every right to question his every word, every move.

The baby's face reddened, her mewling cry growing stronger as her hunger went unabated.

"You'd best feed this little one before she wakes the house."

No censure in his voice. He sounded almost as if he were teasing her, and didn't care who the baby woke. Erin shook her head. She wasn't thinking clearly. This was Mace, not the man of her dreams.

"If you'll leave—"

Mace shook his head, silencing her. He brushed the back of his hand across her flushed cheek, then rose to fix the pillows behind her. Before Erin could ask what he was doing, he eased her up so that she rested more comfortably.

Shielding herself with the edge of the sheet, Erin opened her gown's ties and put the baby to her breast. She winced at the strength her daughter showed, yet a feeling of deep contentment stole over her. Her daughter, she repeated to herself, gently rubbing one finger across her baby's forehead. Closing her eyes, she tried to block out Mace's presence, but he seemed to reach out and make himself a part of this most precious time. She owed him more than thanks for fighting to bring her this child. Without Mace she didn't think she would have survived.

Emotions stirred inside Erin as the child suckled. She fled from the embarrassment of knowing that both Mace and Ketch had helped her give birth. There was just a flare of annoyance that it didn't bother Mace at all. Thinking of her promises to both herself and the unborn baby, she began to doubt her capabilities to carry them out. But, for now, she put that worry aside. All she knew was that love seemed to be overflowing with the passing of every moment that she held her baby.

A dreamy smile played over her lips before a sigh escaped and she cuddled the child closer. Mace had not abandoned her as she sometimes feared he would. He was here, offering his help, and she now understood the depth of the commitment he had made in claiming this child as his own. There were so many questions she wanted to ask him, but they wouldn't form into spoken words.

The melding sound of their breathing made her open her eyes to look at him. Somehow, she wasn't at all surprised to find him still watching her.

"Do you know how beautiful you look right now, Erin?"

Whatever she expected him to say, it wasn't this. How could she appear beautiful? She dropped her gaze to the quilt, feeling the weight of the baby, tiny as she was, begin to sap her strength.

Mace reached out and brushed a loose tendril of hair from her face. "You are, you know. To me, seeing you now is to see the precious circle of life renew itself, renew me," he said, hearing the huskiness in his voice and for once uncaring of the emotion it revealed. She was, with each second that passed, chasing away the nightmare he had lived with so long. He had helped this child to have life, but more, much more meaningful to him, was that Erin was alive.

The gaze he bestowed on Erin when she looked at him held a soft, strange expression. She had seen desire's hot fire waiting to snare her, she had witnessed fury and cold contempt from his dark eyes, but never this... Warmth without passion's heat, a tenderness that made her wish it was love. Erin felt herself coming apart. She had promised the Lord she would ask for no more if He kept Jake safe, and she had kept that promise through the hours she had struggled to bring her child forth and have life. But she was greedy now; she wanted Mace's love... wanted it with every fiber of her being.

Still holding her gaze, he reached over to lower the sheet, his rough callused hand cupping the baby's head. "Don't shy away," he pleaded softly. "There aren't many men who are given a second chance, Erin. I'm one of the lucky ones."

"Mace, I—"

"Hush, there's plenty of time for us to talk. I just wanted you to know that I stayed in case you fell asleep again."

"Did I? While holding her?"

A smile broke his lips, a smile that coaxed one from her. "Don't worry. She's stronger than she looks. Most babies are. And don't be blaming yourself," he reassured her, seeing that her eyes filled with dismay. "You had a rough time of it. But you'll be strong again, Erin. I promise that."

Joy bubbled up and spilled over inside Erin. Could her prayer be answered? His husky voice made her think he really cared, and the tender look of his eyes seemed somewhat deeper.

There was no shame now to know that he watched her with the baby. That surprised her and yet, reflecting upon it, she knew this is what she wanted; a real marriage. One that had no fear, no shame. Erin decided to test it before she was overcome by the need for sleep.

"You know more than I do about babies. I'll depend on your help."

Was this trust she was offering him? Mace asked himself. "If that's what you want."

"Have done toying with me, Mace," she demanded, covering his hand with one of hers. "Tell me what you want. Don't let me dream and find out that I'm fooling myself."

He wondered if she knew what she was asking. The yearning for honesty between them overcame all other feelings inside him. And Mace found that the words weren't all that hard to say. "Yes," he admitted, turning his hand so that he held hers. "I want to raise her as mine. With all the rights of a father." *And those of a husband.*

Erin was startled to see the color rise in his cheeks. Her gaze once again drifted down to look at her baby.

"Have you thought about a name for her, Erin?"

"Maddie. I want to call her that," she whispered, her eyes gazing at the soft downy hair that covered her baby's head.

"Isn't that your friend's name? The one that took you in?"

"Yes." A feeling of peace, of sharing with Mace as she never had before made her add, "I didn't know my mother's name. There is no one else to—"

"Don't remember what hurts you, Erin." He squeezed her hand, leaning closer, wanting the sadness gone from her. "Maddie Dalton sounds fine to me. Now Jake and Becky have a name to call their sister."

Gripping the baby tighter, Erin had to look up at him. "Sister?" she repeated. "Is that their idea?"

"I thought so. I hope so." Trust me, he silently implored, afraid to say the words and break the fragile spell being woven around them. He released her hand and moved to crowd her on the bed, coming to sit near the headboard so that he could enfold both of them within his arms.

A possessive feeling rose inside him. He wanted Erin as his wife and wanted to see her swollen with his child. He would never deny little Maddie a place in his heart, he vowed, for he had brought her into the world and that made her his. He would be the one she came to, the man she would call Papa as Becky and Jake did. He was the one who offered his protection and caring to her.

Rubbing his chin over Erin's hair, his gaze touched upon the lush fullness of her breast, where Maddie's rosebud mouth was losing its grip.

For Erin, the cherishing feel of his arms holding both herself and her child made her brave enough to take another risk. "Mace?" she asked softly, biting her still swollen lip, hesitant but needing to know. "Does it bother you that they call her their sister?"

"No." And he knew it was true. There would always be a haunting sense of loss for Sky; she was his first love and— Finish it, a voice demanded. And until now, his only love. But the pain had been easing, easing all these months that he had known Erin, and he hadn't even realized how much until this moment. The passion he felt for Erin was fierce, a driving force that never left him. He had to admit once more, and then let it rest, that Sky had never made him feel this way.

"Be sure, Mace. Be very sure," she warned, feeling the way his body tensed behind her. It mattered a great deal to her that what he said was true, but it would matter more for her helpless child.

"I'm sure, Erin. I wouldn't have said it otherwise. Jake and Becky's accepting her makes it easier for us."

Us? Erin turned the word over in her mind. For so long she had been alone that she repeated the word over and over to herself. Us. Together. With Mace's warmth and the strength of his body surrounding her, Erin rested her head against his chest.

"Erin," he whispered after a few minutes of contentment. "Little one is satisfied." He felt her watching as he used his fingertip to wipe a dribble of fluid from the corner of Maddie's mouth. He wanted to bring his finger to his lips, but he knew that would shock Erin, for she was rigid as could be as he drew her nightgown over her breast, leaving the ties undone.

"Let me take her," he offered, wanting her to give him the baby, feeling that he needed to know she fully accepted him at his word to make Maddie his own.

"I want to hold her," Erin said in reply. "I want her to know that I'm always going to be there to hold her and show her all the love she could ever want."

There was so much longing in her voice that Mace couldn't speak. And when he finally answered her, he spoke between pressing kisses to her hair. "She'll know. Maddie will have all the love she needs. From all of us," he added. Then, because he knew she was tired, he said, "If you don't let me have her she'll start fussing before long."

After a moment's hesitation that showed how little strength she had, Erin told him to take Maddie. Her gaze was pinned on the way he lifted her and placed her tummy down against his shoulder, patting her bottom with his hand that covered it. He began to rub the baby's back, and he smiled when she burped.

Erin protested when he started to put Maddie in the cradle. "Won't it be easier to let me hold her until you move the cradle to my room?"

"Your room? Why would you think I'd put—" He cut himself off. Shaking his head, he fought down anger. "Erin, you need to sleep here, and so do I. You can't be getting up with her at night."

"But—"

"No buts. That's the way it is."

"I can't let you do more. You can't go without sleep."

"Why not? You're my wife, Erin. Maddie is my daughter. If not me, who has the right to care for you both?"

His face had become harder, more intent, and his eyes dared her to argue. Erin surprised him, just as she surprised herself, by nodding meekly, lowering her head to hide her smile.

"If that's the way you want it, Mace."

"That's the way."

She thought about slipping beneath the quilt and hiding the flood of tears that his words brought. But not for long. The moment he turned back after settling Maddie, she called him. "Mace, please come and hold me. I'm frightened to be this happy. I—" She couldn't say more, for he was there, stretching out on the bed beside her, holding her in his arms.

"I'll make it last, Erin. I promise you. We've both had sorrow enough."

Within the sheltering he offered, Erin released tears that carried joy and sadness. She knew there was goodness in Mace, knew her loving him had been right, and now he had given her more hope than she had dreamed of to build on for the future.

Sleep could no longer be held at bay, but Erin nestled her head against the beating of his heart and asked one last thing of him. "Will you write to Maddie and tell her about the baby?"

"I'll tell her. Maybe she'll come and visit. You'd like that, wouldn't you? Having a woman friend here?"

But Erin never heard his offer. Mace smiled to himself. He'd surprise her.

Chapter Twenty

True to his promise, in the next six weeks that followed, Mace showered Maddie with love. Erin, unable to completely trust him not to hurt her again, retreated from him. Not entirely, she told herself. Her dream would not allow that to happen, but her days were sometimes shadowed by his continued refusal to talk about his first marriage and Sky's death. She, in turn, longed to tell him of her own past and how she had been befriended by Maddie.

It was difficult to keep her distance when Mace was so tender and concerned about her welfare even now that she was able to take over her chores again. And best, there was that enchantment with little Maddie and everything she did that spilled over to all. Jake and Becky adored the baby.

Then, too, there was the matter of her remaining in Mace's room. After feeding Maddie, Erin was finding it almost impossible to slide into bed where Mace waited to gather her into his arms. She spent many sleepless hours, far too conscious of his strong body, the warmth that beckoned her close and the ache that was once more building inside her as each day brought her healing from the birth.

This night was no different. As she resumed her place by his side, Mace turned to her.

"Is that little piglet full enough to sleep a few hours?"

"I hope so," she answered with a laugh, for the baby at times seemed insatiable.

Nuzzling his chin against her cheek, Mace realized that Erin was tense. "Did you see the stunned look on Jake's face when she smiled at him tonight?"

"I thought he was going to drop her. But you're all silly to think she's smiling. It's gas."

"Smiles, Erin," he growled, pinning her in place with his arm crossed over her body. "Maddie smiles for all of us, woman, and don't you dare keep denying it."

Erin wasn't laughing. She was holding her breath, for Mace's arm brushed across her sensitive nipple, swollen from feeding the baby. She couldn't believe the heat that spread in her body, nor the inner tremble that built and pooled so that she clamped her thighs together.

Mace stilled. Every night he had taken her into his arms, racked by need, by a fierce desire to make love to her. It was far too soon. He knew that. Yet the sweet scent of her rose to cloud his mind. His body tautened with need and he knew that tonight Erin was very aware of him as a man, just as he had been always aware of her as a woman.

Tension spiraled up to enfold them. Neither spoke, nor did they move. He hovered above her, his heartbeat drumming like his blood, hotly and with a demand he was having difficulty fighting.

It was too soon...but he couldn't cease the need to trail kisses to the corner of her mouth. Her skin was flushed, and her mouth trembled. Her hand rose and cupped around his forearm, but she didn't push him away. Her breath was his, and his was hers, and then with aching tenderness he fitted his mouth to her lips.

Warm and giving, Erin opened her mouth for his kiss, inviting the deeper intimacy. She wanted him. Wanted to give him all the love she had kept bottled inside, love that had grown with every day, every hour since Maddie's birth. She needed to have Mace accept her love, as he had accepted her baby. For these were the only gifts she had to give him.

Gifts of her heart. Gifts of love.

Mace sipped sorrow from her mouth, took regrets for what had passed between them and burned them away in the welcoming honey sweet taste of Erin. Silently, he gave the love that remained unspoken, gave it to her with a kiss that flamed hotter and brighter as her healing spread through him.

His hand slid beneath her shoulder to cup her head, tilting her face upward to feed the hunger that ravaged him. Healing is what Erin gave, healing that began in his soul with her acceptance of whatever he had to give her of himself without asking for more. He wanted Erin's love. He needed to hear her say the words aloud, to know that the look he often caught in her eyes was love.

She shared with her heart, becoming his haven from the past and his joy for the future.

Erin cradled his face between her palms, sensing a deep need inside him that she longed to fill. Her yearning to give all of herself, all that she felt for him, made her bold.

"Mace?" she whispered, tearing her lips free. "Tell me you feel more than need for a woman. Tell me you want—"

"You," he finished, stringing kisses down her neck, nudging aside the gown. "I want you, Erin. Have from the first minute I saw you." His mouth tasted skin as sweet as spring rain, as warm and as silky. She filled his senses as he wanted to fill hers.

He knew he was fast losing control, and once again the
arning sounded that it was too soon to make love to her.
ut she felt so good in his arms, her small cry telling him
aat she enjoyed the discovery his mouth made of her
ewly lush figure. He wouldn't touch her, he promised
imself. Only with his mouth. But Erin made it impossi-
le for him to keep that promise. She lifted his hand and
laced it over her breast.

"Touch me," she pleaded in a tremulous whisper.

Mace lifted his head, staring down at her. Neither one
ad blown out the lamp, and by its soft flame he saw the
eed in her eyes.

"Erin, it's too soon. I'd hurt you. I don't want that. I
on't want to hurt you again."

Erin looked into his eyes. Passion burned within the
ark depths, passion and an emotion that brought fever
oftly stealing inside her. She began to shake her head,
eeling restricted by the way his fingers tangled in her hair,
nd knew she had to tell him.

"You won't hurt me, Mace. I'll..." Say it, she told
erself, realizing that she had no defenses left. How could
ie, when she loved him? "I'll hurt more if you don't."

"Erin." A visible shudder ran through his body.

She traced his lower lip with her finger, feeling that
iere were more truths to be said. Truths that had to come
rom her first. Yet she hesitated, for Mace had closed his
yes and without seeing that fierce glitter of passion within
iem, she was afraid that he didn't want her love.

"I trust you, Mace," she whispered, cupping his cheek.
I love you enough to trust you that you won't hurt me."

A burden and gift in one, he thought, lowering his
ead, taking her mouth.

He couldn't return the words. He didn't understand
hy he couldn't, but he showed Erin with touches that

were careful to arouse without injury, with kisses th
learned each woman's secret she offered, slowly bringi
her up to match the fire that burned in his body. When h
demand would no longer be denied, he eased his body
join with hers and she gasped, not in pain but with ple
sure, and he felt as if he had returned a small measure
her gift.

He held himself back, satisfying her time and aga
before her cries begged him to come to where she waite
He arched into her with a broken cry, surrendering to tl
need that tore his control, that seared him and then join
him with Erin, soul to soul.

When he found the strength to ease himself away fro
her, Mace rested his head on her breast and knew he ha
not given Erin enough of himself. It was more than pa
time for her to know about Sky.

"I need to tell you about Sky and me, Erin," he whi
pered. "I loved her for so long and we both gave up
much to be together." In a sometimes breaking voice,
the quiet of night he told her of Sky, cleansing himself
the guilt he had carried for so long. He understood, wh
Erin lifted his head and gazed into his eyes, that Erin ha
untold strength and love unmeasured.

"No woman, Mace, could ever ask for more than y
gave. Sky accepted your love. She couldn't have kno
what would happen, just as you can't know that lovi
her as you did caused Jake to come early. There cou
have been other reasons. I want another baby, Mace.
want lots more, but I want them to be your children. W
you tell me," she begged, feeling the tears gather, "th
if I have another child, I must do without your loving m
I'd die if you made that demand of me. Can't you see,
she pleaded, between pressing kisses to his face, "that

woman who loves a man would ever make such a choice?''

"Good Lord, Erin, I want to believe you. You don't know how much I want that.''

"You will, Mace. Trust me this much. Let my love and time show you.'' She brought his lips to hers, sliding her hands down the hard muscles of his back, drawing him to her once more. Love and time, that was all she needed.

"Erin, where are you? There's a letter from San Francisco for you.'' Mace found her in the parlor, on the floor, with Maddie on a blanket between Jake and Becky. The baby's arms and legs were working furiously as the children cooed their own baby talk to her. But as his gaze settled on Erin, her smile instantly warmed, the remembered rapture of last night visible in her gaze.

He walked to her side and helped her to stand, kissing her as if he'd been gone for days rather than a few hours to Walla Walla. She was breathless when he let her go and his smile reflected a deep male satisfaction that it was for him alone.

"Your letter,'' he said, handing it over. Dropping to his knees, he spoke to the children and let Maddie grab one of his fingers.

Erin tore open her letter, knowing that it was from Maddie. She scanned the first few lines of how thrilled she was that Erin named the baby after her.

"It's from your friend, isn't it?'' Mace asked.

"Yes,'' she answered absently, reading.

Your letter took so long to reach me because I've moved, Erin. Got me a new place where the gents got money and manners.

"She tell you why it's taken her so long to answer?''

"She moved, Mace.''

Now Erin, don't get angry, but that man of yours didn'
know what he was doing inviting me to visit. How woul
that look? You can't be having a woman like me around
But I admit to wanting to see your baby.

"Well, is she coming to visit?" Mace lifted the baby
but Erin's silence made him look at her. "What'
wrong?"

She looked up from the letter but didn't look at Mace
What was she going to answer? She had never told hin
about Maddie, about herself. After that night he ha
made love to her, she couldn't bring herself to destro'
what they were building. How much trust would he hav
if he knew what Maddie did for a living? How much trus
would he give her, when he knew that she had lived there'

"Erin?" he prompted.

"I don't think she'll be able to come. Not now, at an
rate." She folded the letter and slipped it into her apro
pocket, planning on finishing it later when she was alone.

Mace set the baby back on the blanket and came to hi
feet. "You don't seem happy to hear from her. Is ther
something wrong? If she needs the money to make th
trip, I'll send it to her."

He felt Erin withdrawing from him and was helpless t
stop it.

She turned then, offering him an absent smile, still un
able to meet his gaze. "I don't think money is a problem
Don't worry about it." To Becky she said, "I'll be in th
kitchen if Maddie fusses."

"I'll sing to her—" Becky started to answer.

"I'll whistle—" Jake broke in.

She nodded, leaving them. Maddie would be fine i
their care for a little while. She needed to be alone.

Mace wasn't so easily put off. He followed her into th
kitchen. "This is likely going to make you mad as hell, bu

I've got to ask. Are you ashamed of Becky and Jake? Are they the reason you don't want Maddie visiting us?"

"How dare you!" She flew at him, ready to strike him, when she stopped herself and realized what she was doing. "Mace, don't ever dare think such a thing. I've never, you hear me, never been ashamed of calling Becky and Jake mine. I never will be. I love them. Having Indian blood makes no difference to me. But since you brought this out into the open, there is something I want to say."

Erin rushed to the doorway to make sure that the two children didn't overhear her. Coming back to stand in front of Mace, she took hold of his hand and dragged him off to the pantry.

"When you wrote to me, you never told me about Sky or Becky or Jake. You should have, Mace. I know it wouldn't have made a difference to me. But I could have hurt those children that day I walked into this house. It wasn't fair to them."

"No."

"No? Is that all you have to say?" Folding her arms across her chest, Erin tapped her foot, feeling righteous and wanting satisfaction.

"Yeah, that's it."

"You're not angry?"

He drew her up against him. "How the hell can I be angry with a woman who loves the way you do?" Nibbling on her tempting lower lip, he smiled at Erin's breathless little sound and backed her up against the shelves. "I can't ever seem to get you alone anymore. If Becky isn't tied to your apron strings, Jake is demanding your attention. Or," he noted, laughter filling his eyes as passion deepened his kisses, which covered her face, "Maddie needs feeding or changing. As if having these three takes you away from me, I've got Ketch fussin' or one of the men has mending or some gift for the baby.''

Caressing her back, swinging her body back and forth so that she couldn't mistake his need, Mace teased her mouth with brief searing kisses. "If you really love me, you'd stop starving me."

"Mace Dalton, for that you pay." She controlled his lips, holding his head still, taking them both where they wanted to be, locked in passion's embrace. Erin was the first to pull away. "Mace, please, it's daylight. The children—"

"One more kiss to keep me until tonight," he coaxed, already taking her mouth.

But Erin's protest summoned the children and Scrap.

Becky's "Oh, Papa," made them spring apart, Erin hastily smoothing her apron, Mace giving a heartfelt sigh.

"Maddie's wet, Erin."

With a shrug, Erin started for the pantry door, but gave him a kiss blown over her shoulder. "The joy of having a family," she said, waving him off.

Mace glared down at this daughter, son and the still pint-size dog sniffing at his heels. Privacy was in damn short supply. "There are times..." he began. Becky giggled and Jake followed. Mace fell back against the shelf, laughing himself. Yes, there were times, but he wouldn't trade them. Not one.

Later, after supper, while he helped Erin finish the dishes, he suggested they all make a trip into town.

"But Maddie's so young." Erin didn't want him to know how much she feared having people count on their fingers and give Mace knowing looks that would offend his pride.

"I want us to go. Together. If what you said today was true—" She shot a glare at him, and Mace held up his hand. "I'm not saying that you lied to me, Erin. I just want us to be together. You can't hide Maddie. She's mine and sooner or later everyone's going to know. I've got to go to a Grange meeting about the Nez Percé Indians. More and more of their reservation land is being given to white men. I can't ignore that. 'Sides, it'll give you a chance to shop and be away from chores."

His engaging grin had her smiling. Mace was proud, she knew. Could she have pride less than his? It would be nice to walk and see shops. She still had that twenty dollars saved.

"You could get fitted for a few new gowns. Becky's growin' out of her clothes and Jake needs shoes." Mace tossed aside the cloth and slid his hands around her waist, turning her to face him. "Tell me yes."

"Yes," she whispered, unable to refuse him.

Intending to spoil Erin, Mace installed her in the same hotel where they spent their wedding night and took the adjoining room for the children. He wanted time alone with Erin, but for now, this would have to do.

Maddie was such a good baby that, once fed, she settled quietly for a nap. Mace took Becky and Jake in hand, telling Erin, "These two come with me. You spend the afternoon with a hot bath and rest."

"What hot bath?" Erin asked.

"The one I'm on my way down to order."

The desire in his eyes made her nod, her own growing warm as she watched him leave with the children. A whole afternoon to herself. Bathwater she didn't need to heat or carry away. Mace loved her, she was sure. She only lacked the words from him to make her joy complete.

Mace told the desk clerk what he wanted, but was distracted by the entrance of a tall, lushly figured woman.

Mace was as much a man as the next. The stylish cut of her clothes marked her as a stranger, but her walk...well, that told him she was a woman who knew her attractions to a man and used every one of them to her advantage. He stood aside as she approached the desk, idle curiosity in his eyes.

After she sized him up and indicated her approval with a slow smile, she asked for a room from the young desk clerk.

Her voice was husky and rich, bringing to mind warm whiskey and messed sheets. Mace grinned to himself at the thought. A look at the clerk showed that the man was trying hard to swallow.

"Is there a way to get a message to a friend of mine?"

"Oh, I'll take it for you, ma'am."

"Not here in town. Matter of fact," she said with a laugh, "I'm not sure exactly where she lives."

Jake tugged on Mace's hand, drawing his attention away. Becky was motioning to him by the door. "Please excuse me, but I need one last thing sent to my wife's room," he said to the honey blonde, who once more smiled at him. Mace ignored the practiced invitation in her eyes. She might be better dressed than some, but a whore's offering held no allure for him.

He ordered a light meal for Erin, cautioning the clerk to make sure he did not wake the baby. He thanked the woman for waiting and turned to leave.

"Now, about my message," the woman said.

Mace no longer listened. He thought about the present he was getting for Erin and left the hotel.

"Good-lookin' man," the woman remarked.

"That's Mace Dalton. He's here with is wife and baby. And those two are his. First marriage. Indian, she was."

The clerk stopped, sensing that he had lost the woman's interest.

"Ma'am? I'll need you to sign the register."

"Yes. Yes, of course." With a flourish, Maddie Daring signed her name. So that was Erin's husband? And Erin was here in the hotel? She took the key handed to her, glanced at the room number and then up at the attentive clerk.

"I couldn't help hearing him order a meal for his wife. Would it be possible for me to do the same? I mean if our rooms aren't too far so that it won't be too much trouble for you."

"No trouble. You're on the same floor. They have three ten and eleven and you're down the hall, three sixteen."

Maddie couldn't resist. She reached out and pinched his cheek. "You're a sweetheart. If you'll bring my bag, I'll see to a nice tip for you."

Flustered as she knew he would be, Maddie hoped he would forget that he gave her Erin's room number. She had no idea how long Erin's husband would be gone, but the chance to see her and the baby was too strong to resist. With a little luck she would be in and out and Mace Dalton would never know about her.

Erin expected the knock at the door. But when she opened it and found a woman standing with her back toward her, she started to close it.

The woman turned and Erin could only stare, clinging to the edge of the door. "Maddie?" she asked after long moments. "Is it really you?"

"None other."

Erin flung herself into Maddie's open arms, crying and hugging her tight. "Oh, I've missed you so!"

Maddie didn't doubt it, but she was aware that anyone passing in the hall could see them together. She managed to get them both inside, moved to a few tears herself when Erin, without asking questions, took her into the adjoining room to see the baby.

Little Maddie's hair was as dark as her mother's. Fair skin, a small nose and a thick sweep of lashes had Maddie whispering how pretty she was.

"And chubby, too," Maddie added, longing to hold the child.

"Don't you want to hold her, Maddie?" Erin asked. "It's all right, you know. She'll stir a bit then go off to sleep. She's a good baby."

Tempted as she was, Maddie put the idea aside and turned to Erin. "I know you must be wondering why I've come. When I wrote you, I wanted to see you, but got to thinking that maybe I'd spoil it for you, Erin."

"Spoil it for me? Maddie, I don't understand. Here, come and sit on the bed with me. Mace won't be back with the children for a while. And I've so much to tell you."

"I saw him, you know. Down in the lobby. He's a fine-looking man. Young, too."

Erin smiled, but saw that Maddie cast another longing glance at the cradle where the baby slept. Patting the other woman's hand, she rose and lifted her daughter, bringing her to Maddie. "Hold her. She won't break. She wouldn't be here but for you and your help."

"Don't be saying things like that, Erin. You'd have found a way without me." But she reached out for the baby, feeling a hunger of her own stir.

The knock Erin had been expecting came and she went to open the door. Two maids brought in hot water for the tub behind a screen in one corner of the room. Since they had to make another trip with more water, Erin told them she would leave the door open for them, and returned to sit with Maddie.

"Tell me, what made you decide to come?" Erin asked.

"I left almost a month after you. Couldn't take working for Jaffery. He got mean. Ugly and mean. The church ladies demanded they clean up the coast. More than a few places got closed down. I guess I got to thinking that I could do better and found out I was right. So much better, Erin, that I've got a gent of my own paying my way."

"Are you happy, Maddie? I wished you had come with me right from the start. It was so lonely without you. I thought of writing to you, but so much was happening that I just couldn't. It wouldn't have been fair to burden you."

"It wasn't good at first, was it, Erin? He didn't beat you or anything?"

"No, nothing like that. But he never gave me any time to tell him about the baby, and that night..." Erin lowered her head, twisting her hands together as the memory crowded her mind. "He was furious when he found out that I lied to him."

"And now? He didn't look like an unhappy man to me. I would know best, wouldn't I?"

That brought a smile, then a laugh from Erin. She looked up and saw that the maids had returned and were leaving, but she didn't bother to get up and lock the door after them.

She wanted to tell Maddie all that happened, and did, but found that some things were too private to share. With a quiet smile of contentment, Maddie listened, enjoying Erin's descriptions of Ketch and the other men, her learning to do ranch chores and finding her way with Mace's children.

"I know that he loves me, Maddie," Erin finished. "I dream only of hearing him say the words now. These last months since little Maddie was born have been the best of my life."

"Aren't you glad you didn't make the choice I once told you was there? Marry a stranger, you said to me. Be something that was bought. Well, it turned out for the best, didn't it, Erin? You never would have been able to bed half a dozen men a night and turn around to do it again. I knew that the first time I saw you."

"I haven't told Mace. I wanted to explain it all so there would be no more secrets between us, Maddie, but I never told him."

"That's why I wasn't going to come. And that's why I think I'll leave you now." She handed the baby back to Erin. "She's a precious child. You see that you take care and love her so she never winds up like me."

Erin placed the baby in her cradle and returned to stand in front of Maddie. "I'm not ashamed of you. I don't want you to leave. Mace will understand."

"Erin, you don't know men as well as me. Don't bet on that. If this man of yours knew that you worked in a place like Jaffery's, putting up with stinking drunks pawing you, he'd be gone so fast you couldn't draw breath. Trust me. I know."

"You're wrong, Maddie. Mace wouldn't care if I worked upstairs at Jaffery's. I know he wouldn't. I told him the truth about the baby. And about losing my position. He believed me."

"Why wouldn't I believe you, Erin? You're my wife."

"Mace!" Erin found it agonizing to look at him standing in the open door that adjoined the rooms. How much had he overheard? And why was he here?

She moved toward him, praying she would not find contempt in his gaze, but his eyes revealed nothing of what he was feeling or thinking. "I didn't hear you come in."

"Aren't you going to introduce me, Erin?" he asked instead of answering.

She turned to gesture Maddie forward, but all the while sensed that he knew exactly who she was. "Mace, this is my friend, Maddie Darling. The one I told you about."

"I wish I had known who you were when I saw you at the desk, Maddie. I would have brought you up to see Erin."

With a knowing smile, Maddie nodded. "Yes, I have a feeling you would have done just that."

"Mace, where are Becky and Jake?" Erin interjected, her feeling that something more was going on between Mace and Maddie puzzling her.

"They're down at the bookstore around the corner, looking for a book for you."

"You still haven't told me why you came back." Erin sent him a pleading look and found he refused to meet her gaze.

"I had something for you and didn't want to wait for you to see it." He then addressed Maddie. "Will you be staying long?"

"No. I came to make sure that Erin was all right and to see the baby."

"And have you?" Mace asked, walking into the room and coming to stand near the cradle. "She's smart and pretty, isn't she, Erin?"

It felt ridiculous to stand there, as Mace went on to brag about the baby, all the while telling herself this was not happening. Mace should by rights be furious—or at the very least, angry. He was neither.

And what was Maddie doing, going to his side, nodding and listening to every word he said? Erin backed away from them, suddenly afraid that Mace knew what Maddie was. If he had heard them talking about Jaffery, if he thought that she sold herself, she could lose everything that mattered to her.

Maddie turned to look at her, saw she was upset and hurried to her.

"I hope I haven't made trouble for you, Erin. If I have, I'm sorry. I never meant for him to know. I'll leave—"

"No, Maddie. You're the only friend I've had. I won't let Mace chase you off."

"He's not. Believe me, Erin, he's not. But it's best that you forget about me."

"Why? Why are you telling me this?"

Taking one of Erin's hands between hers, Maddie gave a quick shake of her head. "Listen to me. I won't be in San Francisco for long. My gent and me are going to Santa Fe. He's been telling me that he's got a place that needs a woman's touch. Maybe I'm being foolish, but I believe him. You have a new life here, Erin. You don't need the likes of me in it."

Before Erin answered, Mace came and slipped his arm around her waist. Her rigid posture forced him to plant a kiss on her hair before he spoke to Maddie.

"Erin told me that you took her in and cared for her when she had no one to turn to."

"That's right, I did. Erin's a good, hardworking woman. Decent and kind. She deserved better than she had." Maddie met his hard, direct gaze with one of her own. She was almost of a height with Mace and refused to allow him to intimidate her. "Whatever Erin told you was the truth."

"I never said that it wasn't, Maddie," Mace answered with a wry smile. "Matter of fact, I don't understand why you feel you can't see or write to Erin. She claims you're her only friend."

"The hell you say!" Maddie was ready to take off her kid gloves. "You don't know what you're offering and what's more, you don't know what I am."

"Maddie, please." Erin turned to look up at Mace. She was angry that he was daring to embarrass Maddie.

"No, it's all right, Erin," Mace said. "I know what Maddie is." And the look he exchanged with Maddie made sure that she had no doubt he spoke the truth.

"And you're still making that offer?" Erin asked. She knew Mace's pride, and this gesture had been given at its cost. Love, she realized, could keep growing, for hers did for him at this moment. The look he bestowed on her left no doubt that he meant every word. She planted a quick shy kiss on his cheek and freed herself from his light hold.

"Let me say goodbye to Maddie."

"I'll be waiting, Erin."

At the door Maddie leaned close and whispered, "You know what love is now, don't you?"

Erin looked at Mace, smiled and nodded.

"It was the right thing that you did in getting away, Erin. I told you you'd never find love in that place. I'm happy for you. Now keep your fingers crossed for me. Maybe some of that Irish luck will rub off."

"It's not luck of any kind, Maddie. Just love. The giving of love brings its own gifts back to you."

With a last hug, Erin let her go, then closed the door. Turning, she faced her husband.

Chapter Twenty-One

"You're not condemning me, Mace? I know you heard us talking. I'm just not sure how much you know."

He nodded, watching her carefully. She leaned against the door as if barring his exit. He puzzled over the strange gleam in her eyes.

"Once before, in this very hotel, I made a confession to you. I need to make another."

"Only if you want to tell me, Erin. I don't need—"

"But I need to tell you. You've given me so much, Mace. I have nothing to offer you but myself and little Maddie."

The sudden lack of spirit in her voice alarmed him, but he made no move toward her. Erin had to find her own way back to his side. But nothing would stop him from answering her.

"The offer of you and the baby are more than enough for me, Erin. The two of you come with love. What man wants for more?"

"And what about truth? You want that, too, in a wife, don't you?" she asked, trying to understand why he was so calm. Or was he?

"If you want. Only if you want."

Gripping the doorknob behind her, Erin buried her
ear. She couldn't look at him as she began to talk. "You
now that I grew up in an orphanage, Mace. I don't know
ho my parents are. I don't even know if my name is re-
ly Erin. I was left there. The woman who worked at the
rphanage told me my infant gown was trimmed with
andmade Irish lace. Since I was a few months old and
ad the coloring of an Irish lass, she called me Erin. When
was able to read I stole the last name of Dunmore from
book. Once I was old enough, I was sent out to work as
maid. You know what happened with Silas."

Mace found he wasn't very strong. He couldn't keep his
solution to let Erin come to him when she was ready. He
ad to hold her. When he had her in his arms, Mace knew
hat she needed to hear from him, and more important,
hat he needed to say.

"Erin, there's no reason for you to drag all this up."

"Yes," she insisted, arching her head away from his
ps. "I was out on the street, trying to get away from two
en, when Maddie found me. She took me with her to
affery's but I only worked as a maid there." It was hard
 talk with Mace nibbling on her ear. She tried to move,
ut his body gently pressed her against the door. "Are you
stening to me?"

"Always," he said, tracing the whorls of her ear, then
miled when he felt her shiver.

"Mace, I want to tell you everything. I sang at night in
ie parlor. I served whiskey…Mace…" The tiny love bite
n her lobe was more than distracting; she couldn't get her
noughts together. "I never went upstairs with any of the
ien. Jaffery tried to threaten me. He said—"

"Shall I find him for you?"

He was slipping the pins from her hair and for a mo-
ent Erin didn't know what he said until he repeated it.

"No. That's all over with. He's—"

"I'm so glad," he whispered, trailing kisses down h
cheek to the corner of her mouth.

Erin began to sag against the door. "You've got to sto
I was desperate when Maddie came up with the idea—"

"Ah, more thanks to Maddie," he murmured, de
fingers unbuttoning the back of her gown. "Erin, o
love, your skin's so sweet and—"

"And you're not . . . really . . . listening," she manag
to say brokenly, passion rising with the light way
cupped her shoulders and arched her into his body.

"I'm listening to every word. You're desperate. To k
me? Love me? What, Erin?" He tilted her face up t
ward his. "Do you think I care? It's the past, Erin. I swe
that to you. It doesn't matter to me where you came fron
or what you've done." Her chin needed a kiss, then h
temple. He held her close, waiting for the tremor to pas

"I never sold myself, Mace."

"I never thought you did."

"But—"

"Don't know you know that what matters to me is wh
you are now? My wife, Erin. The mother of my childre
The woman who looks at me and makes me feel loved.'

Erin felt dizzy. She grabbed his upper arms to stead
herself. She no longer was puzzled by the look in his da
eyes.

"It's taken me a long time to say this, but I love yo
Erin. Love all that you are, all that you've come to mea
to me."

He kissed her slowly, telling her how much he che
ished her in the best way he knew. He kissed her deepl
with hunger, to show her how much he needed her. H
drank the hot glide of her tears and heard her broke
whisper of love. He swept her up into his arms a

rought her to the bed. In her arms and with her love, he new the shadows of the past were truly gone. As he told Erin, what man could ask for more?

Erin silently echoed his words. She had no choice. With Mace's unquestioning acceptance of her gifts of love, he ad given her his own in return. What woman could ask or more?

*   *   *   *   *

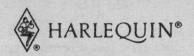 **HARLEQUIN®**

THE TAGGARTS OF TEXAS!

Harlequin's Ruth Jean Dale brings you
THE TAGGARTS OF TEXAS!

Those Taggart men—strong, sexy and hard to resist...

You've met Jesse James Taggart in FIREWORKS!
Harlequin Romance #3205 (July 1992)

Now meet Trey Smith—he's THE RED-BLOODED YANKEE!
Harlequin Temptation #413 (October 1992)

Then there's Daniel Boone Taggart in SHOWDOWN!
Harlequin Romance #3242 (January 1993)

And finally the Taggarts who started it all—in LEGEND!
Harlequin Historical #168 (April 1993)

Read all the Taggart romances!
Meet all the Taggart men!

Available wherever Harlequin books are sold.

HE CROSSED TIME FOR HER

Captain Richard Colter rode the high seas, brandished a sword and pillaged treasure ships. A swashbuckling privateer, he was a man with voracious appetites and a lust for living. And in the eighteenth century, any woman swooned at his feet for the favor of his wild passion. History had it that Captain Richard Colter went down with his ship, the *Black Cutter,* in a dazzling sea battle off the Florida coast in 1792.

Then what was he doing washed ashore on a Key West beach in 1992—alive?

MARGARET ST. GEORGE brings you an extraspecial love story next month, about an extraordinary man who would do anything for the woman he loved:

#462 THE PIRATE AND HIS LADY
by Margaret St. George
November 1992

When love is meant to be, nothing can stand in its way... not even time.

Don't miss American Romance
#462 THE PIRATE AND HIS LADY.
It's a love story you'll never forget.

PAL

HARLEQUIN ROMANCE®

**Harlequin Romance
invites you to a
celebrity wedding—or is it?**

Find out in Bethany Campbell's
ONLY MAKE-BELIEVE (#3230),
the November title in

THE BRIDAL COLLECTION

THE BRIDE was pretending.
THE GROOM was, too.
BUT THE WEDDING was real—the second time!

Available this month (October)
in The Bridal Collection
TO LOVE AND PROTECT
by Kate Denton
Harlequin Romance #3223

Wherever Harlequin Books are sold.

WED-7

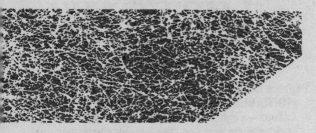

· HARLEQUIN · HISTORICAL

CHRISTMAS

· STORIES · 1992 ·

Capture the magic and romance of Christmas in the 1800s
with HARLEQUIN HISTORICAL CHRISTMAS STORIES
1992—a collection of three stories by celebrated
historical authors. The perfect Christmas gift!

Don't miss these heartwarming stories, available in
November wherever Harlequin books are sold:

MISS MONTRACHET REQUESTS by Maura Seger
CHRISTMAS BOUNTY by Erin Yorke
A PROMISE KEPT by Bronwyn Williams

Plus, this Christmas you can also receive a FREE
keepsake Christmas ornament. Watch for details in all
November and December Harlequin books.

**DISCOVER THE ROMANCE AND MAGIC OF THE
HOLIDAY SEASON WITH HARLEQUIN HISTORICAL
CHRISTMAS STORIES!**